D1126573

THE SHINING SEA

KOJI SUZUKI

Translated by Brian Bergstrom

The Shining Sea
A VERTICAL Book

Editor: Michelle Lin
Production: Grace Lu
Proofreading: Micah Q. Allen

Published by Vertical, an imprint of Kodansha USA Publishing, LLC.

Originally published in Japan as *Hikari sasu umi* by Shinchosha, Tokyo, 1993, and reissued in paperback by Kadokawa Shoten in 2010.

Translation based on the updated paperback edition.

ISBN 978-1-64729-118-1

Printed in the United States of America

First Edition

Kodansha USA Publishing, LLC
451 Park Avenue South, 7th Floor
New York, NY 10016
www.kodansha.us

CONTENTS

WARNING: This book contains references to suicide. If you or someone you know has suicidal thoughts or feelings, you are not alone, and there is free, 24/7 help.

National Suicide Prevention Lifeline offers confidential support for those in crisis or emotional distress. You can call 1-800-273-TALK (8255) or go to SuicidePreventionLifeline.org for free, 24/7 help.

PART I In the Mirror

1

If you stood on your tiptoes and looked out the examination room's window, you could see, spread out before you, the gourd-shaped surface of a lake. They said the mud at the bottom of this lake stuck to the legs of anyone who waded into it, pulling them down into its depths never to emerge again...or at least, that was how local legend had it. The proverbial bottomless swamp. Though in truth, Toshitaka Mochizuki didn't know of anyone who'd ever actually drowned that way. He didn't recall any local newspaper articles to that effect, either, at least not since he was old enough to be aware of such things. The words "bottomless swamp" conjured a rather formless, monstrous image for Mochizuki. As a child, he'd have nightmares in which he'd be playing in the water and his legs would end up stuck in the mud. These dreams of being sucked inexorably down into a world of fathomless darkness scared him much more than any dreams about being chased by monsters or falling from cliffs.

But over the years, land development had changed the view of the swamp, where he'd spent his youth chasing crayfish, to the point that it was nearly unrecognizable. There were stands of reeds here and there, and the dark specter of bottomless swamps that used to haunt the area had shrunk to near non-existence, transformed into the man-made ponds that decorated the stylish new housing developments surrounding them. The mystique was gone, and if anyone called them bottomless swamps these days, surely no one would believe them.

It was a landscape Mochizuki had grown used to over the past forty years and more. He used to play at the muddy edges of the swamps as a child, and even now, after a period spent as part of the medical staff at the Hamamatsu University School of Medicine before becoming the assistant director of the Department of Neuropsychiatry at Matsui Hospital, he still looked out upon it, though this time from on high. There was a time when he regretted leaving his alma mater in Tokyo, but he moved past that and now felt satisfied with how things had turned out. The assistant director position he'd steadily worked his way up to over those forty years was nothing to sneeze at, after all. And when he'd look down at the surface of the lake from the penthouse of the sixteen-floor condo he'd bought three years ago, he would feel a sense of peace at the sight that was much different from how he'd felt growing up. He had a daughter just entering sixth grade, and his relationship with his wife he'd met through a go-between was perfectly fine. Everything had gone according to plan, and there was nothing in particular he longed for anymore. He was enjoying a peaceful life. The zeal he'd felt at the beginning of his psychiatric career had yet to disappear, though it would be wrong to say it hadn't lessened a bit. Still, it was no tragedy for the passions of youth to quiet with age.

Mochizuki sometimes thought of his patients' psyches as comparable to the swamps. Everyone carried a piece of bottomless darkness somewhere in their heart. And if the odors wafting up from these depths began to bother the people around them, that was when patients came to this hospital. It wasn't a physician's role to fill in the swamp. It would be impossible anyway—he'd always thought the best strategy was to surround these bottomless swamps with stylish housing developments until the odors they exuded were perceived as perfumes. Though whether building such mansions around these mysterious swamps actually helped his patients achieve happiness felt like a separate question entirely.

It was an afternoon in late July, and the outdoor air-conditioning unit clattered ceaselessly in the oppressive heat. The air was being cooled, but the direct sunlight near his window still made him sweat. Mochizuki removed his glasses and wiped his face with his handkerchief, then sat down at his desk to pick the one-page report up from where he'd set it down.

Here lay another bottomless swamp.

Every section—not just the family and medical histories, but also the address, name, and age—was blank. The only reason he knew anything about this patient's situation at all was because a friend had handled her case as the attending physician at the general hospital she'd been transferred to from the emergency clinic.

Possible case of temporary global amnesia. Though it could also be something else in disguise, like schizophrenia.

This was the opinion of the attending physician after examining her.

Eight days ago, when the attractive woman who appeared to be in her mid-twenties was found attempting to drown herself in the turbulent waters off the Nakatajima Sand Dunes at ten in the evening, she wasn't carrying anything that could help identify her. Further, she made no effort to explain herself once she was rescued, and so she remained unidentified as she was transferred under the financial auspices of the mayor's office to Matsui Hospital. Anyone could see she was suffering from memory loss, but it was still hard to tell if her uncommunicativeness was due to an illness or an unwillingness to speak. This was the female patient who was about to enter Mochizuki's examination room for diagnosis.

According to the physician's report, the woman was over five months pregnant. Mochizuki was already constructing an all-too-familiar story in the back of his mind: she got pregnant and ended up dumped by the lover. But it was too late for an abortion now that she was past five months. In the end, her worries led to a nervous breakdown, and on impulse—or as a form of revenge on the man who'd left her—she threw herself into the sea. Perhaps the man already had a wife and child, or perhaps... Mochizuki laughed wryly as his mind conjured up various possibilities. He'd read about something similar from a gossip column in a weekly tabloid, and it suddenly struck him as all rather funny.

The tangled relations between men and women often lay at the base of mental disturbances. But you could also say that such disturbances would almost never occur if people had someone of the opposite sex who sincerely loved them with all their heart. He'd held this belief ever since he first chose to specialize in psychiatric medicine. But he'd found, during the two decades he'd spent in this profession, that it was impossible for a psychiatrist to provide enough love to a patient during their one-on-one sessions to cure what ailed them. The problem, quite obviously, was that there were so many more patients than there were psychiatrists. The national average ratio was fifty patients to every psychiatrist. That might work if you were running a tuberculosis ward, but with mental illnesses, the length of time you could spend directly with a patient determined the treatment, and that amount of time was extremely short. Naturally, medication became the solution, but truth be told, Mochizuki didn't have that much faith in its efficacy.

This was the source of the only real dilemma Mochizuki faced in his career—the reason why his zeal for the job had lessened. He felt that medication had to be accompanied by heart-to-heart communication with the patient, but there was no time for that. And realistically, it was impossible from a management perspective to double or triple the number of psychiatrists available to shoulder the load. In short, there was really nothing he could do but try to overcome the dilemma by treating every patient with as much good faith as possible.

Sensing that it must be about time, Mochizuki turned toward the examination room door. The chair revolved as his body moved, emitting a harsh screech.

So—an amnesiac woman, is it?

Looking at the door with his chin in his hand, Mochizuki recalled a male patient he'd treated about two months ago. The patient had arrived at the hospital unidentified as well, but ended up leaving after only three days. Hospitalized due to amnesia brought on by acute alcohol intoxication, this sixty-three-year-old man was quickly identified via a missing person report placed by his family. In cases of temporary amnesia, even a small trigger could release a flood of blocked memories. In this man's case, it took just three days for things to return to normal. Mochizuki hoped that it'd be like that this time as well. She was a young woman, only in her mid-twenties, so surely she had a parent or guardian out there. If they filed a missing person report, she could be identified easily by the police and released into her family's care. But so far, he'd yet to receive such a notice from the police.

The examination room door was open, but the woman didn't enter.

"Go ahead now."

The accompanying nurse pushed her gently on the back, and the woman finally took a hesitant step into the room. She managed the five or six steps necessary to reach the chair. Stretching her elbows out, she sat down and leaned slightly against the backrest. Her slim, well-proportioned body and round face reminded Mochizuki of some celebrity he'd seen on television, though he couldn't recall exactly who.

The woman's expression hadn't changed from when she'd first entered the room, and now, sitting in the chair, she stared blankly ahead at the pen in Mochizuki's hand.

Mochizuki greeted her and asked if she knew the day's date, but she didn't reply. He followed up with more questions, asking her name, address, basic addition and subtraction, and so on. The woman slowly raised her eyes to look at him.

"Do you understand what I'm saying?"

Mochizuki met her gaze. Looking straight into her eyes, he sensed no antagonism, only a sense of calm. The corners of her eyes were slanted downward slightly, which suited the charming double-folds of her eyelids, and it struck Mochizuki that while she looked rather haggard at the moment, with a little make-up, she'd be a knockout. He held her gaze for longer than was natural, but she made no move to look away.

It's unclear to what extent, but her consciousness seems clouded.

As he scribbled in his notepad, the woman shifted her gaze to his hand and blinked.

"Please tell me your name."

Mochizuki slowly repeated his question from earlier. The first step of treatment would be to clarify whether she knew who she was.

Memory can be broadly divided into three main types: sensory memory, short-term memory, and long-term memory. Sensory memory refers to memories of events that just happened. You can test it by showing a patient a card with a number written on it, then hiding it and asking for the number right away. Short-term memory is the ability to remember what took place within the last hour or so, and long-term memory is the storage of information from much longer ago—weeks, months, or years in the past. Therefore, to ask someone if they remember who they are is to test their long-term memory. Suspense TV shows feature amnesiac characters who can't remember their own names and get wrapped up in webs of crime, but in reality, that kind of thing almost never happens. The brain stores information like your name and basic common knowledge in multiple places as a result of overlearning, and those traces are extremely difficult to erase.

Seeing that the woman wouldn't tell him her name, Mochizuki thought again of the term "temporary global amnesia." It's a condition that can arise due to shock, such as that brought about by suddenly jumping into the sea. Based on the testimonies of the two youths who pulled her out of the water, it seemed very likely that such a shock was the cause of her condition. Temporary global amnesia isn't particularly dangerous. Like a strong wind, it arrives suddenly, but it usually departs by itself in a matter of hours and within a day or two at most. In her case, though, it had already been a full week since she'd been engulfed by the sea, but her memories remained cloaked in darkness.

Mochizuki considered another possibility: aphasia. A person with this condition can have trouble expressing their thoughts with words. Alternatively, they can struggle to understand the language used by others. The two functions are governed by separate areas of the brain, so it was hard to imagine that both would be impaired at once. He'd have to determine whether it was motor aphasia or sensory aphasia, but communicating with the patient was necessary to make such a judgment.

Thinking that one way to soothe the woman's distress, even just a little, would be to talk a bit about himself, Mochizuki got up from his desk and began walking around the examination room. This was a longstanding strategy of his. It struck him as unfair to expect patients to tolerate his insistent and intrusive questions without having to divulge anything about himself. And so, especially when he couldn't get the conversation flowing, he'd talk about things like his family and hobbies in an economical, lighthearted manner.

"It's all right, I'm on your side. I would love it if you'd tell me the truth—please don't hold back. That way, we can get you back to your family."

The woman's expression remained unchanged. Mochizuki walked over to the window and looked out. There were several patients in the hospital's courtyard. Almost every patient in the hospital was looking forward to the day they could return to their family. But in rare cases, patients might be unwilling to leave or their family would refuse to have them discharged.

Could one of those scenarios be the case for this woman? Or does she not have any relatives at all?

Mochizuki snuck a look at the woman's profile, then changed

the subject.

"On that evening eight days ago, you weren't just going for a night swim in the sea, right?"

Mochizuki sat down in the chair beside her and bent over slightly to look up at her downcast face. She was wearing a white, short-sleeved t-shirt that the hospital supplied. But when she had walked into the rough waves off the Enshunada coastline, she'd been wearing a denim jumper dress. Perhaps she'd chosen a loose garment to hide the pregnancy that was just beginning to show. Mochizuki tried to imagine the woman as she'd been dressed the night she tried to kill herself.

Being denim, the dress had probably been blue, and she'd worn a red t-shirt beneath it with a pair of white sneakers. Had she worn any accessories? How had she done her shoulder-length hair? The outfit was a little on the childish side, and he visualized the silhouette of this sweet-looking woman with a baby in her belly. Had her expression clouded over already, or had her eyes glittered with unusual brightness?

Mochizuki had been to the Nakatajima Sand Dunes many times. They undulated gently in all directions, and if not for the sound of the waves, you'd think you were in the middle of a desert. At ten o'clock that evening eight days ago, the weather had been clear, the tide just beginning to ebb. The woman had to cross over several dunes before she made it to the wet sand at the edge of the sea, where she stood for a while. A group of four young adults who'd been shooting off fireworks in the dunes had seen her standing there. Even from a distance, they could apparently tell that she had the air of someone who was contemplating suicide. The woman had slipped off her shoes and gathered up the hem of her dress as she walked on the sand. She was the only thing moving around there. The weight of herself and the life inside her bore down on the sand as she waded through the seawater, and the waves eventually reached up to her knees.

The four people in the dunes saw that the woman's actions were truly out of the ordinary, and while one of them hurried to the nearest payphone, the two men, who were confident swimmers, began running across the dunes toward the beach. As they did, they saw a tall wave break over the woman's head, and when it receded, she was no longer there. If those local youths hadn't happened to be nearby setting off fireworks, the woman most likely would have gotten her wish and lost her life. In the end, her rescue was quick enough that she was still breathing when help arrived, and not only her life, but also that of the child inside her was saved. Maybe she didn't have a bag with her, or perhaps it was carried away by the waves, but they couldn't find anything that had her name or address in the area.

Mochizuki replayed in the back of his mind the incident that had unfolded at the border of the nighttime sea in vivid detail. He knew the Nakatajima Sand Dunes so well that even though he was only recreating the scene in his mind, he could almost feel in his hands the weight of her dress soaked in seawater. It was as if he'd experienced it himself: he could picture the resuscitation efforts of the first responders who rushed to the scene, the night sky she must have looked up at as she vomited the seawater she'd swallowed.

Mochizuki remembered walking along the same beach while holding his father's hand as an elementary school kid. Once, they'd stumbled across some sea turtle eggs. There were ten in total when he'd counted. He'd wanted to incubate and observe them in their backyard, and he'd asked his father if they could. His father had responded that if they filled a plastic bag with enough sand that they could recreate the beach conditions, then it might be possible. Excited, Mochizuki had dug all the eggs out, but his father had cautioned him, saying it'd be too sad if the mother turtle returned to find all of her eggs missing, and persuaded him to put at least half of them back. But Mochizuki had wanted more than anything to see a turtle egg hatch in their own backyard, and the chances of that happening with ten eggs was much greater than with just five. He'd sat down in the sand as if throwing a tantrum in a toy store and refused to budge until his father relented and filled the bag with sand and all ten eggs.

Had that spot where he'd discovered the turtle eggs all those years ago been where this pregnant woman had lain gazing up into the sky, covered in her own vomit? Had she waded into the sea at that very spot expressly to lose her child in the waves? Mochizuki couldn't help but wonder.

As he got older, the sadness that the mother turtle must've felt out in the South Seas waiting in vain for her children to swim out to her pained him more and more. It was a sorrow he couldn't understand as a child but understood all too well now as a parent. Why hadn't his father scolded him more harshly and forced him to put those eggs back where they belonged? He even came to hate his deceased father a little for that. In the end, the eggs they brought home never hatched. They simply rotted.

Does this woman want to give birth, though?

The question came to him suddenly. A woman who wanted more than anything to have her child would obviously not attempt to kill herself while pregnant. Of course, if he still couldn't communicate with her, then they'd have no choice but to ensure the safe birth of her child regardless of her wishes. She would be transferred to an open ward for the duration of the pregnancy, then to the university hospital's maternity ward for the birth itself. If her consciousness remained clouded even then, the child would be temporarily placed in a baby-and-infant welfare institution. And if neither her family nor the child's father could be located, then the child would remain in the institution indefinitely.

Mochizuki noticed that he'd been staring at the woman's stomach, where her pregnancy was just starting to show. The dark ocean seemed to foretell the future of the baby growing inside her, and he felt his mood darken, too. The woman didn't seem to mind his gaze as she sat there with her hands folded loosely on her knees. But when she absentmindedly turned them palms up, Mochizuki couldn't help but catch sight of the bumpy brown scars running up her left wrist. He gently took it and lifted it up. The woman didn't resist in any way, even when he held her hand. The wounds looked relatively new—perhaps three or four months old, certainly not more than six. They were deep, and if they'd not been discovered immediately, she certainly would have died from blood loss. This wasn't the first time—she'd tried to take her own life at least once before. And judging from the depth of the wounds, it had been no mere cry for help.

It occurred to Mochizuki that perhaps he could identify her this way. He'd just have to look for her amongst patients who'd been brought to the hospital for a suicide attempt with a slit wrist in the past six months. It didn't seem like much work if he restricted the search to the Hamamatsu area.

But this was based on a preconceived notion. Right before walking into the sea, the pregnant woman had been dressed simply—she had worn a pair of white sneakers and a denim jumper dress. And since she carried no bag or wallet with her, Mochizuki assumed she'd come from somewhere nearby. But he was forgetting about something that had happened earlier. A patient suffering from schizophrenia had escaped Matsui Hospital and ended up in Tokyo three days ago. He, too, didn't carry a bag, wallet, or anything with him. Yet, he traveled almost three hundred kilometers before he was found. It was still unclear what modes of transportation he took to end up there.

In the end, the woman remained completely silent for the entire thirty-minute interview. There was no way to make a diagnosis. But now that he knew she'd tried to take her own life not once but at least twice, the open ward was out of the question, and she was transferred to a room in the locked ward so she could be monitored through the night.

2

The woman ended up spending only that first night under supervision before she was transferred to the open ward the next day. Her consciousness remained clouded, though, for the next two weeks. Mochizuki had treated patients who'd fallen into such states several times before, but compared to them, her mind seemed clear, and her condition wasn't as serious. For example, there was Tomoko Nakano, a patient who'd fallen ill two years ago and was still hospitalized. She failed to respond when spoken to, and her face registered no emotion at all. She couldn't go to the restroom or eat by herself, either. It was as if she had erased her feelings and was passively refusing to live. She'd been full-figured when she was admitted, but she had lost so much weight that by now, she was nothing more than skin and bones. Recovery seemed nowhere in sight, and she'd aged into an old woman in just two short years. There was nothing left to do but wait for her to die. It was certainly ironic seeing her return to a kind of infancy during this wait, wearing disposable diapers and having soft, easily-digestible food spooned into her mouth. Tomoko had once had a small daughter of her own. And just when her child had outgrown the need for diapers and could feed herself without help, she'd drowned during a moment of inattention on Tomoko's part—not in one of the bottomless swamps visible from the examination room window, but in a small reservoir near their home. Tomoko had blamed herself, crying out in sorrow and pain. As nightmares manifested and loomed inside her, she steadily lost her grip on her mental processes, and her psyche collapsed. So now, she wore the diapers her daughter had just stopped needing, as if out of nostalgia for their smell and feel. She wouldn't speak, laugh, cry, or even get angry. Her grief was so great that she'd had to eradicate every mental function—every desire and any capacity for love—in order to bear it. There was really nothing Mochizuki could do for someone with a psyche so frail. Medication didn't help, and as frustrating as it was, he could only slow the decline in her health. And even if she somehow improved, she had no one to rely on. Her husband had filed for divorce when he admitted her to the hospital, and by now he'd remarried and even had another child.

Mochizuki wouldn't be able to bear it if the young woman who'd been admitted two weeks ago ended up going down the same path. In her case, while she resembled Tomoko in that she didn't speak or express any emotion, she was able to use the restroom by herself, seemed to have a bit of an appetite, and took regular walks in the hospital courtyard. So there was reason to hope that something would trigger a sudden improvement in her condition.

Mochizuki was mulling these matters over as he walked through the breezeway connecting the open ward to the locked ward when he heard his name being called excitedly by a patient—one Takeshi Sunako.

Takeshi Sunako had been brought in ten days ago after an attempted suicide. His chart said he suffered from a neurotic disorder. He'd graduated from college at twenty-three and landed a job at an appliance manufacturer in Tokyo, but he'd ended up taking time off and coming back to Hamamatsu to stay with his family due to insomnia and a lack of appetite.

Takeshi had been hanging out in the breezeway, leaning against the wall, and watching the other patients playing croquet in the courtyard for the past hour or so. Their faces were slick with sweat, and they would straighten up to stretch their backs and dab at their brows with their towels. Takeshi didn't like sports, and he felt a distinct revulsion at the sight of the patients willingly breaking a sweat. Naturally, it hadn't occurred to him to join the game, and he was content to shelter from the mid-August sun under the breezeway's roof. He was reflecting on the events ten days ago that had led him here. Had he really wanted to kill himself? It was as if a stranger's hand had suddenly reached for the nape of his neck and pulled him toward the valley of death. The feeling of that hand had been so real, and it seemed to have had nothing to do with his own will—he hadn't thought of himself as someone who wanted to die. But perhaps this was how it felt for anyone on the brink of suicide. There was no reason to think he was a special case.

He didn't talk much with the other patients, so there was no one with whom he was particularly close. Time had passed so slowly when he'd first been admitted, but lately, it seemed like it would be time for lights-out before he knew it. Of course, lights-out here was rather early, but it was also because it took more time than he'd realized to contemplate the course his life had taken up till then.

Early that morning ten days ago, he had tried to bring that life to an end. He'd acted on impulse, but he remembered his own actions clearly enough. Dawn had yet to break when he'd left the house, driving out east in his father's car. He couldn't remember where he'd been heading. Judging from the direction, it seemed like he was returning to his apartment in Tokyo. Takeshi shook his head at the thought—that couldn't be it. There was no reason for him to return to that apartment. He'd felt so cornered and oppressed there. So where had he been going? Takeshi's head had been cloudy, a white blank. A little past four in the morning, the eastern sky had just begun to brighten when he'd flipped off his headlights. That much he remembered. He couldn't recall if he'd switched to parking lights or turned them off completely, but he did remember thinking it was rude to have his headlights blaring at the morning sun, and he had switched them off.

You don't have a place in this world.

He'd heard the voice distinctly, like a whisper in his ear. He stepped on the accelerator, and his range of vision narrowed as the dimness ahead slid by and disappeared behind him. He was driving up a gently sloping curve. As he crested the hill, the river of lights flowing down the Tomei Expressway spread out below him. The world seemed to have given him what felt like his due: nothing. *There's no seat for you to take.* Again, the voice whispered in his ear. Without quite realizing it, he'd drifted over to the left shoulder.

His car made contact with the guardrail and shook violently, making Takeshi cry out. He'd meant to release a long, loud scream, but his body was being rocked side to side so hard that all that emerged was a frog-like *ga ga ga ga*. The road then began to bend to the right, and there seemed to be no way he'd make the curve. But his car separated from the guardrail and Takeshi stomped on the brakes before he could collide with it again.

Having ricocheted off the guardrail and cut across the centerline, his car shuddered to a stop right as its nose smashed into the opposite rail. The car's battered body and the steam billowing up from beneath the hood attested to the severity of the collision. There was little traffic in that area at dawn, and Takeshi spent the next few moments passed out, his face against the steering wheel. Eventually, he heard the sound of sirens—someone must have called an ambulance. He seemed to have struck his face hard, and the knees of his jeans were wet with blood flowing from his nose. All things considered, though, his mood wasn't so bad. He tried to tilt his seat back so that he could go to sleep, but the rapidly approaching sirens kept him awake.

When the police asked him what had caused the accident, Takeshi told the truth.

"I heard a voice. Someone was whispering in my ear. I took my hands off the wheel just like it told me."

"Someone was in the passenger seat?"

"No, no. I was driving alone."

With his parents' consent, the paperwork to admit him was completed the same day. His injuries from the impact, fortunately, weren't serious, so the problems that remained were all mental. Anyone would reach such a conclusion from the evidence at hand. Takeshi was judged a risk to himself and others—that is, there was a suicide risk—and he spent his first night in the male wing of the locked ward.

Even as he absently watched the game unfold under the bright sunlight of the hospital courtyard, Takeshi found himself thinking back to the despair he'd felt that first night of hospitalization. He remembered not really understanding where he was. The room was cramped, and there was a rigid bed stuck in one corner and a simple squat toilet sprouting up from the floor. It felt like a holding cell. There were iron bars in the window. Takeshi gripped them with his hands and tried to shake them. They didn't budge. Suddenly, he was struck by sadness, an unspeakable loneliness… No, rather than loneliness, it was more like profound regret. The bars in his hands were cold, which somehow made him feel even sadder, and tears welled up in his eyes. Takeshi spent his first night weeping in his room.

This incomprehensible sadness didn't go away. The next morning, as the ward's locked doors opened and he stepped out into the courtyard, Takeshi burst into tears again, falling to his hands and knees on the grass-covered turf. How miserable he'd been. He couldn't forgive himself for trying to end his life at twenty-four—as if to prove how meaningless his life had been. Takeshi struck the dirt with his fist. The smell of the grass was fresh in his nose, and he saw countless ants crawling beneath him. Had his tears been sweet, surely even more would have swarmed from all directions, attracted by the scent.

Takeshi knew he'd never forget how he'd felt ten days ago, the tears he'd shed that evening while gripping the iron bars in his room and then again while kneeling on the courtyard lawn the next morning. He still thought about it now. Was the feeling that had welled up inside him, that unnameable emotion that wasn't exactly sorrow, anger, or remorse, rooted somewhere deep in his body? Was it something that had slept within him since before his suicide attempt, or had it boiled up all at once out of nowhere? It frustrated him that he couldn't figure it out. For it meant he wasn't free, that he was still bound to it. He had no confidence that he'd make it after being discharged. He held Mochizuki, his supervising physician, in high esteem—Takeshi knew he was a kind and broad-minded doctor. But even this great doctor had failed to impart a hope strong enough to banish Takeshi's death wish for good. And Takeshi knew why. He needed more than anything to experience, if even just once, the deep love of a woman.

At that moment, his ears were touched by a melodious humming. It had been going on for a while, but it was like a distant sound rising from the depths of his consciousness, and he only just became aware of it.

It was a clear, resonant female voice wordlessly humming a melody. Takeshi looked around at the faces near him, searching for who it might be. The melody seemed to correspond to a song buried deep in his memories. He was sure he'd heard it before.

Then, it came to him. He realized where the song was from. Memories linked to music tend to root themselves deep in the heart, and the melodies act as a trigger to evoke the old recollections. And just like that, memories from six years ago came to life in Takeshi's mind.

He'd been a junior in high school when he'd first heard this song on the radio.

It had been the end of July, the first week of summer vacation, and Takeshi had heard this song on the radio at the same time every day. In the evening, he recalled. He couldn't remember the name of the program, but it had a Song of the Week feature introducing new artists who'd just debuted, which was why the same song would play at the same time for a week. It was an earnest, ardent love song that expressed exactly what had been in Takeshi's own heart, and it had left a deep impression on him. He had a date planned that weekend with his girlfriend, who happened to be his first crush. Listening to the song as he imagined the good times he'd have with her, he grew more and more carried away, and his banal surroundings shimmered with beautiful colors by the end of the week. To make sure his first date would go smoothly, he even made a reconnaissance mission to the park: this was where they'd drink tea, that bench by the lawn was where they'd sit, this was the joke he'd tell to make her laugh, and that was how he'd casually ask for a second date... While humming the song on the radio, Takeshi drew up a remarkably detailed blueprint of their date in the back of his mind. It was a week filled with anticipation, love, and excitement for his future, and this song brought it all back. In the end, things didn't work out with his girlfriend. But even though it didn't turn out the way he'd hoped, he never forgot how he'd felt for that one lovely week.

Hearing it now in the hospital courtyard, the melody was slower and not filled with the same passion as when he'd heard it six years ago. But he knew it was the same song. Takeshi wondered if it carried a precious memory for the woman just like it did for him—he hoped that it'd spark a conversation with her. The song wasn't a big hit. It had played as the Song of the Week on a commercial broadcast station for seven days, but he'd never heard it anywhere else. He hadn't seen the singer on television, either. Takeshi was overjoyed to discover a fellow patient humming a song that had only played briefly on the radio. Six years ago, the world had been so much brighter, and this woman, wherever she'd been, must've been listening to the same program as he had. And this song must have burned itself into the bottom of her soul, attached to some special memory or feeling. Thinking of the two of them listening to the same song at the same moment in time, Takeshi unexpectedly teared up.

He moved away from the wall he'd been leaning against and walked a few steps down the breezeway before he stopped to scan the courtyard with his eyes. The patients played croquet with a certain languor, and they were watching the balls roll along their paths without raising their voices or getting too excited. There were two benches on the opposite side of the yard, and three patients were sitting on them, immersed in conversation.

Walking a little farther brought into view the flowerbed next to Ward One. And it was from the lawn surrounding the flowerbed that the sound of the humming seemed to emanate. His eyes soon picked out the voice's owner—it was someone he'd never seen before. Her face was pale, and she was singing to herself with downcast eyes and her head slightly tilted. She seemed to be around the same age as Takeshi. Sitting on the grass with her arms around her knees, she was tracing something on the ground with her finger. Humming as her hand moved over the grass, she would occasionally lift her head toward the sun and close her eyes to bathe in its radiance.

Takeshi gathered up his courage and walked toward her. Striking up a conversation with a woman he didn't know was no easy task. He wanted to at least ask her name, but once he'd approached where she sat humming, he found, as he looked down at her downcast face, that he had no idea how to proceed. While he stood there paralyzed, he began to hum the same melody without quite realizing it.

The woman raised her head and looked up at him. Seeing her face straight on, Takeshi was shaken. Was this what they call love at first sight? Even as she watched Takeshi hum the same song that danced on her lips, the woman's expression didn't change at first. But after some time, as Takeshi sang the melody again and again, her expression softened, as if she was slowly opening up to him. It was still a bit awkward, but Takeshi began to smile back. He could feel something bursting up from the depths of his body, and for the first time in a while, the tears he'd shed ten days ago were banished from his mind.

"Doctor!" The voice called out to him again, and Mochizuki stopped in the breezeway. He turned to see Takeshi Sunako approaching, looking more animated than the doctor had ever seen him before. Even more surprisingly, he was humming some sort of melody.

"Doctor! Would you happen to know this song?"

Takeshi asked this with a certain respectful bashfulness.

"Song?"

Takeshi hummed the refrain one more time. It didn't seem like a famous tune. Mochizuki smiled. "I don't think I can place it."

"Look over there. See the young woman sitting on the grass?" Takeshi guided Mochizuki to a spot where she was visible. "Would you happen to know her name?" he asked.

Mochizuki didn't quite understand what was going on, but Takeshi's explanation and his uncharacteristically bright expression piqued the doctor's interest. "Why don't we go talk in the tea lounge?"

There was a space for refreshments in the center of the ward building that was shrouded in tobacco smoke. Patients in this hospital, male and female alike, tended to smoke.

Mochizuki took a cigarette from his pocket and offered it to Takeshi, but he refused it with a wave of his hand.

"So you talked with her?"

Mochizuki cocked his head, smoke wafting up from his mouth. Takeshi seemed to be sitting up straighter than ever before.

"No, I failed to converse with her."

Takeshi's oddly stiff language revealed something of his character.

The night Takeshi was first admitted, Mochizuki had happened to be in the nurses' station observing his room from the surveillance camera display. As a suicide prevention measure, patients were monitored via the cameras installed in the corners of their rooms. As Mochizuki watched, Takeshi acted as if he didn't know where he was. It was common for patients to be disoriented on their first day of hospitalization. Takeshi looked around his tiny room and eventually grabbed the iron bars in the window, trying to shake them. Then, he seemed to have finally understood where he was, and he dissolved into tears. The surveillance camera barely picked up the subtle shaking of his shoulders, but Mochizuki could tell he was crying. He wept not so much because he was sad that he'd ended up in a psychiatric hospital, but because he felt helpless toward life itself. In that moment, the twenty-four years of Takeshi's life flowed into Mochizuki's mind. The skinny frame of this young man as he tried to shake the iron bars seemed too frail to bear the weight of his life. Mochizuki suddenly understood the nature of his pain, his despair. There wasn't a specific trigger that had prompted him to kill himself. His problem was his seriousness, his heavy sense of responsibility, and his inability to let go of small things that bothered him. Even if he understood intellectually that he needed to be a little more thick-skinned and confident in order to live a more carefree life, it was impossible for him to be like that. The past twenty-four years must have passed without major incident, like a flat sea unruffled by storm or strife. He likely had never dated nor felt the true love of a woman. And he probably hadn't struck out on a true adventure or walked boldly down a path he'd chosen entirely by himself, either. Mochizuki had heard the general story from his parents: he'd entered the college his mother had wanted him to and picked the department that seemed like the most natural choice. Then, he went through the motions of however many farcical interviews before ending up hired by an appliance manufacturer. As soon as he was assigned to the sales department, though, he began experiencing insomnia and a lack of appetite. Finally, he failed to come into work at all, spending day after day shut up in his room. Looking at Takeshi's tears, Mochizuki felt them fall deep within his own heart. As an adult man still riven with guilt for stealing a clutch of turtle eggs from their mother, Mochizuki saw in the younger man a kindred spirit.

"So you didn't actually exchange words with her."

Mochizuki muttered disappointedly to himself. But knowing she'd been humming a song was already a victory. Just like how people with amnesia still knew how to talk, they could also remember music they'd listened to or sung several times in the past. It was also relatively common for patients with aphasia to retain their sense of music. So this was precious information.

"Can you sing it for me again?"

At Mochizuki's request, Takeshi straightened in his seat and began humming the melody, a determined look on his face. Mochizuki shook his head. He'd never heard the song before.

"Who sings it, do you know?"

Takeshi waited until he'd reached an appropriate place in the music to stop before he answered.

"Actually, I don't know the name of the song or the singer."

"But you remember the melody?"

"Yes," Takeshi answered, and then explained why he recalled the melody so clearly.

"I see..."

Mochizuki nodded as he listened, but he remained dubious. To remember a song that only played briefly on the radio six years ago, it would indeed have to be connected to a lasting and impactful memory. He understood how it had happened to Takeshi, but it seemed like too neat of a coincidence for the same thing to have happened to the woman, too.

"Who is she, Doctor? What's her name?"

"You know, I can't..."

"Surely, just her name would be okay."

"That's the thing. I have no idea what it is."

Takeshi's expression hardened, his jaw thrusting out. It was his turn to be dubious.

"When you say you don't have any idea..."

Mochizuki gave Takeshi a short summary of the woman's situation: that she'd been admitted two weeks ago, and that she remained unidentified and unresponsive.

"No one's filed a missing person report?"

"We haven't heard anything from the police, so it's possible no one has."

"I see..."

Takeshi let out a sigh. Her situation seemed significantly more serious than his. While his mother was a pain, she was the overprotective type who'd file a missing person report if he disappeared even for just one night.

"Doctor, promise you'll tell me her name if you find out what it is."

He said this with a grave expression on his face. Mochizuki knew well the importance of concern for others. Interest in the opposite sex was a good barometer of mental health as well.

"Understood. As long as it doesn't interfere with her treatment."

"Thank you for indulging my request."

Takeshi bowed at a perfect forty-five-degree angle and said, "Please excuse me." Midway through his departure, though, he stopped and turned back, his expression now oddly childlike.

"I wonder... Is there a patient here who knows about such things?"

"Such things?"

"Japanese pop music."

There were many patients in the hospital who possessed some kind of special skill or expertise, and Mochizuki often found himself rather taken aback by their talents. It seemed that Takeshi was beginning to realize this as well.

"You might be right. There's Tomita, for example, in the open ward. He listens to the radio all day, and people say he knows everything about the music world."

"Perhaps it wouldn't hurt to ask..." muttered Takeshi.

"Ask what, exactly?"

"Ah, it's been bothering me that I can remember how the song goes but not its name or the singer... Maybe he can help me with that."

Mochizuki laughed.

"Well, if you figure it out, please let me know. We can share our findings with each other."

Takeshi nodded and returned Mochizuki's smile. "Please excuse me," he repeated, then bowed and walked away.

What a polite young man. He seemed to have nearly recovered his mental wellbeing. Mochizuki thought perhaps he should discuss a discharge plan with him and his parents within the next few days.

He stubbed out his half-finished cigarette in the alumite ashtray and stood up. As he did, a new doubt suddenly arose in his mind.

Did Takeshi not notice that she's pregnant?

3

Tomita never took off the headphones connected to his cassette player, not even during dinner. He tended to hum along with the songs on the radio, which meant he also tended to dawdle over his meals, irritating the kitchen staff.

Takeshi quietly sat down next to Tomita and waited for a good moment to speak to him. Since he seemed to be enjoying the music, Takeshi couldn't help but worry if it'd be bad to interrupt him. Tomita was a small-framed man who looked around fifty, and Takeshi didn't know what had brought him here. Chubby and round-cheeked, he didn't have the air of someone suffering from depression. Was it alcoholism? Takeshi busied himself with guesses as he worked up the nerve to break the ice.

"Excuse me, sir, forgive me for bothering you while you're listening to the radio..."

As always, Takeshi's approach was painfully polite. Still humming, Tomita turned and studied Takeshi from head to toe. Then, without a change in his expression, he simply looked back ahead and stopped humming. An awkward silence ensued. Takeshi felt his body stiffen as it stretched on. *I'm not going to get anything out of this guy,* Takeshi chided himself. *And now, I lost the chance to stand up and leave!* As long as Tomita failed to respond, Takeshi felt unable to either say anything or excuse himself. His anxiety ratcheted higher and higher.

"You want something?"

Without warning, Tomita removed his headphones. Takeshi relaxed his posture and closed his eyes, letting out a sigh of relief.

"Nothing big, it's just that Dr. Mochizuki told me you're very knowledgeable about music..."

"And?"

"So there's this song that I know the melody of, but I don't know the name or the singer..."

"Sing it."

Takeshi looked around, then began to sing. Acutely aware of the other patients sitting around them in the cafeteria, his voice grew softer and softer.

"Can't say I know it," said Tomita rather dismissively. "You sure that's how it goes? Maybe I don't recognize it 'cause you're tone deaf."

"Um, please don't worry, it's all right if you don't know it..."

At this point, Takeshi just wanted to leave.

"Hold on a sec. Here, let me show you something."

After the rather condescending lead-in, Tomita leaned over and whispered a command into Takeshi's ear. "Go over there and bring me that notepad, will you?"

"Notepad?"

"Yes, yes, the notepad. And a pencil, too."

Irritated, Takeshi nonetheless did as he was told, fetching the paper and pencil and bringing them to Tomita.

"Where did you hear this song of yours?"

"Six years ago, it was a Song of the Week on the radio."

"Okay, write down the dates you heard the song on this paper."

"I don't know the exact dates."

"Whatever you remember."

Takeshi wrote, *Six years ago, during the last week of July.*

"Now write down any lyrics you remember."

Takeshi could only recall fragments.

...In the mirror...your back to me...don't turn around...if only the light were stronger... Where have you gone? You're so cruel... That was about it.

"How does this look?"

Tomita brought the paper so close to his face that he looked ready to lick it. Quite a case of nearsightedness, it seemed.

"That's it?"

Takeshi inhaled as Tomita spoke and wrinkled his nose at the stench. He held his breath.

"I'm sorry."

Tomita waved the paper in his hand. "Well, let's give it a try."

"Give...what a try?"

"We're gonna put it in the mailbox."

Takeshi had no idea what Tomita was talking about. *I knew this would be a waste of time.*

"Are you in a hurry?"

"...Sorry?"

"I'm asking you! Are you in a rush to know the name of the song and who sings it?"

"Oh, well... Yes... Of course..."

"All right, then let's get to it."

"U-Um, get to what, exactly?"

"You're gonna write this information down on a postcard and put it in the mailbox."

Takeshi suddenly felt quite silly. He realized what Tomita was going to say next: that if he wrote his question on the postcard and put it in this special mailbox he knew, he'd get an answer. In other words, it was a delusion, a convenient system that only existed in his mind. He might even call it his god. Takeshi imagined himself clinging to a god someone had dreamed up and felt an awful revulsion at the ridiculous farce of it all. Not knowing what to do, he simply remained silent.

"So tell me, what is this song to you, anyway?"

"Oh, it's nothing..."

Tomita was short enough that his legs swung free beneath his seat, and he used one now to kick Takeshi on the shin.

"Huh? What do you mean by that?"

"Ah, it's just, well..."

"Listen. If you have a memory associated with this song, write it down. Be as dramatic as you can. They like that."

There seemed to be nothing left to do but see this through to the end. The singer at the time had probably been around seventeen or eighteen, so Takeshi added that to what he'd written on the notepad.

"You must have more than that."

It looked like Tomita wasn't going to let Takeshi off easy. Resigning himself to his fate, Takeshi wrote that the song likely played around the time of the singer's debut, and that she'd released two singles, and then seemingly disappeared from the entertainment world altogether.

Tomita looked at what he had written, then patted him on the shoulder and said, "Guess that'll do. I'll take care of the rest." He then ripped off another piece of paper and carefully wrote the digits one, six, two, and nine on it.

"Tonight at six, tune into this AM station and see what happens."

With that, Tomita put his headphones back on. The conversation was over, and he didn't look in Takeshi's direction again even once.

After dinner, Takeshi returned to his room. The note Tomita had handed him was folded in his pocket. The numbers written on it did look like a radio frequency. Figuring that his first encounter with the song happened by chance on the radio, Takeshi decided not to dismiss Tomita's suggestion entirely, and when six o'clock rolled around, he tuned his radio as instructed. As he listened, the program switched to a Songs We Remember format wherein the hosts would read aloud postcards sent in by listeners describing memories associated with certain songs. If the listener didn't know the song title or artist, the radio station staff would make it their mission to figure it out from the information on the postcard. Their retellings of these investigations were rather amusing and interesting, and it was the detective work, rather than the songs themselves, that seemed to be the main meat of the program.

To his surprise, Tomita had told him exactly how he could

search for the name and singer of the song lingering in the back of his mind that he couldn't place. He felt ashamed of having written him off as delusional.

The next day, Takeshi bought a pack of thirty postcards and wrote different accounts of his memories on each one, carefully leaving some time between them as he sent them out. He had the feeling that spreading them out, rather than sending them all at once, would make it more likely for one of his postcards to be picked.

Takeshi spent the next three days watching over the woman, sometimes from afar, sometimes after summoning up his courage and sitting down next to her. He knew his discharge was imminent, so he resolved not to waste any moment he had left. And while he tried his utmost to bring a smile to her face, communication was as impossible as ever. Humming the song would soften her expression slightly, but not to the point of actually smiling. Left with no other option, Takeshi made do with sitting beside her and talking about himself: about his high school days, his time at university in Tokyo, his work at the appliance manufacturer after graduation, his terror of dealing with clients, and his eventual dread of going to work... The woman listened without nodding her head, allowing the conversation to be completely one-sided. Takeshi began to feel heavy-hearted as the stories he had left to tell approached the present day.

When and how did life take such a dark turn?

During high school, things had still been good. Even when he was preparing for entrance exams, he didn't remember feeling particularly anxious about the future, and he had fun hanging out with his friends. It was partway through his first year of college that things got rough. He didn't know what had changed, but that was when he began to retreat further and further into his shell.

While glancing sideways at the woman who would sometimes start humming to herself out of the blue, Takeshi found himself comparing their situations. Something in her past must've triggered her mental decline, too. He wanted, if he could, to find out what it was.

Every evening at six o'clock, Takeshi turned on the radio. His chest swelled with anticipation at the thought that this might be the night they played his request. He wanted more than anything to find out what he and the woman might have shared six years ago. He knew how inadequate his current memory was—all he remembered was the melody and some scraps of lyrics. But if he knew the title, he might be able to put his hands on a copy of the song itself. Then it would be his, truly his... It felt like a chance to regain his old self from those bright days six years ago, a chance to get to the heart of what he had lost. And so, as if clinging to a lifeline, he listened to the radio at the same time every night.

Takeshi was discharged after two weeks of hospitalization. The reason for his rapid improvement, Mochizuki thought, lay not in the medication he'd prescribed, but rather in the young man's reawakened interest in the opposite sex after six long years. Because of that, he had regained the energy to live. "Feel free to come back anytime," Mochizuki half-joked to his patient as he walked him out of the hospital.

Takeshi now spent his days relaxing in the room where he'd lived until graduating from high school. His mother, worried about her only son returning to his job in Tokyo, was reluctant to let him leave. His boss had told her that they'd keep his post open so he could take all the time he needed to recover. But she was unwilling to let him live somewhere out of her sight again. What she really wanted was for him to find a new job in Hamamatsu. Takeshi, though, wasn't ready to decide on his future just yet. For the first time in his life, he was allowed to spend every day doing nothing in particular.

Every night at exactly six o'clock, Takeshi switched the radio on. Counting the postcards sent from the hospital, he'd probably mailed in over a hundred by now. His accounts of the memories he associated with the song grew more and more dramatic, and he even tried changing his style of writing to grab the reader's attention. Perhaps due to this embellishment, or perhaps just by chance, the day he'd been waiting for arrived. On a Tuesday near the end of August, he heard the host say, "Takeshi Sunako from Hamamatsu." Takeshi froze where he sat, straining to listen with every fiber of his being as the host read out the memory he'd written on the postcard. It was strange to hear the words coming out of someone else's mouth, as if the memory was someone else's as well. The host boasted about the hard work the staff had put into finding the song using the fragmented lyrics and the fact that an unknown radio station had featured it as a Song of the Week in July six years ago. And then, finally, the host went on to introduce the artist.

Sayuri Asakawa, the singer-songwriter, had indeed been eighteen at the time of her debut. She released her first single, "In the Mirror," and a follow-up titled "Lovecat," then disappeared completely from the entertainment industry. Some time later, she apparently joined a small theater troupe, but never attracted much public attention in that world, either...

Takeshi hurriedly grabbed a pad of paper and began taking notes, writing down the names of the singer, the song, and the record company.

After that, they played it: the song Sayuri Asakawa wrote herself, "In the Mirror." It felt so nostalgic to listen to. Yet, the fresh, youthful voice of this eighteen-year-old singer sounded somewhat different from the voice in his memory. Takeshi held his breath and listened intently as the first part of the song unfolded.

It was in many ways a typical love song. Two lovers wake up together in the morning, and the man goes to brush his teeth in front of the mirror. The narrator of the song sneaks up to him, admiring him from behind, and then notices that the fluorescent light behind her is casting her shadow faintly onto his back. The lover begins to turn toward her, but she blurts out, "Don't turn around!"

This was the story told in the opening verses. It overflowed with the emotions of a young woman trying so hard—pathologically hard, even—to protect the fragile love between them. Rather than painting an optimistic picture of their future, the songwriter chose instead to over-emphasize the uncertainty in their relationship. The narrator in the lyrics saw even the slightest coincidence as a sign of luck, and she took it upon herself to protect it. That morning, her shadow falling incidentally onto her lover's back seemed to symbolize the future of their union, and she had to preserve it at all costs.

Takeshi wondered if the singer-songwriter Sayuri Asakawa had been inspired by the Greek myth of Orpheus and his wife Eurydice. Orpheus followed his wife into the Underworld after her death, charming the gods there with the beauty of his music. The gods then agreed to let him lead Eurydice back out, provided that he never glanced back at her until they'd both emerged into the land of the living. But Orpheus couldn't resist the temptation to look at his wife, turning back just steps away from the exit, and Eurydice was dragged back into the Underworld once and for all. The tragic scene of Orpheus losing his beloved wife forever must have flashed in the narrator's mind as she cried out to her lover not to turn around.

This was what Takeshi was musing over when the song reached its end. The singer hummed the refrain over and over again as the music faded out, and he suddenly sat up from his habitual slouch at the sound of her voice. Sayuri Asakawa sounded exactly like the woman at Matsui Hospital. The music now ended, and the program shifted to another segment. Takeshi hurriedly flipped the switch to turn the radio off.

He compared the voices in his mind again and again. They really sounded similar. It even began to seem more likely to him that the woman he'd met at the hospital was Sayuri Asakawa rather than someone who happened to know the same song as him. After all, that song had only played for a brief time on a radio station, and it had to be a big coincidence for him to bump into someone like that in the tiny space of a hospital.

The more he thought about it, the surer he became. It didn't seem like a flight of fancy or a delusion—it was as if he could actually hear the pieces of the puzzle click into place. He decided to return to the hospital as soon as possible, perhaps even tomorrow, to discuss his revelation with Mochizuki.

If she really was Sayuri Asakawa, how had this eighteen-year-old singer who sang her love song with such a clear and beautiful voice become, in six short years, a nameless woman attempting to take her own life, a woman who seemed to have no one around to look for her or even notice she was missing? Takeshi was all the more intrigued by what might have happened. Surely, it had to be something much more terrible than anything that had happened to him. How else to explain such a drastic change in circumstance? Takeshi, for a third time, felt ashamed of his own weakness and the trivial reasons for his suicide attempt. And he found himself consumed with the need to know what had happened to this woman.

4

Takeshi went to Matsui Hospital to meet Mochizuki the next morning at ten. Ostensibly a trip to get his prescription refilled, his true purpose was to report his speculations from the previous evening.

He waited until noon to grab lunch with the doctor. Instead of the hospital's tea lounge, they went to a hip café that was about a two-minute walk away. The place was bustling with activity and crowded with white-collar workers who had flooded out of the offices nearby. Around when they'd both finished their meals and were contemplating getting coffee, Takeshi gradually steered the conversation away from his own situation and toward the woman.

"Have you found out anything about her condition?"

Mochizuki had to admit that he sometimes found talking with Takeshi trying. For example, he obviously had something he wanted to discuss today since he'd gone out of his way to arrange this meeting, and while he could've just cut to the chase, he'd spent all their time talking about anything but that. It got on his nerves. But what irritated him even more was to be asked about the condition of this particular female patient, whose consciousness remained clouded. Examining her thus far had revealed that whatever was ailing her wasn't caused by a blow to the head or any other kind of external injury. There were no significant abnormalities in her brainwave patterns, and it was extremely difficult to narrow down her diagnosis—was it a neurotic disorder like hysteria? Catatonic schizophrenia? Depression? For his part, Mochizuki suspected that it was a psychosomatic clouding of her consciousness, technically closer to obtundation than stupor. But she could also have been suffering from schizophrenia, perhaps even before her suicide attempts, and it was hard to determine a proper course of treatment in the absence of any background information. And indeed, there had been no progress on that front, either. Her identity remained as much of a mystery as ever. So no matter how many times Takeshi pressed him for details, Mochizuki had nothing to tell him. And it always put Mochizuki in a bad mood to have to voice a pessimistic view—not to mention that it injured his pride as a physician not to be able to even give a name to her ailment.

Mochizuki grimaced and took a sullen sip of his coffee, and Takeshi, noticing the change in the doctor's demeanor, hurriedly apologized.

But this meaningless apology only irritated Mochizuki more.

"Why are you apologizing?"

He tried to keep the harshness out of his tone, but there was still an edge to it.

"I shouldn't have asked something that was none of my business..."

In lieu of responding, Mochizuki simply checked his watch.

"Um... To tell the truth..."

Prodded by Mochizuki's impatient behavior, Takeshi blurted everything all at once—that the previous night, the song of a singer-songwriter named Sayuri Asakawa had played on the radio, and that her voice had sounded extremely similar to the female patient's. Takeshi was trepidatious at first, worried that there was no way Mochizuki would entertain such wild speculations. But his apprehension disappeared as he continued talking, for Mochizuki was leaning almost all the way across the table as he became more and more absorbed in Takeshi's tale.

Mochizuki was thinking about his other patient with a clouded consciousness, Tomoko Nakano, as he listened. The image of her unresponsive figure lying in her hospital bed appeared in his mind. Her condition was much worse than that of the younger woman—she was virtually bedridden and unable to feed or relieve herself without a nurse's assistance. Yet, he had seen her many times tapping her fingers rhythmically on the white sheets of her bed. Mochizuki knew right away what he was seeing: Tomoko had studied piano since she was four years old, eventually graduating from music school, and during the eight years between getting married and giving birth to her daughter, she'd given piano lessons to the children in her neighborhood. *She must be teaching piano to her deceased daughter somewhere in her clouded mind*... He remembered being so sure of this when he observed the weak movements of her fingers. It was no rare thing, after all, for daily routines and habits to suddenly resurface.

In this case, it was obvious that the song the younger woman kept humming had some sort of outsized significance for her. It was probably a song that she'd sung repeatedly at some point in her life. If she'd been a singer and this song had been her debut single, it made sense that it would end up engraved deep in her heart. Amnesiacs usually don't forget how to speak or drive, and in the same way, this song must have worn a groove somewhere in her consciousness that allowed it to surface even in her present condition.

Mochizuki thus thought it deserved careful consideration whether the woman currently living in the open ward was indeed the same person as this singer-songwriter named Sayuri Asakawa, who'd debuted six years ago at the age of eighteen. She was a bit gaunt at the moment, but it was easy to imagine her as a former idol.

"So what do you think, Doctor?"

Mochizuki pulled back from the forward-leaning posture he'd fallen into and rested his head against the back of his chair as he looked up at the ceiling. Takeshi waited for the doctor's opinion, but all Mochizuki provided was an inarticulate, "Hmm..."

The idea that the woman's identity could be found in such an unexpected way surprised, even appalled, Mochizuki. Nothing had turned up when he checked with the police and other hospitals in Hamamatsu. So to think that all the pieces—from her nonchalant humming to the open-ward patient Tomita's idea of sending in a request to a radio show—could fit together so neatly and yield such valuable information...

Finally, Mochizuki spoke.

"There's no way for us to confirm it, though. Even if we try to ask her, with the state she's in..."

"Um..."

Takeshi hesitated.

"What is it?"

"Would you like me to go to Tokyo and find out what I can about her?"

"You?"

Mochizuki was much too busy to run off to Tokyo to investigate unsubstantiated suspicions about a patient's identity. But if he had evidence connecting this patient with Sayuri Asakawa, he'd be willing to go through the trouble and make a trip to Tokyo. Moreover, he wanted to see for himself how effective it'd be if he, as a psychiatrist, could focus all his attention on the care of a single patient.

"Ah, I have other reasons to go, too. As you know, my apartment in Shimo-Ochiai is just as I left it. I need to go back, tidy up, and maybe vacate it soon. It's been bothering me for a while now. And I figured, since I'm going anyway, I could look into this, too."

Takeshi was careful not to let Mochizuki think he was going up to Tokyo solely to find out about her.

"What sort of lead do you actually have to investigate?"

"I have the name of the record company that put out her single."

Takeshi figured he'd be able to find at least one or two people at the record company who remembered her. Still, this was his only lead.

"But it's not going to be as easy as you think."

"That's okay. I have nothing to do, anyways."

Mochizuki thought that he should applaud the courage of someone as maladroit as Takeshi plunging himself into a morass of complicated human relationships. It wouldn't be a terrible thing for Takeshi to play detective, regardless of whether he ended up succeeding or not. Of course, if luck was with him and he did manage to find out something about the woman, then that would certainly help in her treatment. As it was, with everything in her background shrouded in impenetrable darkness—including her family, medical, and social histories—he had no way of even diagnosing her. But equally as important, it was also his duty as a psychiatrist to support Takeshi in his passion for helping this woman.

"Well, if that's the case, I think you should give it a try."

Mochizuki patted Takeshi on the shoulder, and he blushed, murmuring, "Okay."

"I'd really appreciate getting updates from you as you find things out..."

Mochizuki handed Takeshi his card, which had his home phone number and the hospital's fax number printed on it.

"Understood."

Takeshi almost leaped to his feet. He looked like he was going to head to the train station right there and then.

"Oh, wait..."

Mochizuki had noticed it was Takeshi's infatuation with this woman that was driving him. And if this woman really was Sayuri Asakawa, his investigation at some point would surely reveal her past relationships with men.

I should tell him now so it doesn't shock him later.

"You might not have realized it, but she's pregnant."

Loath to watch Takeshi's face darken with disappointment, Mochizuki kept his eyes on his now-cold coffee as he brought it toward his mouth. He then shifted his gaze even lower toward Takeshi's legs. The movement of his body rising from his chair seemed unusually slow. The way he placed his hands on the table and shifted to leave his seat from one side appeared awkward, too.

"Understood," Takeshi repeated once he stood next to his chair. His habitual slouch seemed worse than ever as he walked out of the café. His chin sunk into his chest, and he reached up to hold the rim of his glasses with his fingers.

The whole conversation left Mochizuki feeling somehow exhausted.

5

There were only four days left in August, yet the temperature in Tokyo was well over thirty degrees Celsius at two in the afternoon. It was still hot in Hamamatsu, too, but it always felt more stifling and uncomfortable in Tokyo because of the humidity.

Takeshi got off the train at the Shibuya JR station, then crossed National Route 246 and headed south on the road running alongside the railway. He was relying on the address that the record company had given him and checking the address signs on the utility poles one by one as he passed them. The man at the company had told him it was a five-minute walk from the station.

It took even less than that. The production office was a room in a six-story building next to the railway. The previous day, he'd ridden the train up from Hamamatsu right after his conversation with Mochizuki, and this morning, he'd visited the record company and gotten the address of Sayuri Asakawa's production company and the name of the person who'd been her manager.

"If you want to know about her, Miya at Ken Production's your best bet," the man had said and told him the manager's name was Miyagawa.

Things were moving quite fast for Takeshi. He'd been gripped by anxiety when he walked through the doors of the record company, and he was now feeling unnecessarily nervous as he ascended the stairs to the production office. Yet, he wasn't as horribly insecure as he usually was. He'd shown photos of the woman at the hospital to a mid-level employee at the record company and had found that she almost certainly was Sayuri Asakawa. He was happy that his suspicions were confirmed and was able to act rather decisively from there on. He wanted to uncover the truth as quickly as possible. The more he hesitated, the longer it would take. So he hurried up the three flights of stairs, willing to break a sweat if it meant he'd find something to report back to Mochizuki even one second faster.

The office was a mess. "Excuse me?" he said from the doorway, and a female staff member looked up from her work.

"Yes?" she answered.

"Mr. Maruyama at Columbia Records sent me. Would the manager named Miyagawa happen to be in today?"

Takeshi handed over his business card, as was his habit. It bore the name of the appliance manufacturer where he'd worked until a month ago. It was a small scrap of paper that made his voice and hands tremble whenever he held it up to people he met for the first time.

"Oh..."

The woman took the card, seemingly a bit befuddled to imagine the connection between a production company and an appliance manufacturer. "Miyagawa is at our studio in Nishi-Eifuku at the moment..."

"When do you think he will be back?"

"Well, yesterday he pulled another all-nighter, so I really can't say."

"I see."

Takeshi sighed.

"Um, would it be too much of a bother if I were to visit the studio in person?"

Takeshi asked this question rather hesitantly. Unfamiliar with the music world, he imagined the studio to be a place where people rushed about as if their pants were on fire. But the woman casually replied, "No, I think it'd be fine.

"Recording with Jun takes forever, so I'm pretty sure Miya's just waiting around bored."

"Is that so? If it's not too much trouble, could you let me know how I might get there?"

To Takeshi's surprise, his decisive behavior was paying dividends. The woman was sketching a map on a piece of paper, and as he peered over her head, he realized something. He'd been told this by several people multiple times in the past. The moral of the day seemed to be that before falling into a sea of anxiety, he should speak out and act. People weren't nearly as bothered by him as he typically assumed they were. He now saw that they were telling the truth.

Miyagawa was lying on the sofa, fast asleep in the lobby of Studio Attic in Nishi-Eifuku. The lady at the reception desk confirmed to Takeshi that this was indeed the manager he was looking for. He cautiously crept up to the sofa until he found himself standing next to it. The man had a receding hairline and was snoring lightly. For a short while, Takeshi simply stood there and looked down at him. He remembered the woman at the production company telling him that Miyagawa had pulled another all-nighter. The word "another" made it seem like he'd pulled one not just last night, but the night before that, and perhaps even the night before *that*... Takeshi grew steadily more apprehensive as he imagined the accumulated fatigue and the annoyance Miyagawa would feel if he was forcibly awakened after all those sleepless nights. He would be angry. He might even hit him. The tiny worry in his head escalated and grew into something close to terror. This was how it always went.

Takeshi debated a little longer on whether to call out to him, then gave up and sank into the adjacent sofa. The best way forward was simply to wait for him to wake up naturally. The moral of the day forgotten already, Takeshi sat there feeling disgusted by how weak he was.

The air conditioning was blasting in the lobby, and it was getting more cold than cool. Takeshi slipped on the jacket he'd been carrying with him. As he did, he reflexively slid his hand into the pocket and found the photos of the woman he now knew to be Sayuri Asakawa. There were six in total, and he took them out to look at them again. How many times had he stared at these photos since he'd been discharged from the hospital? They were all taken in the hospital's courtyard, though each featured a different pose. She looked lonely in every one. There was a picture of her leaning against a white wall, another of her sitting with her legs stretched out on the lawn. She looked like she'd just been plopped there when she sat like that. Her eyes would be unfocused, as if gazing off at something that wasn't really there. It made Takeshi all the more curious about what she was looking at. The future? The past? He was sure that once he figured it out, he could save her.

He was in love with Sayuri, even knowing it was completely one-sided. How many times had he fallen in love like this since being dumped by his first girlfriend? He would fall in love, get dumped, fall in love again, get dumped again, over and over.

His first date had been during the summer of his third year in high school, making him a late bloomer compared to his classmates. She'd been no great beauty or anything—just a plain, ordinary girl. The date he'd worked up the courage to ask her on had ended in utter disaster. She'd stopped speaking partway through, and Takeshi, not knowing why or what else to do, began apologizing. They'd parted awkwardly, and then, as soon as he got home, he'd called her. The girl simply answered the phone but didn't respond. Takeshi, once again, found himself apologizing. *If I say sorry, she'll forgive me...* He had no real idea what he had to apologize for, but it seemed to him that there was no other way to fix whatever had broken between them.

"Takeshi, being with you makes me so tired."

The girl, who had left him hanging for so long, blurted out these words and then hung up the phone. Takeshi couldn't understand how things had gone so wrong. He'd tried to be considerate of her feelings during the whole date. Enough that it had exhausted him. By contrast, she hadn't displayed any interest in his feelings at all. Yet she was complaining that he made her tired.

I'm the one who's tired!

Takeshi looked in the mirror. How did this happen? Nothing really stood out to him as he studied the narrow features staring back at him. Was this a face that tired people out? He opened his eyes wider and mussed his hair into a different shape. As he stared at himself, an intense feeling of disgust began to well up within him, and the sight of any part of himself became painful. The slender, delicate lines of his shoulders seemed less charmingly naive than just unhealthy. The longer he looked at himself, the more his will to live left him. And this was the first time he remembered asking himself the question that ended up haunting him ever since.

What's the point of you living?

"Isn't that...Sayuri?"

Takeshi heard a man's voice, and a bald head suddenly appeared in front of his face.

"I'm sure of it—that's Sayuri."

Miyagawa had apparently woken up at some point and was now looking down with bleary eyes at the photos in Takeshi's hands.

"Oh, I'm sorry, I didn't mean to wake you..."

As soon as he said it, Takeshi chided himself for apologizing. The man had obviously woken up by himself.

"Tell me, the woman in these pictures—that's Sayuri Asakawa, isn't it?"

Takeshi handed the photos to Miyagawa. He was grateful that he didn't have to begin the conversation himself.

Miyagawa leafed through the six photos and then, with a nostalgic look on his face, he flipped through them again, this time lingering on each one before moving to the next.

"Forgive me, I was just surprised. I didn't expect to see her face here..."

Miyagawa seemed reluctant when he handed them back to Takeshi.

Holding his business card up to Miyagawa, Takeshi quickly introduced himself. He explained that Sayuri was suffering from amnesia and was hospitalized in Hamamatsu at the moment. He then told Miyagawa that he had gotten his name from someone at the record company and that was why he was here at the studio. Saying that Sayuri had amnesia was to save him from describing the condition she was in. After all, it was impossible for Takeshi to explain all of it in detail.

"Amnesia? Did she hit her head or something?"

Miyagawa's expression was serious.

"No, I actually don't know the details."

"I see, but it's still a bit of a shock to see her here. How old is she now, by the way?"

Since she'd debuted right after graduating high school, Takeshi figured that she must be about a year older than he was.

"She should be twenty-five."

Miyagawa began muttering to himself, calculating something under his breath.

"So that would mean it's been six years. Dang, no wonder I'm getting old..."

Miyagawa rubbed his forehead. It had surely been covered with hair back when he'd been Sayuri's manager.

"Well, so, the thing is..."

Takeshi forced himself to get to the point.

"Oh, yes, of course. What do you need from me?"

"You see, the hospital's in a difficult position because she doesn't seem to have anyone looking for her. I was wondering if you would happen to know where her family might be?"

Miyagawa stared at Takeshi as he spoke.

"And you came all the way here from Hamamatsu?"

"Well, yes, but I had other business in Tokyo, so I thought I'd look into it while I'm here."

"I see." Miyagawa made a somewhat sullen face, then added, "The fact is, Sayuri's parents are no longer with us."

"You mean they passed away?"

"I'm afraid so."

It finally sunk in. Sayuri had no family, and that was why no one had filed a missing person report for her.

"If I remember right, her father died just after her debut."

"Was it an illness? An accident?"

"Hmm, how should I put it?" Miyagawa was strangely lost in thought. "Well, it seemed to be a suicide."

"Seemed to be? Does that mean it might not have been?"

"No, it had to be." Miyagawa shook his head with certainty. "It was suicide, no doubt about it. It wasn't an accident. It's just, there was no reason why he'd do it. And I heard he didn't leave a note."

Takeshi took out his notepad and held it in his hand. He felt like a magazine reporter.

"If it's not too much trouble, could you tell me more?"

If only we knew her family or medical history... Takeshi remembered Mochizuki's frequent lament. The fact that her father had apparently ended his own life seemed like an important thing to know about.

Miyagawa proceeded to share all that he knew about Sayuri Asakawa, and Takeshi jotted everything down in his notepad, careful not to miss even the smallest detail. He planned on summarizing it all into a report that he could fax to Mochizuki right away. Not only did he manage to identify the patient, but he also found information that shed light on her family background and medical history. Takeshi was itching to let Mochizuki know as he nodded along to Miyagawa's story.

6

Mochizuki finished the simple dinner he'd heated in the microwave and shut off the television. The otherwise empty three-bedroom apartment seemed all the lonelier without its noise. His wife and daughter were away, staying with his wife's family in Inazawa. Pressured by their daughter, who'd wanted to see her grandma one last time before the end of her summer break, his wife Naomi had suddenly announced the day before yesterday that they were going to Inazawa. Mochizuki's parents were no longer living, and his older brother, who'd taken over their family business and ran an internal medicine clinic in the city, had no children of his own. So it made sense that the home in Inazawa, where her grandma and three cousins lived, was a fun place to be for their only child. Neither Naomi nor Mochizuki had the heart to refuse her when she begged to go.

Mochizuki was holding the fax he'd received from Takeshi when he jerked his head up. He thought he'd sensed the elevator open at the end of the hallway leading to his door. He strained his ears, but they didn't detect the sound of high heels that should have followed. *I'm imagining things,* he thought, nestling back into the sofa and putting his feet up. Since a while ago, he hadn't been able to calm down. He couldn't figure out Akiko Nonoyama's true intentions, and he'd even tried soaking in the bath, but to no avail. It wasn't like he could call her house, so he'd been distracted, turning on the television only to turn it back off, pacing around the room, and trying to read the report. He would catch himself staring at his telephone, which doubled as a fax machine, willing it to ring. Sure, he'd been a bit drunk, but he still remembered what she'd told him the previous evening.

I'll call you tomorrow night.

He'd seen Akiko Nonoyama several times at the hospital during the day, but she'd remained impassive and mentioned nothing about last night at all. Mochizuki, for his part, lacked the courage to ask her and even felt foolish for wanting to know what she was thinking, so he'd let it be. But now, it was late, and he could feel his chest tighten. It had been twenty years since he'd last felt anything like this.

Two months had passed since Akiko Nonoyama had voluntarily transferred to Matsui Hospital from the Hamamatsu University School of Medicine, where she'd been working as a psychotherapist. She was thirty-three years old, married for four years, but had no children.

With her charming features and cheeks that dimpled when she smiled, Akiko seemed like the epitome of a good wife and wise mother. But Mochizuki could tell that she was a woman who would never be satisfied by her domestic life. In the midst of her psychotherapeutic sessions, there were times when she would be overcome with bouts of inexplicable anger. Faced with a recalcitrant patient, she would suddenly grow stonily silent. Running her hand through her long hair, she'd avert her eyes to spare her patient from seeing the rising irritation in them. Her expression would distort, and at times like that, she'd give off a sexual allure that was even more powerful compared to when she was calm. As a clinical psychiatrist, she was extremely knowledgeable and had an intuition that allowed her to choose almost instantly the best treatments for her patients. However, Mochizuki oftentimes couldn't help but wonder, as he observed her, if she was cut out for therapeutic work.

In any event, he couldn't deny his attraction to Akiko. There were times he found himself held in that defiant gaze of hers, completely absorbed by her wide and unblinking eyes. He'd forget to listen to what she was telling him and instead grow captivated by the hints of her body just visible through the white cloth of her uniform. His ears would block out her words, and his chest would grow full with the allure of her flesh.

He'd had a vague premonition that this would happen when she came to Matsui Hospital. Her presence piqued his interest for some reason. His domestic life had proceeded smoothly up till then, with nary a ripple in its placid surface, but Akiko possessed the type of charm that could blow it all apart. The moment he had first met her, he'd vowed to do whatever he could to prevent himself from succumbing to her spell.

But last night, this was the very woman with whom he'd gone out drinking until late in the evening. He'd had dinner with her and a female caseworker, who also worked at their hospital, and then someone had suggested drinks. They ended up sitting in a row along the curved bar of an American-style pub downtown: Mochizuki, the caseworker, and then Akiko. The women were having a discussion between themselves, and it began to grow a bit edgy all of a sudden. Akiko had said something rather nasty about a hospitalized patient, and the caseworker, provoked, had responded, "You're a bit of a wolf in sheep's clothing, aren't you?" Things escalated from there, and neither of them was able to keep their emotions in check. The argument became so heated that they began to attract the attention of the other pub patrons. In particular, the caseworker tried a few times to get Mochizuki to back her up, but he kept his responses noncommittal and vague, staying above the fray as he watched and smiled wryly at the two of them.

At one point, Akiko tried to get the caseworker to leave, saying, "I'm tired of your face. Why don't you just go home already?" Mochizuki didn't realize the element of same-sex rivalry in Akiko's aggression at the time, and he wondered why she wouldn't leave herself if she couldn't stand looking at the woman's face.

"If you don't want to be here, you're free to go." The caseworker didn't give in easily, however, and she made no attempt to leave her seat.

In truth, Mochizuki secretly welcomed the conflict between the two women. This caseworker who'd jammed herself between them was as much of a bother to him as she seemed to be to Akiko. He understood she was a sincere person, but bringing up work over drinks and asking this and that about patient care tired him out. If only the shower of insults she was receiving would offend her and make her leave! Then, he and Akiko Nonoyama could have some time alone. He feared that once it was just the two of them, he wouldn't be able to defend himself against her boldness and lose control. Yet, he remained quiet, and while he knew Akiko was the one being unreasonable for picking a fight, he found himself taking her side. The argument had started over an ethical disagreement about how patients should be treated, and judging from his usual conduct at work, Mochizuki should clearly have been on the caseworker's side—it was only natural that she'd look to him for backup. But Mochizuki kept his silence.

After a while, the caseworker got up to go to the restroom. Akiko followed her in, but then returned to her seat before the caseworker. From how quickly she'd come back, it was clear she hadn't actually needed to use the restroom. So why had she gone? It occurred to Mochizuki that she must have followed the caseworker so that she could say something to her and deliver the finishing blow. Akiko probably couldn't say it in front of him—it must have been something so extreme that anyone who overheard her would question her character. And indeed, the caseworker returned to her seat paler than before. She sat thinking and trembling for a few seconds with her bag resting on her knees before getting up again and muttering, "I'll go home now." Turning on her heel, she then headed for the door. Akiko, with a hard expression on her face, peered over her shoulder and watched the caseworker go. But when she turned back to look at Mochizuki, she was suddenly all smiles.

Pushing her hair back, she glanced up at him with big, innocent eyes that seemed to say, "Got rid of her good, didn't I?"

Mochizuki found himself both appalled and attracted by how

swiftly her expression changed. Lowering his voice for some reason, he asked, "Did you say something to her in the restroom?"

Akiko just giggled and replied, "It's a secret." As it should be, he reflected. After all, she'd walked all the way there because she didn't want to be overheard. It wouldn't make any sense if she told him now. And so he never learned exactly how she managed to get the caseworker to leave that night.

Akiko moved over to take the caseworker's seat, noisily dragging the long-legged barstool toward Mochizuki. They spent the rest of the evening shoulder-to-shoulder, talking about anything and everything until the pub closed.

"Should we get going?" It was close to midnight, and just when Mochizuki was about to rise from his seat, Akiko grabbed his hand tightly.

"When am I going to see you again?" she whispered in a low, intimate voice. Her eyes were opened wide, as usual, and filled with irresistible passion.

Almost reflexively, Mochizuki sputtered, "I'll be alone tomorrow evening." He had been determined not to fall into her trap, yet he was raising his foot to step into it himself.

"Okay. I'll call you tomorrow night," she replied, loosening her grip on his hand.

Returning to the train of thought that had been interrupted by the sound he had heard, Mochizuki looked down at the fax in his hand. It was Takeshi's report on Sayuri Asakawa. But every time he tried reading it, Akiko's image would flash in his mind, and he couldn't concentrate at all.

I should just say no.

He figured she would call him with a proposition to meet, and he steeled himself to refuse her. It would be easy. All he had to do was invent an errand to get out of it. But Akiko's relentless persecution of the caseworker the previous night haunted him, and he felt his resolve waver as he recalled her fervor.

Looking back down at the report, Mochizuki chewed the end of his ballpoint pen as he read on. He couldn't help but be impressed by the amount of information Takeshi had managed to dig up in just a single day. He felt certain that once Takeshi overcame his mental weaknesses, his abilities would allow him to rejoin society and do well in life. At any rate, Takeshi had succeeded in uncovering the identity of his female patient.

Mochizuki quickly scanned the first page of the report. The second page was a simple timeline, but at the moment, most of the entries were blank. The next step of the investigation would be to start filling those in, it seemed.

Born in November twenty-five years ago in Ota, Tokyo, Sayuri Asakawa was an only child. She lost her mother at a young age, and as she was graduating high school, she debuted as a singer under Columbia Records. Her second single was released that July, and she was touring the country on a summer campaign when she reportedly grew more and more depressed. According to her former manager Miyagawa, she would shut herself up in her hotel room and not eat her meals properly. Then, on the fourth of September, her father took his own life. Sayuri canceled the rest of her promotional tour and returned home, but perhaps due to the shock, she never resumed her singing career. Miyagawa claimed not to know the reason for her father's suicide, and Takeshi had made a note, saying, *I will have to ask Sayuri's father's former business partner, a person named Nagata, to find more details regarding this matter.*

So her father died of suicide... What did this mean? Mochizuki took the pen from his mouth and underlined those words. He knew it was an important clue that would shed light on the darkness in Sayuri's heart. Was the condition plaguing her now caused by her father's suicide? He had so many questions and so few answers. Like Takeshi, Mochizuki wanted to get to the bottom of this mystery as quickly as possible. But could they really discover the cause of her father's death six years later? The world was awash in new singers trying to break through. Even if a singer lost their father to suicide, the mass media surely wouldn't take much more than the most perfunctory notice. It'd be featured in the human-interest section of a newspaper at most. Mochizuki didn't know how Takeshi planned to continue his investigation, but he suddenly hoped he didn't end up entering a territory he shouldn't and harming himself irreparably.

Right then, his doorbell rang. Mochizuki startled, looking over at his phone, and then realized that it was indeed the doorbell. Shifting his gaze to the door, he could more or less guess who was standing on the other side. Akiko had told him she'd call, but ambushed him in person instead. The boldness of her showing up without making sure his wife and child were away angered Mochizuki. Throwing open the door with the intention of upbraiding her for her unannounced visit, his eyes fell upon Akiko Nonoyama as she stood there in the dim light of the hallway. The first thing that drew his attention was her hair.

She's got snakes on her head.

That was how it looked to Mochizuki. Akiko had twisted her long hair into braids and wrapped them around her head. He had the impression that once she unpinned them, they'd slither down like glossy serpents.

Mochizuki forgot the words that had been on the tip of his tongue and simply stood there, holding the door half open with his hand.

"Whoops—I'm here."

Akiko spoke in a whisper, her face breaking into a mischievous grin as she looked up at him. The unexpectedly childish expression on the face of a woman in her thirties threw him off balance, and he found himself returning her smile. Then, with his conflicted feelings still congealed into that smile, he invited her in.

7

Having faxed the report he had finished writing to Mochizuki, Takeshi headed to the bookstore in the shopping mall. He was looking for a book Miyagawa had told him about: *A Guide to the Theater Troupes of Tokyo.*

As the title suggested, it was a book that introduced Tokyo-based theater troupes with profiles, anecdotes, and lists of the core members. Takeshi found it among the periodicals and bought it right away.

Sayuri seemed to have been suffering from some sort of neurological condition since that summer six years ago that rendered her unable to continue her singing career. Miyagawa had looked pained when he talked about how miserable Sayuri seemed at the time. He must have felt for her, but above all else, as her manager, it must have been difficult watching the lucrative career he'd finally managed to discover and nurture fall apart before his very eyes. Sayuri had no choice but to give up on pursuing her dream of becoming a singer. Miyagawa assured her that if she ever felt up to it, she was always welcome to come back, but she never took him up on the offer. However, just half a year later, he saw her on stage in a production put on by a small theater troupe.

"It was ridiculous—she didn't even get a penny! Maybe she was there because of some man she'd met." Miyagawa's voice was filled with bitterness.

Had she recovered from her emotional wound and then ended up on stage, or had theater and trying something new been what helped her overcome the pain in her heart?

Since her relationship with the production company ended there, Takeshi had to look for the theater troupe she joined in order to find out what happened after that.

The Wind Theater Company.

This was where Miyagawa had seen Sayuri perform a singing role. However, the company no longer existed. Actors and production staff had started leaving the troupe until it split into two groups: Panic Theater and the Low Blood Pressure Theater. Miyagawa naturally didn't know which of these Sayuri had joined, so Takeshi was left with little choice but to investigate both.

He left the department store and went to a phone booth, then punched in the number for Panic Theater. A young woman answered.

"Excuse me for calling out of the blue like this… I was wondering if a woman named Sayuri Asakawa is a member of your troupe?"

"What?" The woman spoke loudly. "There's no one here by that name."

Takeshi felt like apologizing and hanging up right away, but he continued his inquiry. "This would have been about five years ago. I was told she played a singing role."

"Huh? I wouldn't know, I just joined the troupe this year."

If you don't know, why not just hand the phone to someone who does?

The woman's high, tinny voice began to irritate Takeshi.

"Perhaps I can speak with the director?"

"He's in rehearsals at the moment and not here. If it's an urgent matter, please call Space Ten in Kichijoji. The number is 0422-22-35XX."

The young woman said this in a manner that seemed well-rehearsed, almost as if she'd been told by her superiors to respond this way if anyone called. Takeshi confirmed the number and wrote it down. He was about to hang up when the woman's voice stung his ear once more.

"Oh! Wait a minute, are you talking about the woman who was an idol singer at Columbia Records?"

"You know her?"

"I knew it! I'd heard rumors, but they were kind of hard to believe. Who'd think a real singer would end up in a little troupe like this? I laughed when I heard it. What's her name again?"

"Sayuri Asakawa."

"Yep, that sounds right."

"So the director should know about her, right?"

"I think so, he's been here for a long time."

"Do you know what time rehearsals are over?"

"Ten o'clock."

"Understood. Thank you very much."

Takeshi hung up the phone. Kichijoji was only about thirty minutes away from Shibuya. Thinking it wouldn't do to interrupt their rehearsal, Takeshi decided to grab dinner first.

Truth be told, he felt a bit hesitant going. The very words "theater rehearsal space" conjured up preconceived notions of places where enigmatic and weird people gathered. And these young people, with thoughts and feelings completely different from his own, were able to perform love scenes in front of everyone without batting an eye, and sometimes even nude scenes... No matter how hard he tried, Takeshi couldn't imagine how anyone would be able to do such things. Their courage was inconceivable to him, and they became objects of envy—and fear.

Looking at the time, he decided it would be impossible to follow up with the other theater troupe that night as well. Or rather, his mental fatigue had reached the point that he knew poking his head into the Panic Theater rehearsal space would take all the energy he had left. It was clear that his character was unsuited to sales or business. But he'd never thought about it back when he was graduating from university. In fact, he'd never even considered what kind of work he *was* suited to. He'd just studied diligently until he managed to get into a third-rate university, a result that satisfied him at the time since he had done better than he'd expected. Thinking that things would work out one way or another if he put in the effort, he applied himself to his job and didn't voice a single complaint even when he found himself assigned to the appliance manufacturer's sales department. However, the more he met and pitched his company's products to people, the more resistance he felt within himself, less at the psychological level than the physical. His body felt sluggish, his appetite decreased, and he struggled to wake up in the morning. At first, he pushed himself and ignored these symptoms, blaming them on the heat as spring turned into summer. But in the space of only three months, he'd lost the ability to leave his apartment altogether and began skipping work without even calling in. All in all, it was obvious he wasn't suited to work in sales. Then what was he supposed to do now? As he threw himself into investigating Sayuri's past, he was probing into his own future as well.

Takeshi picked out an affordable place to eat in the restaurant area, and while he sat there waiting for his food, he thought about not only Sayuri but also himself. He felt a tingling sensation of affection well up within him as he wondered why he was starting to take an interest in his inner self now, of all times.

An aphorism-like thought formed in his mind.

People who don't care about others also don't care about themselves.

8

Akiko Nonoyama sat down on the sofa, crossed her legs, and pulled at the hem of her tight blue skirt. Her top was a short-sleeved blouse, and overall, it was a simple outfit. In her case, it didn't matter what she wore—as long as it fit, any clothing she chose only served to accentuate her allure. She seemed to know this about herself and pointedly avoided anything flashy.

"Would you like something to drink?" asked Mochizuki.

"I'd like beer." Akiko's response was immediate. It was a hot, humid night, and there were beads of sweat on the nape of her neck. Small pearl earrings shone from her earlobes like white, lustrous counterpoints.

As Mochizuki fetched the beer, Akiko picked up and started reading the fax lying on the table.

"And what do we have here? A love letter from your wife?"

Mochizuki was appalled by how rude she was not to ask before reading a fax—even one left out on the table—that was obviously addressed to someone else. "I thought you were going to call first," he said with reproach in his voice.

"I'm thirty-three. I don't have time to mess around."

Mochizuki forgot what he was going to say, momentarily baffled by the number thirty-three. He belatedly realized she was talking about her age, but he still didn't see what connection it had to her decision to come here without phoning first.

It wasn't like she was dodging the question—there was a clear connection and it made sense in her head. But Mochizuki, of course, had no way of knowing. He changed the subject to the fax in her hand.

"Seems like we now know the identity of my unresponsive patient."

"Singer-songwriter? Oh, she was a singer?"

"Looks like it."

"Who did this investigation?"

"I think you know him. Remember a patient named Takeshi Sunako? We discharged him about ten days ago."

Akiko thought for a moment, searching her memory.

"Ah, that guy who couldn't kill himself."

Mochizuki already knew Akiko was foul-mouthed. The fight last night with the caseworker was touched off by a similarly crass choice of words. As soon as her white coat came off, jokes and comments making fun of her patients seemed to fly in a constant volley from her lips. Mochizuki, goaded into a bit of psychotherapy himself, chalked it up to some form of frustrated desire. He was seized with a temptation to dig up and expose what was lurking deep inside her, and he found this even more titillating than the thought of her disrobing.

"You should watch your choice of words," Mochizuki said gently.

"Why? This is your home, not the hospital. We should be honest here."

Akiko didn't display the slightest hint of remorse. Kicking her crossed leg playfully, she thanked him for the beer and delightedly poured it down her throat.

Mochizuki studied Akiko. He was looking for a weakness in her as if she were an enemy combatant, though less to prepare for battle than to find a way to resist her...

"Don't look at me like that, Conscientious Assistant Director."

A conscientious psychiatrist. Akiko had come across those words in a book she'd read about Matsui Hospital. It was written by a former reporter at a major newspaper headquartered in Tokyo and was titled *Modern Psychiatry.* As the title implied, it was an examination of psychiatric care in the modern age. In the book, the author argued that the humanity of mental health professionals played a large part in the quality of hospital care, starting at the top with the director. It mentioned horrifying incidents, such as of nurses ganging up on and even killing patients, and also described a number of problematic hospitals. But these critical accounts of care were balanced by profiles of institutions whose practices were rooted in good conscience. In fact, the positive profiles made up about seventy percent of the book. Matsui Hospital ranked second among this "conscientious group" and was introduced in great detail. There were photographs of the director, Doctor Matsui, who had retired from Hamamatsu University School of Medicine to open the hospital, and of Mochizuki, the assistant director. Akiko first laid eyes on his picture more than two years ago, which meant she'd been familiar with Mochizuki's face and name well before her arrival at Matsui Hospital. The photo was actually quite a bit more flattering than the real thing, overflowing with the mesmerizing goodness of a principled doctor in his prime. The simple fact that he was featured with a photo in a book put out by a major newspaper was enough to inspire Akiko, who hailed from a tiny city like Hamakita. Though intelligent, Akiko had an oddly childish side that made her easily dazzled by fame and power. Despite being married, she'd carried a torch for Mochizuki and had counted the days till she'd have the chance to work at Matsui Hospital herself. And two months ago, her wish had finally come true.

Of course, Mochizuki had no clue about Akiko's calculations and never suspected that her sudden visit was the culmination of more than two years of machinations. If he'd known, though, it would have made things clearer. Akiko had looked at him with the glittering eyes of a predator locking in on its prey when they'd first met. Thinking back on it now, she had clinched her victory right there and then. To have a woman look at you with such passionate and alluring eyes—it was impossible to resist. The frankness of her interest, coupled with her beauty, would make any man fall into her trap. A sensible person probably wouldn't get involved if she weren't so flirtatious. Mochizuki, struck by her piercing eyes, had felt his entire body stiffen, and his heart had raced so fast that he was forced to look away.

Akiko softened her gaze and slowly looked up from the fax.

"He did a good job investigating all this."

"Yes, I'm impressed."

"Will it help in the treatment?"

"Of course."

"Why don't you sit down?"

Mochizuki was still standing next to the sofa, and Akiko beckoned him to sit beside her. The guest was now acting as the host.

Had Mochizuki spent the last two months secretly hoping for this turn of events? Leaving his fate to the gods, he sat down on the L-shaped sofa so that he was facing Akiko's right profile.

"Introduce your husband to me sometime."

He deliberately brought this up, hoping to remind her of her status as someone's wife.

Pressing the chilled beer against her cheek, Akiko answered, "I don't want to. He's pathetic." She took a sip, then continued.

"I'm too embarrassed. He's nothing I'd ever show off to anyone."

She spoke of him as if he was a piece of interior decor that didn't suit her taste. Mochizuki couldn't help but imagine that her husband, despite having such an attractive wife, found his domestic life unsatisfying.

"So, Doctor. Don't you think this Sayuri Asakawa woman is pulling one over on us?"

"What do you mean?"

"It's not like she can't speak. She's just refusing to."

"You think so?"

"That's how it looks to me, at least."

Perhaps Akiko meant that Sayuri was exercising what agency she had by refusing to engage with the reality she'd found herself in.

"Why would she do that?"

"Because she has nowhere else to go."

Akiko probably came to this conclusion after learning from the fax that she had no family.

"I mean, Matsui Hospital is a nice place, right? Comfortable enough that patients might want to stay for as long as they can. Both you and the director are good people, after all."

The truth was, if Sayuri's condition failed to improve, it would be quite difficult to ever discharge her.

He hadn't noticed when it happened, but the top buttons of Akiko's blouse had come undone, exposing her cleavage. She was facing sideways, and her hand was resting on Mochizuki's knee.

Still, Mochizuki tried to keep the conversation on work. He felt this was the only way to keep the situation under control. But he already had a raging erection. He'd only ever slept with one woman besides his wife, and that was before he'd met her. She was a fellow student he'd dated for three months in medical school.

"You know, Doctor, I saw your face in a book."

Akiko brought her face close to Mochizuki's neck and shifted her gaze to the copy of *Modern Psychiatry* sitting on the sideboard in front of them. Her mention of the book troubled Mochizuki. He felt ambushed by the saintly portrait it painted of him. The author's hyperbolic descriptions of Mochizuki's "humanity" as an "excellent psychiatrist" jarred with the reality of his present situation. In a valiant attempt to conform to that version of himself, he tried to sit upright. But there was still the matter of the erection, and it wasn't the zipper that was restraining him. Instead, it was his high ethical standards, social reputation, and the resulting overly positive self-image that was strapped on to him like armor and holding him back. Despite all the pressure in him to resist, though, his erection stubbornly persisted, and Akiko's hand, as it traveled along his thigh, was coming dangerously close to crossing the line. At just that moment, the phone rang.

The tension in the air dissipated. Mochizuki twisted his body away from Akiko and reached for the receiver.

"Hello?"

His throat was parched, and he swallowed once.

"Doctor, it's me. Did you receive my fax?"

The call seemed to be from a payphone, and Mochizuki could hear cars passing in the background. It was Takeshi.

"Ah, yes, of course. Thank you... I looked it over."

"Were you sleeping, Doctor...?"

"No, no, nothing like that."

"I apologize for disturbing you at such a late hour. I was going to wait until tomorrow, but then I thought perhaps you'd want to hear from me as soon as possible. Should I hang up now and call again in the morning?"

Mochizuki glanced at the clock. It was only ten.

"No, not at all. Don't worry."

"All right... Was there anything in the report that seemed unclear, by the way?"

Mochizuki picked up the fax. Akiko, who was next to him, leaned her face close to his and looked down at the report from almost the same angle. It was like he could feel her cheek against his, and he found it hard to maintain his train of thought.

"Let's see... It says here that her father died by suicide on September 4 six years ago, but that her mental condition started declining two or three months before that. Shouldn't it be the other way around? That she became depressed after her father's death...?"

"No, I checked with Miyagawa about that. He said Sayuri began feeling worse and worse starting the end of July, partway through their summer promotional campaign."

"Do you have any idea what he meant by 'feeling worse'? How did she act?"

"She'd stay shut up in her hotel room, refuse to eat..."

"Anything else?"

There was a small interval before Takeshi replied.

"Please excuse me, I didn't think to press the issue. I'll make sure to ask next time I see him."

"That'd be great... Oh, and when you do, make sure you don't ask this Miyagawa person for his subjective opinions. Stick with objective facts, okay?"

It was hard for Mochizuki to diagnose someone in a depressed state of mind even when he observed them directly. So he didn't expect much from this investigation, since he'd be learning about her through two other people.

"Understood. By the way, does it bother you?"

"What?"

"The reason why Sayuri's father killed himself."

"Well, of course. But we still don't know much about it, right?"

"We know that her father—his name was Shuichiro—tied a rope to his balcony and hanged himself from it."

Takeshi was planning on going first thing the next day to visit the office of Stage Loop, a theatrical lighting company, located out in Yotsuya. This was the business Shuichiro had run with his friend, Nagata. Takeshi had gotten Stage Loop's address from Miyagawa.

"If you want to learn more about the suicide, the best thing to do would be to talk to Nagata directly," Miyagawa had suggested.

"So you're going to investigate it?"

"Yes, starting tomorrow. Doctor, do you think finding out the secret behind it will help save Sayuri?"

"Hmm, yes... Perhaps I should've made this clear, Takeshi, but a person's psyche is no simple thing to try and save. Knowing more about her family history, though, can at least give us some insight into a part of her that might be otherwise inaccessible, and in that way, it can help us understand the cause of her condition."

"Understood."

"So don't run yourself ragged over this."

"And this is something I just found out, but... Are you ready to write it down?"

"Yes, go ahead."

"05357-8-06XX, Yoichi Maki. *Yo* like the Pacific Ocean, *ichi* like the number one, *ma* like truth, *ki* like tree. I don't have his address just yet."

Mochizuki wrote the number and name down on the fax.

"Sayuri appeared on stage with the Wind Theater Company in April five years ago, and in July that year, she started living with Yoichi Maki, who was a full-time actor at that company. Three years later, in the fall, they both left the troupe and apparently cut off all contact. The number I just gave you is his parents' house. The troupe's director happened to have it written down in the address directory..."

"05357... Isn't this the area code for Kosai?"

"That's correct."

Kosai was a city that lay to the west of Hamamatsu, on the border of Lake Hamana.

"That means...there's a good possibility Sayuri might have left Tokyo and come here to visit this Yoichi."

"Yes. Ah, and one more thing—it's about that song she was humming in the hospital courtyard... Apparently, it was an important song for the two of them. They danced and sang it as a duet for their first performance together. It was during the course of her teaching it to him that their relationship grew intimate...or at least, that's how the director put it."

Mochizuki felt for Takeshi. It was clear the young man was

taken with Sayuri. But the song she'd been humming was inspired by memories of a past lover. Even if he'd been able to sing with her, Takeshi would never be able to enter the world of her memories.

"In any case, did you try calling his family?"

"Yes, just now."

"And what happened?"

"Yoichi Maki's mother answered."

"Was he there?"

"No."

"He wasn't home?"

"...Where do you suppose the man is right now?"

Takeshi surprised the doctor by asking a question of his own.

"Somewhere far away?"

"Well..."

A chime rang, signaling that Takeshi's phone card was running out.

"He's on a boat. A tuna boat called *Wakashio Maru No. 7.* He's probably somewhere off the coast of New Zealand as we speak."

Takeshi spoke quickly, but stopped there.

"A tuna boat?"

"I'm so sorry, my phone card is running out—"

And then the line went dead.

The discovery of Yoichi Maki, a man who hailed from a city near Hamamatsu, was a major advance in the investigation. It was clear that there was a connection between Sayuri's suicide attempt and her relationship with this man. Further, it seemed very likely that the baby she was carrying was his. But to think that, with Sayuri four months away from giving birth, he would be out at sea...

"That was a long call."

With her ear against the other side of the receiver, Akiko had been listening the whole time.

"And how devoted you are to your work! Look, you've gone all soft."

While saying this, Akiko brushed her hand against the zipper of his pants. Mochizuki closed his eyes. The faces of all the patients he'd treated for maladies caused by their complicated relationships with women floated up before him. In an attempt to collect himself, he lit a cigarette and took a puff before setting it on the ashtray. He then pretended to read the fax, but Akiko, without even turning to look at the ashtray, snuffed the cigarette out as if she was crushing a bug.

"A man like yourself shouldn't smoke."

What hit Mochizuki first wasn't anger but pressure, and her words burned themselves into his mind.

On the sideboard facing them, right next to the copy of *Modern Psychiatry,* was a picture of him and his family taken during a trip to Hawaii. This image of the husband, wife, and daughter burned warmly, as if on a banked fire, and he watched the smoke from the just-snuffed cigarette waft up in front of it. *That's probably how she'd do it. She'd smash that triad without a second thought and take whatever piece she wanted.* Mochizuki felt an alarm bell sound deep inside him. He had to do something before it was too late...

Mochizuki had no idea when Akiko had loosened her hair. The locks that had been coiled around her head now flowed down over the swelling of her breasts. It was as though a single serpent had split into a thousand. Using her fingers like a comb, she smoothed them into submission. Mochizuki knew exactly what was going to happen next. He'd imagined it over and over in the back of his mind from the moment his doorbell had rung and he'd discovered her standing there, and it was a scene that never failed to make his body swell... He tried one last time to stave off these feelings, summoning images of his peaceful life with his family, but even that couldn't stop the waves from crashing in. He slid his left arm around Akiko's waist and pulled her toward him. As if anticipating it, Akiko pressed her lips on his. Their mouths overlapped and just as their tongues found each other, Mochizuki felt the countless serpents coil around and suffocate his sense of reason.

PART II The Tuna Boat

1

Yoichi Maki was on the bridge of the 379-ton longline tuna fishing boat *Wakashio Maru No. 7* as it reached the 180th meridian east off the coast of New Zealand. The International Dateline jogged to the east to include this patch of ocean, so it was still the same day as it was in Japan, but if he were to go only a little farther east, he'd be greeting today for a second time. It was slightly past 11:30 p.m., a time difference of three hours from Japan. The sea lay before him like the smooth surface of a black mirror. Yoichi had been standing watch for four hours now, and he found himself staring at the wheelhouse floor, fighting sleep.

There was an empty aluminum cup sitting in front of the shelf where the navigation equipment was housed. He tried to will himself to refill it with coffee, but his body refused to respond. The cramped, glassed-in wheelhouse cabin was suffused with uncharacteristic quiet. This was the first time since he'd begun his voyage that the sea was so eerily calm.

His fatigue was reaching a breaking point. The cabin was quiet now, but his ears still rang with the frenzied clamor from earlier. It replayed in his head at the slightest provocation, the silvery scales of the tuna as they jumped dazzling his mind's eye. Only a few hours earlier, the deck of the boat had been like a war zone. They were pulling up southern bluefins measuring over two meters in length one after another, and every fisherman's eyes were bloodshot. They'd nearly finished hauling in the fishing lines when seven of the great fish came up. Fishermen for whom this was hardly their first time on the floor ran around the deck, barking at each other, "We're rich! We're rich!"

Yoichi's head drooped even as the brightness and noise of the day came back to him in vivid fragments. He caught his head mid-nod, and his hand brushed against the blood that had dried on his right cheek. It sent a surge of dull pain through the side of his face, and simultaneously, he felt a wave of anger toward a veteran fisherman named Miyazaki, who'd punched him while he was struggling with a shark that had come up with the tuna catch.

It was the newest crewmen on the boat who got the job of dealing with the sharks that mistakenly bit onto the branch lines. They killed the sharks by flipping them over and plunging a large T-shaped spike into their vital spots, and then they cut off their fins and threw them back into the sea. The fins were hung up to dry around the boat and sold to specialized dealers back in Japan. The money was divided equally among the crew members. As a key ingredient in Chinese shark fin soup, the fins generated a significant amount of supplemental income. So while tuna fishing was their main job, shark finning was, so to speak, a kind of side hustle. The income from the tuna catch was distributed according to a hierarchy, with the largest amounts going to the top: the skipper, the first mate, the chief engineer, and so on. The skipper ended up with two or three times the portion allotted to the regular boatmen. But the money made from the shark fin trade was distributed equally among everyone, old salt and newbie alike. And so it seemed natural that such a job would fall to the newbies to do.

There were two such newbies aboard the *Wakashio Maru No. 7*. They were complete amateurs in that this was their very first time on a tuna boat. There was Mizukoshi, a young man who'd left the white-collar world at the age of twenty-four, and Yoichi Maki, a twenty-nine-year-old who, interestingly, used to be an actor in a small theater troupe. The heavy labor on tuna boats meant they were always short-handed, so pretty much anyone who wanted to work was welcomed aboard. Of course, there were those who attended fishery high schools and followed a more traditional track that allowed them to gain hands-on experience before graduation, so the boat was merely an extension of a world they already knew. But for people like Mizukoshi, who'd graduated with an economics degree from a private university and then worked at a local city hall, and Yoichi, who'd pursued his dreams as a stage actor after graduating with his own private university degree in literature, it was a world as different from their humdrum lives as heaven was from earth.

That afternoon, Yoichi, while straddling the shark on its back, had tried to plunge the T-shaped spike into its vital spot, but he missed and the shark's body bucked and thrashed violently. Its tailfin ended up striking Miyazaki, who happened to be pulling up glass floats next to him, on his right cheek. Stunned by a momentary concussion, Miyazaki almost fell overboard, but he managed to stop himself at the last minute. He turned to see what had struck him, then charged at Yoichi and threw a punch at him, yelling "What's wrong with you?! That thing should be dead by now!" Yoichi, who was still struggling with the shark, hadn't noticed that its tail had hit Miyazaki, so the blow came as a total surprise and knocked him off his feet. Looking up, he saw Miyazaki spitting blood in his mouth onto the deck as he walked away to return to his task. It was only then that Yoichi finally realized what must have happened. But was that reason enough to hit him? He couldn't stop anger from rising within him. Yet, he was beginning to understand something about life on a boat: out here on the high seas, with nowhere to get away from each other, the most valuable skill a fisherman could have wasn't physical strength or good fishing instincts—it was the ability to get along with others. If he didn't control himself and ended up returning Miyazaki's punch, the situation could descend into a genuine bloodbath. There were only nineteen men trapped together on this boat, after all.

Yoichi stood up with the urge to shout, "Fuck you!" boiling inside him, and he glared at the deeply bronzed nape of Miyazaki's neck before angrily plunging the spike into the shark. He felt it strike home this time, and he twisted it back and forth until he was sure the shark's life had finally been extinguished.

It was harder than it seemed to find the right place to plunge the spike. The fishermen's way was to give impossible directions and then bark at you when you screwed up. That was surely how Miyazaki had learned the ropes as well. Even the smallest things were potentially matters of life and death, so the fishermen reacted hotly to everything, no matter how trivial. It was just the way things were at sea. But it was also customary to let that anger dissipate as quickly as it flared up. Miyazaki, though, was relentless in his bullying of Mizukoshi and Yoichi, grumbling that this boat was no place for a couple of college boys. There was still more than half a year left of their voyage, and Yoichi had little confidence that it would go by without things between Miyazaki and himself coming to some sort of head.

Tracing the edge of his wound with his finger, Yoichi grew sleepy again. The satellite-enabled navigation system guaranteed that the boat would reach the next fishing area without anyone having to touch the helm at all. With the machines doing the actual work, all that was left for him to do during watch was to stare out in the direction they were traveling on the off chance something unexpected occurred. The main activity during these hours was the simple battle to stay awake.

Some time passed, and then a shudder ran through his body. It wasn't the sensation of falling he sometimes felt in his dreams, nor was it the rocking of the boat. He felt a small electric charge pass through him, somewhere deep within his body. It was as if a heartbeat had traveled like a longitudinal wave through the air all the way to his chest... At some point, Yoichi had begun humming to himself. It was a nostalgic tune, one he'd once sung again and again. And just then, a certain woman's scent came back to him. If his relationship with her hadn't collapsed, he wouldn't be on this boat right now. He still remembered how he had felt when they'd first met, and he could recall the night their relationship first became intimate. It had been five years ago, a night when he could feel the rainy season finally beginning to lift. They had embraced by the sea. Their bodies were intermittently illuminated by headlights from National Route 134, and the distant sound of cars passing provided a soundtrack to their lovemaking. Their desire was so strong, it didn't matter to them that their jeans and underwear were getting soaked in seawater. They embraced in the shadow of an outcropping, pressed up against the wet, slippery rocks as they tasted bliss. Tall-booted fishermen walked in the darkness just above them, but not even that stopped Yoichi. And now, as he floated upon the high seas, he'd find himself reliving that moment from time to time.

Yoichi looked down at his crotch. He was erect. Awakened by the memories, his desire was raising its head beneath the thin cotton of his sweatpants. He hadn't masturbated or even had a wet dream during the entire four months he'd been at sea. Life on the boat took all the energy he had, with none left over for daydreaming about women or anything else. It seemed inconceivable to him, the way his life on land had been ruled by lust, immersed in a web of messy male-female relationships. It was like he was remembering being an entirely different person with an entirely different body. His sex drive seemed so unimportant compared to the desires that ruled him now: the need to eat, sleep, and excrete. The amount of energy devoted to sex was something that increased as civilization advanced. The tuna boat, despite the presence of so much automation and technology, was a world of primitive labor, medieval in its demands on the body and its dependence on the forces of nature.

Yoichi stood up and said a little prayer to the shrine for a safe voyage. While checking the boat's direction, his thoughts drifted northward to Japan. It was the country where the woman he'd left still lived. All that was over. Everything between them had been washed clean with fresh blood. While the memory of their initial encounter had aroused him, that of their break-up never failed to dampen his excitement. Yoichi looked down and couldn't help but laugh to himself.

It had been only four months since this voyage began, and he knew it could potentially continue for another year more. It depressed him to think about it. The sea held such mystery. He'd jumped on the tuna boat as if by reflex—why? To run away? He'd felt as though he needed to be at sea to look back objectively on all that had happened on land. Especially for him, the sea was a place where he could reflect and see where his real problems lay, where he could tease apart the tangled threads... He imagined that the water would render all that was invisible to him visible at last.

Yoichi rose unsteadily to his feet and was recording their current position in the boat's log when the door to the wheelhouse unexpectedly opened. He hadn't heard any footsteps on the stairs leading up to the cabin, which told him exactly who it must be. Akimitsu Miyazaki, the person who'd punched him during the day. He never wore shoes. For some reason, it was his custom to walk around the boat's cabins barefoot. Of course, he wore tall boots like everyone out on the deck when he was at work, but he walked everywhere else with nothing on his feet. And that was why he passed through the cabins silently. Some of his friends called him Ghost. This wasn't a night when Miyazaki was meant to keep watch. He should have been sleeping soundly with the rest of the crewmen, but instead, here he was creeping in the cabins—Yoichi couldn't keep the irritation off his face. This was the third time Miyazaki had intruded into the wheelhouse during one of Yoichi's watches. It wasn't to make sure he didn't forget to record the boat's position in the log or to help him fight off sleep. Whenever Miyazaki made his little visits, he would start a conversation, his words making very little sense, before stopping midstream and returning to his cabin.

This time, Miyazaki crossed the wheelhouse without so much as a glance in Yoichi's direction and peered down at the forward shelter deck. He seemed to have totally forgotten about punching Yoichi earlier that day. But minor skirmishes were an everyday occurrence on the tuna boat. There was no reason to remember each and every one.

Yoichi joined Miyazaki in looking down at the forward deck. A figure was walking up the steps leading from the hull to the bow. It reached the top of the stairs and then leaned against the foremast, where it stopped moving. The fluorescents in the wheelhouse created reflections on the glass that made it hard to see. Yoichi squinted, cupping his hands to shade his eyes. He made out a short, stocky silhouette, which told him it was the skipper, Jukichi Takagi.

"Look at the old man, praying again," said Miyazaki.

He finally turned to face Yoichi. "Hey, you know what he's praying to?"

Yoichi didn't respond and instead continued staring at the skipper, who remained motionless with his left hand against the mast.

Jukichi was the first person Yoichi had exchanged words with when he arrived at the port of Misaki. It was the end of March. He had parked his motorcycle at the pier and gazed at the fishing boats lined up along the docks. As an elementary school kid, he had loved the ocean. There were many times he had dreamed of becoming a ship's captain. Exhausted by life in the city, Yoichi was staring up longingly at the words *Wakashio Maru No. 7* painted across the broadside of the boat in front of him when a short, muscular man walked down the boarding ramp. It was Jukichi.

"Is this a tuna boat?" asked Yoichi as the man approached.

"Sure is," he replied.

"How many tons?" Yoichi continued.

"Three hundred seventy-nine."

Jukichi's answer was brusque, but he followed it up by muttering, "We're so shorthanded, we might not be able to leave next week." His words weren't directed at Yoichi, yet they struck him like a divine revelation. Coupled with the state of his mind at the time, they made him receptive when Jukichi asked, "You interested in joining us?"

"Do you think someone like me would be able to work on that boat?"

"Sure."

Jukichi's initial response was curt, but he took a moment to look at Yoichi from head to toe and, seeming to like what he saw, he added, "You'd be welcome anytime."

It was only a few minutes later that Yoichi found out this man was the *Wakashio Maru No. 7*'s fishing chief—that is, the skipper. Jukichi had taken Yoichi to the office of the shipowner, Wakashio Fisheries, where he had asked Yoichi to confirm that he was serious about working on the boat. It was then when Jukichi introduced himself. To Yoichi, who didn't know the first thing about tuna fishing, the term "skipper" was ambiguous. He could only picture the captain of a ferry. While a skipper of a tuna boat was a position higher than a captain, on this particular voyage, Jukichi was going to act as both skipper and captain. In other words, he would wield absolute authority aboard the boat.

Jukichi was short in stature, but his shoulders were unusually broad. Standing there in his tall black boots, his deeply lined face stared out from the hand towel wrapped around his head. Yoichi had no idea what his real age might be.

This was the man who was currently standing at the bow of the boat, immersed, according to Miyazaki, in prayer. And at this hour, everyone on board was asleep... Yoichi was surprised. Two people who should be sleeping were up and about in the middle of the night. One was soundlessly creeping around the wheelhouse, and the other was seemingly frozen in place on the forward deck.

"Hey, did you hear me? I asked if you know what the old man's praying to!"

Miyazaki lightly struck Yoichi on the shoulder.

It was dark and difficult to make out, but Yoichi had his doubts about whether Jukichi was actually praying. It didn't really look like a prayer pose.

"You really think he's praying?"

"What else would he be doing?"

Miyazaki glared at him with bloodshot eyes. Besides disliking Miyazaki, Yoichi also found himself profoundly unsettled by him. Fixed at close range by that bloodshot gaze, he felt like Miyazaki could see right through him, and he even started to feel short of breath. Talking to him always made Yoichi feel like he was losing his balance. He could never guess what the man was thinking. But once Miyazaki fixed someone in his sights like this, he was never the one who averted his eyes first.

Unable to stand it any longer, Yoichi dropped his eyes and looked down at the deck. Jukichi was still there, in the same position as before. It wasn't like he had his hands folded or anything. But he did have the air of someone immersed in something like prayer.

"This is the first time I've seen him out there like that."

And it was true. Yoichi had had to stand watch countless times during the past four months, but he had never seen the skipper standing motionless on the forward deck for no discernible reason.

"He's always like this."

Miyazaki said this with a look of contempt.

"Do you know why he's praying?"

"Yeah, I do." Laughing a little to himself, Miyazaki banged his fist repetitively on the window glass. "I saw the bastard reading the Bible, even."

As if he found the idea of a skipper reading a holy book ridiculous, Miyazaki increased his strength as he knocked against the window.

"And he told us to change fishing spots even though we caught seven tuna this afternoon."

What possible connection could there be between reading the Bible and deciding to change fishing spots? Yoichi couldn't figure out what context in Miyazaki's mind would make his words decipherable.

Since Yoichi wanted Miyazaki to go away, he chose not to answer. The average age of the crewmen on this boat was thirty-seven, and apart from Yoichi, Miyazaki was the only other person who was twenty-nine. It didn't seem like it, though. It was hard for Yoichi to look at him and imagine they were the same age. Half of his hair had fallen out on top, with what little there was left forming a straggly fringe from the sides of his ears to the back of his head. It was the hair of a man in his sixties. But his skin was glowing, deeply tanned, with not a wrinkle to be found. His back was a bit stooped, his limbs long, and his body skinny, but his shoulders and upper arms were impressively built up. While Yoichi was fairly confident in his own arm strength, he wasn't sure he'd win an arm-wrestling match with Miyazaki. Once, he had seen Miyazaki dangling from the deck railing, doing pull-ups. He'd casually watched him for a while, counting the reps in his head until he reached thirty, then decided to return to his bunk—it was obvious Miyazaki wasn't going to stop anytime soon. And then, there was his habit of tiptoeing around barefoot.

Heat builds up in my feet.

That was his explanation. It was true that he always slept with his feet sticking out from under his blankets even when the weather turned chilly. His bunkmates had touched them out of curiosity in the middle of the night, and his feet had been hot, as if on fire.

You gotta let it out—it's no good to have heat build up in your body.

This was his reason.

Miyazaki, who didn't seem like he belonged on a tuna boat in so many ways, paradoxically struck Yoichi as the perfect symbol of life aboard the *Wakashio Maru No. 7*. He was unbalanced. Something about him lacked harmony. And now, he was saying that the man wielding absolute authority on this boat spent his nights out on the deck, praying. It was indeed another strange sight.

The fact was, Jukichi Takagi was a pinch hitter. The longtime skipper of the boat had been Kota Kimura, a legendary Misaki seaman. But right before the *Wakashio Maru No. 7* was meant to embark on its journey, he'd suddenly collapsed from a subarachnoid hemorrhage. It was Kimura who specifically recommended Jukichi to take his place. Having spent most of his time skippering a ship owned by a man out in Muroto, Jukichi was an unknown quantity for the men on the *Wakashio*. Many questioned his ability to take over the boat, wondering if he really had what it took to run things properly. Kimura pushed for him as forcefully as he could, but he was hampered by his condition, which prevented him from speaking much at all. In the end, the crew had little choice but to accept Jukichi as the great man's pick, whatever the doubts that might linger.

So this was the skipper who'd announced this evening that, despite hauling in seven enormous southern bluefins in a short period of time, the boat would head to a new fishing area. No one spoke against him aloud, but it was clear there was much disagreement among the crewmen. Once back in port, the share of the profits each man received—and whether the catch was bountiful or sparse—were entirely attributed to the talents of the skipper. It was the skipper's job to use his rich experience and intuition to locate and guide the boat to the best spots and let the fishermen discover the riches there. This was how a skipper earned the respect and trust of his men, and it was also how he prevented trouble from brewing on board. At the moment, Jukichi's leadership seemed inadequate. Yoichi surmised that this was what caused Miyazaki to call him "old man" behind his back. Usually, crewmen referred to the skipper using the more respectful term "boss."

Yoichi opened the boat's log and wrote down their position. Only two hours left before the next man on watch would come to relieve him.

"Do you not sleep, sir?"

He asked this without looking up from the log. They were the same age, but Miyazaki had gone to fishery school and then straight onto a boat, so in that sense, he held considerable seniority. It behooved Yoichi to talk politely to him.

"Am I bothering you?"

"Kind of..." Yoichi admitted lightly.

"Actually, I came here 'cause I had a favor to ask."

"What is it?"

"My back's itchy—scratch it for me."

Yoichi looked up, his mouth half-open.

Is this some kind of joke? This bastard, he can't be serious. What kind of freak comes all the way out to the bridge in the middle of the night to find someone to scratch his back?!

"If your back's itchy, you can always rub it against the bedrail, like a caterpillar. That's what I do."

Joke or not, Yoichi didn't feel like engaging with Miyazaki's nonsense. But seeing that Yoichi made no move to help, Miyazaki shot him a dark look and walked backward toward the shelf housing the boat's shrine. Pressing his back against its corner, he spread his legs wide, then started bending and stretching them awkwardly. The talismans, meant to ensure plentiful catches and safety on the high seas, began swinging back and forth in time with Miyazaki's motions, the plates that held rice offerings rattling all the while. Miyazaki's face was seriousness itself as he looked down at the forward deck and glared at Jukichi's back.

"Or maybe the old man's down there begging for his life," he muttered.

The rice-filled plates continued their rattling.

Yoichi was about to respond, but then swallowed his words. Not usually reticent, Yoichi nonetheless found it impossible to conduct a proper conversation when he found himself alone with Miyazaki. Even when he was on the verge of saying something, the timing always seemed off when he tried to actually say it. *If only he'd just go...* Yoichi repeated this wish from the bottom of his heart.

Miyazaki walked over to where Yoichi was sitting in his revolving chair, put his hand on his shoulder, and leaned in to whisper into his ear.

"I heard you're here to get out of some jam you got into with a woman."

With that, Miyazaki opened the wheelhouse door and returned to his bunk. Though he'd been silent when he arrived, Yoichi could faintly hear his footsteps now as he left.

Yoichi spent the next while staring expressionlessly at the door Miyazaki had walked through, waiting for the nearly imperceptible sounds of his feet against the boards to recede completely. Then he spoke, softly and to himself. "How does that asshole know why I'm on this boat?"

2

The days spent moving from one fishing area to another were leisurely aboard a tuna boat. The sea was calm the following day, and its gentle rocking was perfect for soothing the aches and exhaustion of the boatmen. The work that needed to be done shrank to nearly nothing—routine maintenance of the fishing gear, seeing if the line haulers needed repair—which meant that, aside from whoever was assigned to the watch, everyone aboard the boat was free to make the most of these brief periods of rest.

Yoichi had managed to sleep soundly after finishing his watch the previous night, and perhaps that was why he was in a better mood than usual. He never tired of looking out at the open sea on a nice day. The boat's middle deck, usually overrun with tuna that had their tails cut off and their guts and fins removed, was filled instead with men sitting in circles, drinking. Many boats restricted the amount of alcohol available during each month, as it tended to lead to even more conflicts among the crewmen, but the *Wakashio Maru No. 7* was not among them. So in the afternoons, the crew would gather in small groups of friends and start drinking.

But Yoichi wasn't part of such a group. Instead, he was standing on the forward deck, close to where he'd seen Jukichi late last night. He was trying to imagine what thoughts the skipper might have had as he stood there for so long. It was an old habit of Yoichi's to immerse himself in recreating the thoughts of others as if preparing for a role. And this time, he was trying to become Jukichi Takagi. Standing in the same spot and looking in the direction he'd looked, Yoichi mentally blocked out the shining sun and tried to imagine the words Jukichi might have offered to the night-dark sea. But the raucous laughter of the drunk men behind him intruded on his thoughts, breaking his concentration. They were telling a story about when, during the previous voyage, the boat had docked at a foreign port and two crewmen had inadvertently ended up sleeping with the same prostitute.

"And that—*that's* when we realized we accidentally became brothers!"

It was the punchline to an oft-told tale. That was why Yoichi tended not to join in when the men started drinking. It made him weary to have to pretend to be amused by the same old jokes. The world could seem so small aboard the boat, it sometimes made him feel suffocated.

Just then, he heard the sound of metal clanking against metal from below him. Jukichi had finished fixing the line haulers and walked partway up the stairs, and now he was leaning out toward the water, checking the guide rollers. Once he walked the rest of the way up, he caught sight of Yoichi on the forward deck.

"What're you doing up here?" he asked as he sat down, straddling the keel of a nearby lifeboat.

"Nothing in particular..."

Of course, Yoichi couldn't tell Jukichi that he was "playing" him like a role. Despite his vague answer, he was gripped by a need to get things out in the open once and for all, and he added, "Sir, last night when you were out here..." Yoichi glanced up at the wheelhouse window. Through the glass, he saw Miyazaki's profile and only then realized that the man was on watch. Yoichi looked back down and tried to act like he hadn't seen anything, but Jukichi didn't miss the change in his expression.

"You were the one on watch last night?"

"Yes."

"So you saw."

Jukichi stood up from his perch on the lifeboat and walked over to put a hand on the younger man's shoulder. Yoichi felt its meaty weight. In the Wakashio Fisheries office back at Misaki Port, he remembered Jukichi asking him, "Are you actually serious about joining us on the boat?" When Yoichi had answered that he was, Jukichi had followed up by asking, "What if there was someone on the boat you just couldn't stand? What would you do? Would you fight him?"

Wondering what Jukichi really meant by the question, Yoichi had answered, "I would try to put up with him, of course." And that was when Jukichi had placed his meaty palm on Yoichi's shoulder, just as he was doing now.

"I can't put a man on my boat who's not willing to fight."

Yoichi vividly remembered the serious look on the skipper's face as well as the weight of the hand on his shoulder. That was the moment when he realized how much of a commitment boarding the tuna boat would truly be.

Jukichi had often told him this:

"The worst thing you can do is harbor hatred in secret. Conflicts need to be aired out right away so they don't linger. Little fights are bound to break out from time to time, and there really isn't anything to do except look the other way."

So how was Yoichi doing these days? His hatred for Miyazaki seemed to be growing deeper and deeper. Though "hatred" wasn't quite the word—he couldn't pin down exactly how he felt about Miyazaki, who was impossible for him to get along with. In any case, he was someone who Yoichi, if given the choice, would rather never see again.

Jukichi untied the hand towel from around his neck and used it to wipe the sweat from his brow.

"What do you think I was doing out here last night?"

His voice was hoarse.

Yoichi wanted to throw that question back at him.

How do you think you looked to the other men being out here like that?

Was he telling Yoichi to figure out why he'd been staring out at the open sea in the dark? Miyazaki had interpreted it as prayer, and indeed, what other conclusion was there to draw?

"Were you praying?"

He felt somewhat awkward, averting his eyes as he spoke. Jukichi looked surprised and glanced up at the wheelhouse.

"Is that what Miyazaki told you?"

"He visited the wheelhouse during my watch."

"And that's what he said?"

"Well..."

"Did he say anything else?"

Or maybe the old man's down there begging for his life.

Those were the words Miyazaki had muttered under his breath, but Yoichi couldn't bring himself to say them aloud.

"I see."

Jukichi, squinting as if dazzled by the sun, looked out from the bow at an island just visible portside. The crinkles pulled his eyes down at the edges, giving him a kindly look. He wasn't a man prone to laughter, but when he did smile, his face looked just like that.

The piece of land sliding by on their left was one of the small, subtropical islands of the Kermadec group. Suddenly quiet, Jukichi gazed in its direction as he peered deep within himself, at a landscape in his memories.

"Are you a Christian?"

Yoichi tried to imagine this oddly shaped man, with his bulky upper body and skinny legs, lurching his way into a church. It didn't seem right—the image of Jukichi there, with a Bible open before him, seemed as unbalanced and disharmonious as the two halves of his body.

"I used to go to a Catholic church. About twenty-five years ago."

"And these days?"

Jukichi shook his head.

"No, I'm not even baptized."

"But you pray..."

"What, me?"

Jukichi had raised his voice—a rarity for him—and pointed to himself.

"Am I wrong?"

"That's just what Miyazaki said, right?"

"Then what were you...?"

"Searching for a new fishing area, obviously."

It was hard to tell what Jukichi was thinking. Admittedly a newbie, Yoichi nonetheless found it hard to believe that the way to find a new fishing area was to simply stand and look blankly out at the sea at night. Maybe long ago, basic animal intuition allowed fishermen to sense schools of fish beneath the waves. But these days, people used fish finders, sonars, and other scientific methods to locate and determine their fishing areas.

A skeptical expression crossed Yoichi's face as he frowned and looked away. The island had disappeared from sight, replaced by a flock of storm petrels flying past them.

"You can find new fisheries by watching birds, right?"

Yoichi said this as soon as the thought came to his mind. In actuality, the movement of birds often corresponded to that of fish in the sea.

"For me, it's more like I can smell where the fish are. My sense of smell is sharper at night."

If reading the natural laws and movements of the sea involved not only knowledge but also the five senses, then Jukichi's explanation was hardly far-fetched. A veteran tuna boat skipper could read slight changes in the color of the sea, the flow of the tides, the feel of the wind, the sound of the waves interacting with that of the boat engine, the softness of the sunlight, the cries of the birds in the sky... They'd use all of their senses, except taste, to search for the fish beneath the waves. And indeed, one might even say that the unseen movements of the fish touched off corresponding harmonics within the body of a good skipper. A person's sight, by far the most important sense, is muted at night. And because of that, the sense of smell becomes heightened.

Yoichi realized Jukichi had said something to him. He'd heard him clearly through the drunken banter behind them, but the words had slipped right through. "Huh?" Yoichi responded.

What did he say about a baby? Why bring up a baby out of the blue? Is he talking about tuna spawning?

"I asked if you had a child."

So he was talking about me. But what? My baby?

"No, I don't have a child. I don't even have a wife."

He sputtered through this denial, despite its simplicity.

"Huh, okay. I just had the feeling you were a father, that's all."

What Miyazaki had said the previous night before he left the wheelhouse came back to Yoichi.

I heard you're here to get out of some jam you got into with a woman.

"Did you tell Miyazaki that?"

"Tell him what?"

"About me."

"What about you?"

"No, I mean..."

"I barely know the first thing about you."

"But Miyazaki said something to me. That I'd gotten into a jam with a woman."

"Don't be an idiot. One look at you and anyone could tell. It was written all over your face until a while ago. We get people like you sometimes. They hop on the boat to run away from something... And with you, it's obviously a woman."

Jukichi let an interval pass, then continued in a hushed, serious tone, "When you first joined up, you had the sodden face of a drowned man."

Now that he thought about it, Yoichi realized he'd barely seen his own face at all since boarding the boat. Back in Sayuri's apartment, he'd looked at himself in the mirror all the time, preparing for this role or that, but it seemed like he'd discarded the habit completely. He wanted to see what it was like—the face of a man fleeing a woman. He'd played men who'd dumped their lovers countless times before, but never to his satisfaction.

"How does my face look now?"

"It's changed quite a bit."

"How so?"

"Like you finally threw up all that water you'd swallowed and came back to life."

That wasn't how it felt to Yoichi, though. His every waking moment was consumed with manual labor, and he hadn't even had time to think about his future. Living a life pared down to the essentials—eating, sleeping, working—might have reignited a certain spark in his eyes, but that was the extent of it. Still, it made him relieved to hear Jukichi tell him he'd changed. Perhaps a man like the skipper, who was able to find new fisheries with his senses, could see the changes in his heart just by looking at him.

Will I ever be able to find myself?

He wanted to feel that he'd truly changed. And he hoped that he'd be able to see himself as he really was, right down to his very core, and discern once and for all the sort of life he was meant to lead. It wasn't too late, after all. Twenty-nine left him plenty of time.

It was at that moment that Jukichi's eyes unexpectedly clouded over. While he appeared to be looking up at the radar mount on the mast, he was actually staring just below it at the figures moving up and down in the wheelhouse. Compared to the forward deck where Jukichi and Yoichi were standing, the wheelhouse was much higher, and its front windows were blocked by navigation equipment and the like, so they could only see anyone standing inside from about the chest up. Miyazaki, who was completely bald on the top of his head, was standing in profile and staring blankly at something. It was the reverse of the previous night. Instead of Miyazaki and Yoichi looking down from the wheelhouse at Jukichi on the shelter deck, now Yoichi was standing with Jukichi on the deck, looking up at Miyazaki in the wheelhouse. However, Miyazaki was not alone. The black hair of another man bobbed up as they watched, barely visible next to the helm. They could tell there was someone else in the cramped wheelhouse. Miyazaki's mouth seemed to be moving—from the shapes it made, he seemed to be yelling. His hand reached out and grabbed the top of the other man's head, then pushed it down with considerable force. The other man's head sank again, disappearing from view. All Yoichi and Jukichi could see from their position were Miyazaki from the chest up and the other man's hair as it bobbed up and down.

"What the hell is Miyazaki doing up there?"

As if playing a game of whack-a-mole, Miyazaki was forcing the man's head back down every time he tried to get up. It reminded Yoichi of a teacher he once saw administering corporal punishment. He'd been in junior high school, and the student who had forgotten his homework was made to sit on his knees on top of his desk. When the pain in his legs became unbearable, he'd try to sit up, but every time he did, the teacher would press his head down, just as Miyazaki was doing now.

Yoichi looked over at the middle deck, sorting through the faces of the men gathered there to drink. There were only nineteen men on the boat, so it was easy to figure out through the process of elimination who was up there with Miyazaki. He didn't see the chief engineer or the radio operator, but given their positions, it seemed very unlikely it was one of them. So that left Mizukoshi. He was the fellow newbie, a weakling who'd left his job as a local government employee to come work on the tuna boat. He'd thought the hard manual labor would make him stronger, but all it had done was drive him into neurosis.

"The other guy up there—that's Mizukoshi, right?"

Jukichi seemed to have reached the same conclusion as Yoichi.

"I think so, yes."

The scene from last evening suddenly replayed itself in the back of Yoichi's head. Miyazaki had turned his back to Yoichi, asking him to scratch it, but he had refused. He recalled the look on Miyazaki's face as he crouched up and down, rubbing his back against the edge of the shrine's shelf.

Was a back scratch really all he'd wanted?

He felt sick as the thought came to him. Mizukoshi was probably being forced to kneel on the floor before Miyazaki. And Miyazaki was most likely pushing him back down every time he tried to stand.

"You have to do something!"

Overcome with anger, Yoichi hissed this at Jukichi. But the skipper's answer showed how much their viewpoints diverged.

"I'm not in the position to say a word against Miyazaki. Even if he killed me."

Before he could process the skipper's words, a question appeared in his mind: did he have someone in his life he could say the same about—someone he would never say a word against, even if they killed him? He already knew the answer. But he just wanted to confirm it for himself. He'd offered his life up to a woman once. At the time, he'd felt no fear as he did—only happiness and a certain sense of relief. Perhaps he really had wanted to run away. But the feeling had only lasted for a short while. Soon after, a power against his will had risen up within him, and it had knocked down not just his own body, but also that of the woman. Why, indeed, had he spontaneously fled onto this tuna boat? Yoichi realized it was to strengthen the source of that power that had welled up inside him at that moment. Battling a grand, natural force like the sea would surely make him stronger.

The door to the cabins opened to reveal Chief Engineer Ueda's oil-streaked face. He was a forty-three-year-old man who seemed to be the last sort you'd imagine living his life on a boat. His actions were always a bit clumsy and slow, but his natural kindness made him universally adored by the other men. Everyone knew he was someone whose rightful place was elsewhere, but no one—not his family, not his friends, not even himself—knew where that elsewhere might be. So it seemed that Ueda might well spend the rest of his life at sea before anyone figured it out.

Leaning out the half-open door, Ueda called out lazily.

"Hey, I need some help here."

"What's going on?"

The few men sitting nearest to the door turned to look at Ueda. Their cups, stopped midway to their mouths, were filled to the rim with liquor.

"Mizukoshi's lying at the bottom of the stairs, and it looks like he can't move. Someone give me a hand."

Ueda's tone drained the urgency from the situation, and because of that, the men moved slower than usual. His demeanor was the same even when a storm spoiled a catch, paradoxically making him seem dependable.

"Alrighty."

The three men rose to their feet at the same time. Everyone assumed that nothing more serious had happened than Mizukoshi slipping on the stairs and getting the wind knocked out of him.

"Boss, could you come too?"

Ueda waved his hand at Jukichi, who was still standing on the shelter deck. The skipper would have to walk down the stairs and then cross the length of the hull to get from where he was to the cabins. The situation must be more serious than it seemed, and Yoichi, who had been observing what was going on in the wheelhouse, followed Jukichi down the stairs. Ueda never did things for no reason—he would only call the skipper over if it was an emergency.

They discovered Mizukoshi slumped in the shadows at the foot of the stairs leading to the wheelhouse, lost in a daze. He seemed to have lost control of his lower body, and a dark stain spread out from the crotch of his light-green jersey pants.

"He pissed himself," someone muttered behind Yoichi. And indeed, the smell filling the cramped space told the story clearly enough. Jukichi made his way through the three men and ran his hands down Mizukoshi's legs, feeling them from hips to feet. He didn't seem to find anything wrong, no broken bones or strained muscles. Mizukoshi's expression and the way he was slouched on the floor made it seem like he'd collapsed for a reason more complex than a simple fall down the stairs.

"Hey, what happened?"

Jukichi looked squarely into Mizukoshi's eyes. Their color seemed somehow off.

"N-Nothing."

His voice trembled as he answered, and his shoulders shook so convulsively, they seemed like they were about to break.

"Obviously, something happened."

"No, it was just..."

Bracing himself against the wall of the cabin hallway, Mizukoshi tried to get up. Jukichi kept Ueda from lending a hand to the young man and simply watched over him as he struggled. Mizukoshi managed to pull one of his knees out from under himself, but he wasn't able to lift his body any higher.

"Can't you stand up?"

The tone of Jukichi's voice wasn't hectoring, but rather filled with a mix of shock and concern. Mizukoshi looked embarrassed—he couldn't understand what was happening to his body. He should have been able to stand, but he couldn't. Turning his waist, Mizukoshi pushed against the wall with both hands. Their trembling spoke of his frustration at being unable to understand why his body no longer obeyed him.

"Did you fall from up there?"

Ueda slowly raised his chin to indicate the top of the stairs, but Mizukoshi was too occupied with trying to stand to answer him. Finally, the young man's face crumpled, and all the strength left his body. He collapsed to the floor and wept. His face was raw and ugly as he cried. No man had ever looked so pathetic.

"Boss, what happened to him?"

"Did he fall down the stairs and break something?"

"But he doesn't look like he's hurt."

The younger deck crew began to talk. Jukichi, who had his arms held out to stop anyone from touching Mizukoshi, placed his hands on the young man's shoulder.

"Can you stand?"

Mizukoshi let out a howl of despair, realizing he'd lost control of his lower body.

But Yoichi could more or less guess what had happened to Mizukoshi. Turning to face the stairs, he shouted angrily, loud enough for everyone to hear.

"Miyazaki, you bastard! What did you do to Mizukoshi?"

Right then, the wheelhouse door opened, as if responding to Yoichi's words. Miyazaki appeared in the doorway, silhouetted against the late afternoon sun that poured in through the windows behind him. His face was obscured by shadow.

"What's everyone doing down there?" said Miyazaki, his voice casual as could be, as he zipped up his half-open fly.

"Okay, everyone, carry Mizukoshi to his bunk." Jukichi glanced at Miyazaki's face, then looked the other way and ordered, "Make sure you get him into some new clothes, too."

No one but Yoichi and Jukichi registered that it was psychological damage that lay at the heart of Mizukoshi's condition. And they were the only two to realize that this damage had been inflicted by Miyazaki. After all, they were the only ones who'd seen Miyazaki in profile standing in the wheelhouse with Mizukoshi's head bobbing up and down before him.

An old hand on the high seas like Jukichi had seen men in Mizukoshi's condition before. It was a typical psychogenic reaction, so there naturally wouldn't be any visible injuries. In Mizukoshi's case, he had the will to stand, but his flesh refused to obey. Jukichi had seen many men on his boat who'd collapsed and couldn't get up. In rare cases, they even had throat spasms that rendered them mute. Most ended up diagnosed as "unable to adapt to the environment." But in the confined space of a boat, it was impossible to adequately change the "environment" even if someone suffered so much that it caused a psychogenic reaction. Mizukoshi might have joined the boat crew to escape the everyday life he'd hated as a local government employee, but the natural world was rejecting his body outright. Even though the direct cause of his breakdown was Miyazaki's malicious bullying, it had already been clear that Mizukoshi's home was not the sea. He'd most likely recover once he returned to land and the civilization that waited there.

Jukichi clucked his tongue at the prospect of losing a crewman less than half a year into the voyage. It seemed that Mizukoshi's condition wouldn't improve as long as he remained on the boat. The only thing left to do was to move forward in the schedule and load him onto a medical supply ship so he could receive care on his way back to Japan. But Jukichi was torn about whether he should replace Mizukoshi with a new crewman. Even as a relatively unskilled newbie, Mizukoshi filled a necessary role within the tuna boat's hierarchy. Without him, Yoichi would end up shouldering the burden at the bottom alone, which might very well result in losing him to a breakdown as well. Jukichi turned and glanced back in the narrow hallway to check on Yoichi. The men in the front were busy opening the door to Mizukoshi's bunk and carrying the young man's body through it. He saw that Yoichi was standing stock-still at the foot of the stairs, staring hard up at Miyazaki, who was still framed by the open wheelhouse door. Jukichi walked down the hallway and pushed Yoichi on the shoulder, leading him back out onto the sunlit deck. Yoichi looked confused as the skipper guided him all the way to the edge of the hull, where he sat him down next to the line haulers.

"Weren't you the one who said you wouldn't have a man on your boat who's not willing to fight?" Yoichi said indignantly as he crossed his legs.

"You idiot, don't start something with Miyazaki."

"Why not?"

"I don't need to give you a reason. Just don't—he's a special case."

Yoichi was on the verge of asking what made Miyazaki so special, but then swallowed his words. He realized it had something to do with the general disharmony of life aboard the *Wakashio Maru No. 7*. Or rather, to be more precise, it had to do with the relationship between the skipper Jukichi Takagi and Akimitsu Miyazaki. Jukichi seemed to owe some sort of debt to Miyazaki—Yoichi could feel its weight hanging over the whole boat.

"What happened between you two?"

Yoichi decided to press the issue. It was the skipper's duty to address Miyazaki's behavior when he stepped so far out of line.

Though they were two very different types of men, Yoichi had a certain respect for Mizukoshi. He had a seriousness about him, a sincere desire to seek out the most meaningful life he could. His job as a government worker had been stable, but he'd left it anyway to challenge himself to a life at sea that was, without a doubt, completely foreign to anything he'd ever known. To Yoichi, who had boarded the boat out of desperation, Mizukoshi's courage was admirable. Under normal circumstances, Yoichi would never have had the guts to change course so drastically. In the handful of free moments they'd enjoyed on the boat, Yoichi would often seek Mizukoshi out to talk with him. Yoichi was clearly more physically suited to the fishing life than Mizukoshi, but in terms of the struggle to find purpose and meaning in life, Mizukoshi impressed him as far more advanced despite being five years his junior. Everyone is born with different physical and intellectual abilities, but what Yoichi learned from Mizukoshi was that life gained meaning from pushing those abilities to their limits. And now, that same Mizukoshi was covered in his own piss, unable to even stand up by himself. It was too much.

"Do you hate Miyazaki?"

Jukichi's voice was soft as he asked the question.

"Of course. It's because of him that Mizukoshi..."

"You think that was Miyazaki's fault?"

"He's been bullying both of us."

"*Bullying*? Really? Are you kids?"

"What would you call it then?"

"You went to college, figure it out yourself."

What else would you call it?

A grayscale memory rose up in the back of Yoichi's head. It had happened during a storm, and seawater had been pouring into the hull. If they weren't careful, they'd get thrown over the side of the boat and fall headfirst into the waves. Even in that intense situation, Miyazaki took the time to walk over to Mizukoshi, who was fighting his terror while "dissecting" the catch—that is, removing the gills and guts. Miyazaki prodded him in the backside with a hooked fishing spike while yelling at the younger man in a voice colored with clear malice, "Hey idiot, what are you dicking around for? Hurry up, or I'll dissect you!"

"Why is an asshole like him on this boat anyway?"

Yoichi felt his entire body stiffen in anger as he spat out the words. He balled up his fist and drove it into the iron column next to him.

"I admit I've wondered the same thing."

Jukichi stood up and looked around for a place away from the other crewmen. "Will you come with me for a moment?" he asked. Leading Yoichi to the poop deck and sitting down on the capstan, he said, "There's something I think you should hear." Then, Jukichi began relating an incident that had happened twenty-five years ago.

Another island slowly slid by, this time off the boat's starboard side. Though it wasn't the one in Jukichi's story, a remote South Seas island much like it figured prominently in the incident he recounted.

Jukichi told his story haltingly, flames licking up into the sky behind his eyelids as he spoke. The stink of burning meat came back to him, as did the feeling of a blade severing the artery beneath a collarbone. It crept from his fingertips up his arms and toward his heart. Images returned in fragments: a bloody mouth, a set of broken teeth. They were disjointed and disordered as they flooded his mind. But he knew he had to put things back in order so Yoichi could understand his story. The corpse lying beneath the palm trees wasn't the beginning. It was the end. But what *was* the beginning? Jukichi had no choice but to start somewhere in the middle.

Perhaps Jukichi found it hard to remember how things had started because his memories of what came after were so vivid. He could recall what had happened after quite clearly. But why had that man come at him like that in the first place? Had it been his fault, or was it just the habit of putting the blame on the new trainee? Was the other man right? Had he really been smirking? At this point, Jukichi's memory was too faulty to know for sure.

The sky had been filled with clouds from a recent squall, but they were starting to break apart, allowing the clear outlines of the Caroline Islands to emerge as they rose from the sea. Jukichi had been twenty at the time, a navigation trainee on the 135-ton tuna boat *Kaiho Maru No. 2*, and so he hardly had time to gaze idly at the swiftly changing ocean sky. He was hauling in the last fishing line of the day, and bigeye tuna almost two meters in length were being pulled up one after another. Surrounded by wild-eyed fishermen barking orders at each other, Jukichi had thought he'd heard his name and turned to look. But at that moment, he somehow suffered a concussion and fell to the floor. That had been the beginning of it. He'd looked back, and before he'd even had the chance to focus his eyes, a fellow crewman had entered his field of vision, and the next thing he knew, sky and deck had switched places.

"What's so fucking funny?"

The words rang in his ears. He didn't remember smiling, and it took several moments to even realize he'd been punched.

As soon as this catch was finished, they'd have to turn around and start heading back because they had run out of bait. It was hardly a big catch, but they had no choice since they were scraping the bottom of the bait already. The prospect of heading home usually lit up the fishermen's eyes with joy and anticipation, but this time, the atmosphere on the boat was heavy. A sufficient catch at sea could provide an income several times larger than what the fishermen could make on land. But everyone knew the profits this time would be scant. If they'd been scheduled to arrive back at the port just before New Year's, they could have expected a sizable profit even from a small catch due to the market prices during that time of the year. However, it was summer, and the prospect weighed heavily on the fishermen, especially those with families, as the shortfall was a matter of life and death. This pent-up frustration filled the air as they worked to process the last of their catch. Of course, none of it mattered to Jukichi, who was there as a trainee. The simple prospect of returning to Japan after three months at sea filled him with unmixed glee. If he could just escape the floating hell where he never got more than three or four hours of sleep a night, that would be reward enough.

According to the man who hit him, Jukichi had been pulling up a string of floats when he suddenly paused and smirked. Looking back on it, Jukichi guessed that he might have smiled thinking of the lover he'd left back on land. This was the smile that apparently rubbed the other crewman, who had a wife and young child waiting for him at home, the wrong way. It was impossible for him to get along with a trainee like Jukichi, a student at a fishery school who was likely to step into a leadership role on his next voyage. After all, he could end up finding himself on a boat with Jukichi as the skipper. Imagining himself having to work under the newbie was enough to drive anyone crazy. So the crewman took every opportunity to give the trainee a hard time. But looking over and seeing that he still had the wherewithal to stand there smirking to himself pushed him over the edge.

Right as Jukichi fell to the deck after being struck, a wave crashed against the starboard side of the bow, tilting the hull so that he slid on his back across the deck and hit his head against the gunwale next to the gangway. He lay awkwardly there like an overturned frog. Something tingled beneath his eyes, and his hand came away covered in blood when he tried to wipe his face. The sea's spray stung as it fell into the wound. Seemingly unsatisfied with just punching, the man rushed at Jukichi and began kicking him in the crotch as he struggled. This finally broke Jukichi, and he lost his reason entirely. Bending at his waist, he turned himself over and leaped to his feet to defend himself.

"Fucking asshole!"

In an instant, Jukichi's relief at the prospect of returning to Japan after only a little more hardship transformed into an instinctive readiness for battle. Up till then, he had managed to tolerate this man during the voyage well enough. Ten years older, the man was a seasoned crewman, and he strutted around the boat like a master fisherman. But he possessed a difficult personality and a short fuse, which made the other crewmen shun him, leaving him isolated and alone. The skipper, especially, seemed to resent the man's reflexive opposition to his every command and hated him from the bottom of his heart. So when Jukichi stood up to him on the deck, he had that context in mind. He optimistically expected that when push came to shove, his fellow crewmen would have his back. It wasn't a conscious calculation, though. This idea about the balance of power on the boat rushed into his head during the split second he leaped to his feet to shout back at the man who'd hit him.

Seeing Jukichi standing ready to meet his attack, the man paused, but only briefly, before resuming his charge. His fierce expression remained unchanged.

The twenty-four seamen on this old-fashioned freezer troller *Kaiho Maru No. 2* were rough individuals with at least one or two eccentricities each. Many had tattoos, and some spent their days ostentatiously sharpening knives out on the main deck. Others showed off guns they'd smuggled aboard and were careful to keep them out of sight of the skipper. They'd play cards while drinking *shochu* like water, and when the balance of winners and losers got too one-sided, or when they drank too much, fights would break out. When that happened, the other men would do little to intervene at first. The idea seemed to be to let squabbles take their natural course, and only when a clear winner had emerged would anyone step in, saying, "Okay, that's enough." Sometimes, this intervention would be too late, and someone would actually end up dying. But one rule was never broken: no one ever threw another man into the ocean. This was the rule among the seamen, it seemed. They could try to kill each other with knives, but throwing someone overboard was the ultimate taboo. It was strange. But without this unspoken rule, all jokes aside, no one would be left on the boat if an all-out war between factions broke out. In the midst of a brawl, if someone they were facing was in danger of falling overboard, they'd just help him back on board and then continue fighting.

The men around Jukichi and his attacker were content to simply watch when the fight erupted. As it turned out, though, there was hardly time to watch before the skipper angrily intervened.

"If you have time to squabble, you have time to work!"

The skipper's words were loud enough for everyone on the boat to hear. A fisherman stopped in the middle of the gangway with a fish hanging from his hook, and he turned his head when he heard someone shout, "It's a fight!" At that moment, the bigeye in his hand shook itself free, and he found himself clocked on the head by the boatswain. The haulers were clattering as the lines were wound back in, and the fishermen were at their posts, busy removing the fins and guts of the bigeyes falling into the boat. Only Jukichi and the other man stood apart, facing off on the deck.

After exchanging a few blows to the face and head, the two men began to grapple, soon falling together onto the boards. Jukichi headbutted the other man's nose, shoved a knee into his stomach, and then found himself astride the man as they punched each other in the face. His brain couldn't even process the pain, and darkness was beginning to shroud his eyes. From the depths of this darkness came something else—the urge to kill. An urge he felt also in the man he was fighting. In this exchange of blows, where one moment he was attacking and the next being attacked, fear ended up eclipsed by a sense of exhilaration. Right then, Jukichi felt a sharp sting in his thigh, different from all the other pains he'd sustained. He glimpsed a flash of metal in his combatant's right hand and realized the man had slipped a handmade knife out of the boot where he'd hidden it and stabbed him. Jukichi grabbed the man's right wrist with both hands. He knew that he could easily lose his life if he loosened his grip even a little, so he tried his best to bend the man's wrist away from him. As he did, the boat was rocked by another wave, tilting sharply. He heard a voice cry out right next to his ear, then saw gouts of fresh blood pouring over his ears and shoulders. It seemed that the man had lost his balance as the boat tipped, and he'd fallen down onto Jukichi—and onto the knife in the hand Jukichi still gripped by the wrist. The blade slid deep into the man's left shoulder. This development, at last, prompted the approach of the distinctive sounds of seawater-soaked boots as his fellow fishermen rushed over from all sides and pulled the two men apart. Once the man's body no longer occupied his field of vision, Jukichi collapsed onto his back, his chest heaving as sunlight poured down upon him. He hadn't felt the sun in what seemed like ages. His sense of time was paralyzed. The fight had probably lasted only a minute, but it felt as though a near-eternity had passed.

The other fishermen were much more preoccupied with the older man than with Jukichi. They were peering down at his prone form and murmuring, "This looks bad..." Jukichi sat up to take a look himself. *It's just a flesh wound to the shoulder, how bad could it be?* he thought, only to be confronted by the sight of blood spurting up like a fountain from the man's shoulder. The resigned looks on the fishermen's faces as they peered down at the man told the rest of the story: the point of the blade seemed to have cut through the artery running beneath his left clavicle. There was nothing to do at that point, and so the fishermen simply stood there, watching the man as he lay gasping. Soon enough, the man drew his last breath, his blood flowing out to mix with the discarded bigeye guts and fins littering the deck around him.

The fishing work was temporarily suspended, and the skipper, the captain, the chief engineer, and then everyone else on the boat all crowded onto the deck. Everyone was discussing what to do with the body. Newer boats had modern freezing systems that would have made the problem simple to solve—all they would have had to do was freeze the corpse and take it back to Japan. But an old-fashioned freezer troller like this one lacked the ability to do such a thing, and the prospect of transporting a body back to Japan through the heat of the tropics and subtropics filled everyone with dread. A skipper had the power to authorize a burial at sea if a crewmember died during a voyage. But the skipper of the *Kaiho Maru No. 2* hesitated to do so. On a previous occasion, he'd authorized the sea burial of a fisherman who had been killed in an accident, but the family of the deceased had been upset about it and caused a lot of trouble.

The tuna boat happened to be passing by a seemingly uninhabited island in the Caroline archipelago at the time. Glimpsing its outline in the distance beneath the blazing sun, the skipper came up with an idea: they would use a dinghy to transport the body to the island and cremate it there. Then, they could take the bones back to Japan. But who should be made to do such a thing? Perhaps as a form of punishment, Jukichi found himself tasked to complete this mission alone. After all, he was the one responsible.

Early the next morning, the *Kaiho Maru No. 2* dropped anchor and lowered the dinghy into the water. Jukichi felt increasingly forlorn as he looked up at the broadside of the boat that was slowly receding from his seat by the corpse. No, forlorn was the wrong word. He felt ghastly, and his horror colored even the sea itself. He held in his arms a glass jar that had previously stored food preserved in soy sauce, and he had an oil lighter in his pocket. His task was to use the lighter to set fire to the body after setting it atop whatever tropical wood he could gather onshore, then place the burnt bones in the jar to bring back to Japan... Jukichi had seen a body post-cremation once before, but it was long ago, back when he was around ten years old. The cremated body didn't even look human. The colors of the skin and blood were lost, and even its facial features were indistinct amid the blackened pile of former flesh. It no longer seemed to have any relation to a living thing. If the eyes disappeared, so would his dread to some extent. But the corpse lay at Jukichi's feet as he rowed the dinghy toward the island, and no matter how he tried to avert his eyes from it, he somehow felt its gaze on him. He'd taken this man's life with his own hands. The sun began to rise, and depending on the angle, the pale cheek of the dead man sparkled as if he was still alive.

Finally, Jukichi's boat touched the sand of the island's shore.

Just as it had seemed from the tuna boat, the island appeared to be completely uninhabited. Of course, there might have been people living on the far shore or somewhere in the shadows of the mangroves, but as far as he could see, he was alone. Jukichi tied the dinghy with a bowline knot to one of the palms that were bending out toward the water, then pulled it up onto the sand. After parting the mangrove foliage to double-check for signs of inhabitation, he lifted the corpse and the canister of diesel oil out of the dinghy. The sun was inching steadily toward its zenith, and the air was deathly still. The *Kaiho Maru No. 2* lay due east, anchored in wait, and the figures of the men as they worked on the deck appeared a solid black in the sun. It had been fifteen hours since the man at his feet had lost his life. The heat was beginning to make him smell.

Jukichi had no idea how best to cremate a body. It would be one thing to simply burn it to a crisp, but he needed to make a fire hot enough to transform the body into ash-like bones so that they fit in the wide-mouthed jar. Nonetheless, he had to get started, and so he walked into the mangroves to gather the wood.

He needed to light a fire, but the plants were all too green and wet to catch. Looking around, he caught sight of some bougainvillea flowers peeking through the foliage like flames. They reminded him of a story he'd heard from one of the older fishermen. On the return home from a particularly prosperous voyage in the South Seas, the boat had docked at an island so that the men could amuse themselves. They swam to shore with little bottles of hair lotion tied to their heads and then used it on the bodies of the island women waiting for them. They rubbed the lotion into their tanned skin to make it glossy and slick as they played together. *Amazing,* thought young Jukichi as he'd imagined the scene. The bougainvillea flowers the women wore in their hair as they bid farewell to the men returning to the boat now symbolized the flames he needed to conjure, and they bloomed vivid red around him.

Jukichi gathered up as much fallen wood as possible. Despite not really knowing what he was doing, he managed to stack it well enough to create a makeshift pyre. He then slid the slender, flexible branches he had collected from the willow-like island pine through the spaces in the stacked wood. The needles were slightly yellow, a color that seemed to anticipate the flames that would soon consume the structure. He poured diesel oil over the whole thing, and then it was ready: the funeral pyre sat on top of the packed sand of the beach, which itself rested on an unseen bed of coral reef. Jukichi lifted the corpse and set it carefully on the structure, then stood back to check that it wouldn't fall. Gripping the oil lighter in one hand, he walked around to examine his handiwork. He was ready, but he couldn't make himself do it. Once he lit the wood, the body would burn. He found himself looking from every conceivable angle at this man he'd killed. The sun beat down as it climbed higher in the sky above them. Perhaps its heat would burn the body black for him even without the fire.

The smell of oil didn't suit the place. Jukichi re-entered the mangrove and picked several blooming branches of bougainvillea to place upon the corpse's chest. He wasn't wracked with guilt or regret or worried about what might befall him when he returned to Japan. Rather, he was consumed by the sheer sight of the corpse lying there, covered in vivid red flowers, with the palms rising up like a backdrop behind it. The stink of the oil pricked his nose. It filled him with terror to contemplate the absolute disharmony he'd created in this tropical paradise. He felt like he was in the presence of a god. The pale, bloodless face of the man lying on the pyre was otherworldly, divine. Jukichi finally lit the branch in his hand and threw it onto the pyre.

The crackling flames licked up and, for a fleeting moment, breathed new life into the corpse. The man's face twisted, and his head and arms that had been pressed down began to shake and break the branches supporting them. His mouth opened into a scream. Jukichi, standing near his feet, turned toward the man's head to try to hear his words. The man tightened his lips, and his scream turned into sobs. The frizzled hairs stood up from his head. What was he trying to say?

The wind picked up, blowing the smoke and stink in one direction, and Jukichi looked up toward the sky. Clouds moved along the distant horizon. How awful if another squall blew in right after he managed to set this fire! *Become bones already,* he thought, and then poked at the body with a stick. It tore open the seared skin, and intestines unspooled from the resulting wound. They were like a separate organism entirely. Swelling and rising up with the flames, they changed shape and color as they moved. Jukichi watched the body as it burned so closely that every detail—every color, every odor—was seared into his brain. Something within him flared up too. His cells were burning. Wherever the flames died down, he applied more oil to the spot. For some reason, though, the man's toes didn't burn like the rest of his body. They remained untouched at the tips of the blackened sticks of his feet. Prodded by the sight of their flesh, Jukichi splashed oil on them again and again. Even when he pushed them into the strongest flames, the man's nails refused to turn black. His toes remained intact to the very end.

It took around eight hours, but the man's body finally became a pile of blackened bones. The setting sun dyed the sea in the west red as Jukichi rowed the dinghy back to the *Kaiho Maru No. 2*, the burnt bones stowed safely in the glass jar beside him. The dead man had turned black, but Jukichi's hair had turned white. The flames and smell of burning flesh had aged his body and soul in less than a single day, and he hadn't realized it until his fellow crewmen pointed it out to him.

3

"How old do I look to you?"

The question made Yoichi look with new eyes at the deep creases in Jukichi's face and neck. The man's skin had been burnt by the sun and tide, blemished in places by what looked like age spots. From the shoulders up, he could easily pass for seventy. But judging from that question, Yoichi realized that he must be much younger than his appearance suggested.

"I know how I look, but I'm actually forty-five," Jukichi said.

"So young."

"It aged me horribly."

After burning the body and returning to the boat, Jukichi's fellow crewmen had crowded around him, asking, "What happened to you out there?" Filled with trepidation, he'd peered into a mirror and discovered that he'd aged more than ten years in a single day. And it wasn't just his appearance that had changed—the entire trip back to Japan, he hardly spoke a word to anyone. More than killing a man, it was burning a human body all by himself on that tropical island that changed him, body and soul.

"What became of the bones you brought back?" asked Yoichi.

"We gave them to his family, of course. He had a wife and a little kid..."

Jukichi visited the family of the man he'd killed soon after his return. There, in that dimly lit tatami-floored room, he'd offered the man's bones—transferred from the glass jar that had held preserved food to a proper ossuary—to his impassive wife. Her expression was dark, her eyes downcast, but she didn't seem to be mourning her husband's death. As he explained what had happened, her only response was a weak sigh that troubled him more than any outpouring of hatred would have. Had she not loved him, her own husband? Because he'd always been out at sea? But judging from how the man had behaved on the boat, it was unlikely he'd treated her very well at home. She even looked relieved at being allowed to escape his violence. The darkness of her expression at hearing the news seemed to stem solely from her worries about how she'd support herself and her young child.

Even though it had been unintentional, or perhaps in self-defense, it concerned Yoichi that Jukichi seemed to have escaped judgment for taking the life of another. While the crewmen apparently agreed to tell the authorities the man had fallen overboard by accident, someone harboring a grudge against Jukichi could still use the truth against him. But something else bothered Yoichi even more.

What does any of this have to do with Akimitsu Miyazaki?

Contemplating this question, Yoichi recalled the mental image he'd conjured of the mother and the young child sitting next to her. His mind's eye focused in on the child.

"That man's kid... Was it a boy?"

"Yes."

Now Yoichi was sure.

"That boy grew up to become Miyazaki, didn't he?"

As if relieved that Yoichi had finally figured it out, Jukichi turned to look at him.

"Yes. He turned out to be as terrible as his father. But you understand now, don't you? I owe him."

Jukichi shuddered at the thought of the thick blood binding father and son. He knew about Miyazaki's habit of complaining that his feet were hot. Hearing that he liked to sleep with his feet sticking out from beneath his blanket, Jukichi once snuck into the bunk at night to see for himself. Opening the door, he peered in and found that the rumors were true: his toes were sticking incongruously out from the blanket. The sight chilled him to the bone. The blanket was brown, but as Jukichi stared at it, it seemed to turn the color of fire. The stink of burning flesh and the smell of the diesel oil he'd splashed on the toes that refused to burn came back to him as well. It was so raw, this memory of the man's two feet sticking out from the pyre of burning sticks. The heat of the fire that had engulfed his father's feet had been passed down along with the grudge to the son. The sight filled him with such terror that he nearly forgot himself and screamed aloud.

What did Jukichi owe the son of the man he killed? Did he have to shoulder the responsibility for the rest of his life? Perhaps this had more to do with Jukichi than Miyazaki, thought Yoichi. It was a punishment he was visiting upon himself. He'd escaped the law, so he decided that meant he owed fealty to the bearer of the man's remaining genetic material. He was someone who would feel duty-bound to bear the burden till the day he died.

"You may owe a debt to Miyazaki, but I don't. I know what binds you two together now, but it doesn't change the fact that he's a bastard!"

"You're right, of course."

"Things on the boat will fall apart if you keep letting him do whatever he wants. As skipper, you've got to step in and do something."

"Are you talking about expulsion?"

Expulsion: the word struck Yoichi as so extreme. To expel was to remove something unacceptable from a place completely, irrevocably. In short, it was exactly what Jukichi had done to Miyazaki's father all those years ago. He'd killed him, turned him to ash, and erased every trace of his existence from this world.

"That's not necessarily what I mean..."

"Yoichi, listen. I need to look the other way with Miyazaki. I don't have a choice—if I try to discipline him, who knows what sort of hell might break loose on this boat. Twenty-five years ago, I got rid of someone entirely—I *expelled* him. I did it because I thought my fellow crewmen all felt the same way as me. But I can never do something like that again."

Yoichi had nothing to say to that. He knew the power a group could have, as he'd experienced it firsthand as part of the theater troupe. The more closed and isolated a group was, the more extreme the system for expelling a foreign element became. A boat was like a locked psychiatric ward floating all alone on the sea.

"Then what am I supposed to do?"

"Let it go."

"Let it go?"

"Yeah."

"Wait a minute—"

Jukichi laughed.

"Don't try anything with Miyazaki, trust me. One of you would end up dead. And it'd probably be you."

Jukichi wasn't exaggerating. His words rang uncomfortably true to Yoichi. A faint shudder passed through his body. Just the thought of a fight to the death with a man like Miyazaki was enough to shake him to the core. And it would be a dog's death. Boarding the *Wakashio Maru No. 7* had been like getting a second chance at life. He had no intention of wasting it. He'd boarded this tuna boat, an entirely uncharted territory, so that he could experience a whole new way of life. He hadn't come here to die. This was what Yoichi told himself.

4

At the beginning of October, the *Wakashio Maru No. 7* met the four-thousand-ton medical supply ship *Hoyo Maru No. 2* that circulated through the waters of the South Pacific. The purpose was to replenish things like fuel, food, and bait. A tuna boat like the *Wakashio* used not only foreign ports, but also ships that serviced specific routes to restock on supplies. Replenishing at sea regularly allowed tuna boats to complete their journeys without having to dock on shore. However, a boat still had to go ashore from time to time, if only so the men could regain their morale. And so the *Wakashio* only restocked on the minimum supplies necessary to continue its voyage.

A ship like this delivered letters and packages from Japan addressed to the crewmen out at sea, and it provided care to anyone who might have fallen ill. It went the other way, too: the ship received outgoing mail from the crewmen, and they also took in Mizukoshi, who could no longer stand on his own due to Miyazaki's abuse. The ship's doctor diagnosed Mizukoshi with a type of hysteria and recommended he be transported home while receiving care on the way. His inability to stand was traced to an unconscious wish to escape the harsh conditions aboard the tuna boat, and it was likely he'd recover from his psychological trauma once he was home. So it was decided he'd be taken to Auckland and brought by plane back to Japan. Yoichi was relieved to hear Mizukoshi's condition wasn't serious. They had encouraged each other during their time on the boat, and he was sorry to see his comrade-in-arms leave. But they vowed earnestly to meet again once they were both back in Japan, and he saw Mizukoshi off.

Almost all of the crewmen with family back home received letters and packages, but Yoichi expected to receive nothing. All he had in the way of family, after all, was his elderly mother and his brother, a salaryman working in Hiroshima. Yoichi had only told his mother of his plan to board the tuna boat a day before he left. He had called her from Misaki and told her just the boat's name. He tried to hang up before she could say something, but he heard her cry out.

"Wait, you—!"

These truncated words, and the blame they carried, bled from the receiver as he slammed it down, and they echoed in his head even now. He imagined the rest of her sentence to be, "You unfilial wretch!" He'd chosen a unilateral way to tell her that he was leaving so she wouldn't have the time to get angry or change his mind, but it backfired, and his abruptness made her explode with rage. Thinking back on the events leading up to his departure, he supposed her anger was natural. As an unfilial son, he'd only caused trouble for her, and there was no way she'd send anything to him. Yoichi cast a sidelong glance at his fellow crewmen happily receiving their packages, then turned his gaze to the sea as a wave of loneliness washed over him.

Contrary to his expectations, though, Yoichi did end up with a package placed in his hands. It had his name, Yoichi Maki, written on it. There was no mistake. But he didn't recognize the name on the return address.

"Takeshi Sunako." He read it under his breath a few times, trying to recall if he'd heard it before. Rooting around in the recesses of his mind, he strained to remember the faces and names of old friends from elementary or junior high school, then mentally separated the two names in case the surname might have changed due to adoption. But he didn't have a clue who it might be. Seeing it was a Hamamatsu address, he figured it must be someone he'd known in high school or before, as he'd left Kosai at nineteen to attend university in Tokyo.

Yoichi opened the package while he walked along the deck. There was a video cassette and a letter inside. It was common for fishermen at sea to receive videotaped "letters" from their families. He remembered seeing tough crewmen who'd been away from home for a year or more weep while they watched clips of their babies taking their first steps. So receiving a videotape wasn't in itself such a rare thing. But to get one from a complete stranger left him consumed with curiosity. He went back to his bunk and put the tape in the VHS machine there, then leaned forward with his face close to the fourteen-inch CRT television screen as he waited in anticipation.

The image shuddered at first, then resolved into what appeared to be the white wall of a hospital-like building. He could hear cicadas buzzing in the trees in the back of the shot: *oh-zingg-chk-chk!* It was the sound of summer's end. The almost stereotypically Japanese scenery and sounds pricked Yoichi's homesickness. But then, as if to disrupt this feeling, a young woman walked into the center of the frame. Those slow, dreamy footsteps… She seemed thinner than before. Her hair was longer. She was wearing no makeup, and her face was unhealthily pale. Those eyes, fringed with thick lashes, were slightly lowered.

"Sayuri…"

Yoichi almost cried out, but her name caught in his throat.

The screen momentarily went black, and then a new scene appeared. Sayuri was sitting on a bench. Whoever was holding the camera had the sun to his back, and his shadow stretched across the grass almost to Sayuri's feet. A young man's voice came from somewhere nearby.

"Smile, Sayuri!

"That's it, look this way.

"Over here, look here."

It was as if he were talking to a child. But the young man's was the only voice to be heard. Sayuri never said a word. The camera zoomed in on her face, and Yoichi could see how dulled her eyes had become. This wasn't the Sayuri he knew.

Where is this?

Yoichi looked at the name on the package again.

Takeshi Sunako.

Is that who's holding the camera?

The video now showed Sayuri's body from the side, the camera lingering on the area around her stomach before moving slowly up to her face. Somewhere in the distance, two women walked by dressed in white uniforms.

This is definitely a hospital. What's going on? Is she still there? It's been more than half a year.

Yoichi thought about what these images might mean. What was the message behind them? He couldn't figure out why the tape had been sent to him, and it made him angry that the reality he'd meant to leave behind had followed him out to sea. Yet, he was also overcome with nostalgia and love. His heart was split in two, and his conscious mind was unable to keep his body from responding on its own: he broke down, bursting into tears right then and there. It was a completely unexpected reaction. He'd thought of her many times during this voyage, of course, but such was the power of an image. He lost all control and wept so hard it seemed he'd never stop.

Sayuri sat silently on the bench, her eyes blank as she stared into the camera. The light in her bright eyes had been snuffed out completely. Her unfocused gaze rendered any emotion she might be feeling totally unreadable. Yoichi tore his own gaze from the screen and buried his face in his sleeve. A single word resounded in his mind: *regret*. But almost immediately, a different voice also spoke within him. *Perhaps it's for the best,* it said. Just like always, self-indictment was followed by self-justification. Yoichi regained his composure and, springing up to his feet, picked up the letter that had come with the tape.

Dear Mister Yoichi Maki,

Please forgive this sudden delivery. I know it must be quite a shock. Were you able to look at the enclosed videotape? As I am sure you are aware, the woman on the tape is Sayuri Asakawa. She is currently being cared for at Matsui Hospital, a psychiatric hospital located in the outskirts of Hamamatsu. On the night of July 23, she attempted to drown herself off the coast of the Nakatajima Sand Dunes, and she is now suffering from various impairments as a result of the shock, including loss of memory, speech, and the ability to express emotion.

I was a patient in the same hospital, and that is where I got to know her. Since I am not a professional, I am unqualified to say more about the details of her condition. However, even the doctors are having trouble diagnosing her. The only thing that is clear at present is her total inability to communicate. Therefore, it was not from her that I learned of you, but rather from Mr. Ugami, the director of Panic Theater. He told me about the incident that transpired between you. Please know that my inquiries were done strictly in the interest of helping Sayuri's treatment—I never meant to impinge upon your privacy. The doctor in charge of Sayuri's case (the brilliant Dr. Mochizuki) told me that a patient's medical and family history can provide essential information in their treatment. But in Sayuri's case, she has no relatives and is unable to give us any details herself, and it has stalled her treatment's progress. There is a real possibility that she might spend the rest of her life unable to connect and interact with the outside world.

With this in mind, I have written to you with a humble request: if you are willing, could you provide us with as much information about her as you can? According to my research, you are the closest person to her. I understand the presumptuous nature of my request, but I implore you to help as we attempt to shed light on the inner workings of her heart.

There is one final thing I feel obligated to bring to your attention. As you may have noticed in the footage, Sayuri is pregnant. She appears to be about six months along. We humbly ask for your cooperation on this matter as well.

Sincerely,
Takeshi Sunako
September 2

Finishing the letter, it was the last line that bothered Yoichi most.

We humbly ask for your cooperation on this matter as well. What did that mean? What did this Takeshi Sunako person want from him, exactly? Was this a way of asking if Yoichi was the father? Or was he implying that Yoichi should return to Japan as soon as possible to assume his responsibilities to mother and child?

Whatever the case, it was none of this person's business. Yoichi crumpled the letter up in his hands. But soon after, the sheer fact of Sayuri's pregnancy began to sink in. *If she was six months along on September 2...* Yoichi counted back in his head. Indeed, it was not impossible.

That child may well be mine.

His intuition began to work. He thought he understood why she'd tried to drown herself. When she discovered she was pregnant, she'd looked for the father. And when she reached his family's home in Kosai, she'd found out he'd hopped a tuna boat and was somewhere in the South Pacific. She realized he'd run away from her, and she had no way to follow him since he was out at sea. Yet the child within her continued to grow. Finally, she had a nervous breakdown and threw herself into the waves. The Pacific-facing Nakatajima Sand Dunes were a place to die that provided a connection to the man who'd fled from her.

The video had continued to play even as he read the letter. There was no sound, so he'd forgotten it was still running until he looked back up at the screen. Sayuri was still sitting on the bench in the hospital courtyard. Her position was unchanged, as was her expression as she sat with her hands resting on her knees. He turned his attention to her belly, which was framed by her elbows on either side. There did seem to be a slight swelling there. His heart began to beat faster as he stared at it. Overcome by a sudden desire to be free of it all, he punched the eject button on the VHS player, grabbed the tape as it popped out, then ran out onto the deck with it and the wadded-up letter gripped in his hands. He continued running and then threw both the letter and tape into the sea. The crumpled letter hit the boat's broadside and tumbled out to float on the waves, while the tape fell end-over-end in an arc before being swallowed, its passage marked by only a small splash as it disappeared. That was all he wanted, for everything to disappear forever... He'd gotten on this boat so that he could throw away everything in his old life and start a brand new one. Yet, here he was, confronted with these images. He couldn't stand it. And so he cast them into the sea, hoping he wouldn't be reminded of them ever again.

Sayuri has nothing to do with me anymore! I don't care if she's carrying my child!

Even as he told himself this, he heard a voice telling him the opposite. He did his best to shut it out. But memories of how things had unfolded between them kept bubbling up anyway, as if summoned by the needling questions posed by this Takeshi Sunako. Whoever he was, Yoichi couldn't send him an answer now, even if he wanted to. The return address was gone, along with the tape. That didn't stop him from asking himself the question, though: how had things gone so wrong? He recalled when he'd first met Sayuri. That summer five years ago, he was in his final year as a student. Even as graduation approached, he couldn't make himself focus on finding a job. Wasn't there some other option besides becoming a salaryman? He was trying to figure his life out during that time. And, of course, he could never forget how it ended. Six months ago, the life he had with Sayuri got washed away in a torrent of fresh blood.

5

All at once, the cicadas covering the trunk of the tree exploded into flight. Surprised, Yoichi looked up and followed with his eyes as the cloud of insects dispersed, the harsh buzz of their wingbeats dissipating like mist. He sat up and looked over at the redness of the bricks in the library wall next to him that seemed to warm his skin. The sound of passing students talking and laughing grew louder and louder around him, and the noise of the cicadas had disappeared completely. He'd caught sight of a job recruitment flyer posted on a university bulletin board and it had put him in a funk, so he'd wandered aimlessly around the campus, finally ending up stretched out on this bench, taking a nap. The dream of cicadas he had right before he woke up was still fresh in his mind, and he looked up into the sky as he rubbed the sleep from his eyes. He felt like he could still hear them. But their season was still a month away. The dream left him wistful, gripped with inexplicable nostalgia. It would be one thing to long for something in the past, but what did it mean to feel like this about a season that was still approaching? There was something unnatural about it.

It was only June, but the campus was crowded with students. All his friends seemed to talk about nothing but their respective job searches, so Yoichi found himself avoiding them and spending most of his time alone. He stood up from the bench and began to head down the hill toward the campus's east entrance.

As he descended the slope, he saw a longhaired woman standing next to the motorcycle he'd parked in the shade of the trees lining the sidewalk. She seemed to be paying an unusual amount of attention to his modest four-hundred-cc single-cylinder bike, peering at the speedometer and running both hands along the smooth curves of the gas tank. Watching a young woman show so much interest in his motorcycle made Yoichi tremble, as if it were his body she caressed instead. The woman was dressed in a light-pink blouse and a diaphanous green skirt. She didn't really look like the type to be into motorcycles. Her back was to the entrance, so he couldn't see her face. But he could see a flash of pale skin at the nape of her neck where her long hair parted.

Almost as if she was hugging the bike, she continued running her hands over it, seemingly unaware of his approaching footsteps. She gripped the accelerator, gently squeezing and releasing it. Soon, Yoichi was standing right next to her, and he took his keys out of his pocket.

"Um, excuse me."

He twirled the keys around his finger to show he was the owner.

"What?" said the woman as she turned. "Oh, is this your motorcycle?"

"Yeah, it is."

Yoichi stuck the key into the ignition and released the handle lock, then peered back at the woman. Her smile was distorted, as if she was forcing it... Yet it also accentuated her beauty, lighting up the features of her oval face.

"I'm sorry."

She slowly withdrew her hand from the accelerator.

"Don't worry, it's fine."

"Is it fast?"

The woman's gaze had returned to the motorcycle.

"No."

Yoichi's answer was blunt. This four-stroke bike of his would never be *fast*.

"Really? But it looks like it'd be..."

"Even a two-stroke, fifty-cc bike would probably be faster."

"That can't be true."

"Well, it depends on the rider."

"I was thinking of getting my license."

"You were?"

"Is that weird?"

"No, of course not."

Yoichi opened the helmet holder to get his helmet, but then stopped. He found that he didn't want to get on his bike, start the engine, and ride away. And it was because of this free-flowing conversation he was having with this woman—a conversation she herself seemed to be steering.

The woman introduced herself, explaining that she was not a fellow university student, but rather an actress just starting out in a small theater troupe called the Wind Theater Company. She'd come to the university to post flyers on the bulletin boards for their next show, which was going up in a month's time. Her empty hands seemed to signify that she'd completed her task. The mention of the bulletin boards reminded him of his job search, but his anxiety eased as he imagined the flyers for this woman's play posted side-by-side with the dreaded job notices. He had no real sense of what kind of production a small theater troupe might put on, but he nonetheless felt compelled to support this woman in her efforts.

"Give me a ride!"

She asked this without preamble, her eyes filled with yearning. Not only her words but her entire being—her eyes, her face, her body—was alight with her desire to ride his bike, and she'd interrupted their conversation with this rather peremptory request.

"I can't, I don't have a helmet for you."

Yoichi's reply, however, was matter-of-fact. If this were an American movie, she'd be riding behind him on the freeway without a helmet already, but here in Japan, they'd surely be stopped by a traffic cop in no time.

"You can't?"

The woman's whole body seemed to deflate in disappointment.

"I'm sorry. If I get two more citations, I'll lose my license."

"I see."

Her face full of regret, the woman tapped lightly on the bike's gas tank. Their conversation paused right there. He felt like it would end for good if either of them said, "Well then," and a moment of awkwardness stretched between them. Yoichi wanted to invite her to have a coffee, but, not wanting to sound like some guy trying out a pick-up line, he didn't. He had the feeling it would diminish him in her eyes to do something like that. Both his desire to make the most of this encounter and his pride, which wanted her to see him as someone special, stopped him from asking.

But the woman's expression changed suddenly, and she broke the silence between them.

"Why don't you take me to lunch instead, then?"

Yoichi searched the woman's face to see if she was joking.

"Please? I'd love something to eat. I'm really hungry."

Yoichi removed the key from the ignition.

"Are you serious?"

"Yes."

The audacity of a woman asking something like that of a man she'd just met came as a refreshing surprise. It made him feel like they were already longtime friends. And it reminded him of hearing a song for the first time but thinking he'd heard it somewhere before. That sense of familiarity all but guaranteed it would be a song he'd end up liking. Perhaps all this meant, though, was that his tastes had been set in stone long ago.

"Follow me." Yoichi slipped his keys back in his pocket and headed toward his usual coffee shop.

This was how Yoichi met Sayuri. As they ate a light lunch together, they exchanged names and phone numbers. Hearing that she'd once been an idol singer, he was even more intrigued. He imagined all the young men who'd surely had a crush on her... What luck, then, to get the chance to talk with her one-on-one like this! It didn't matter how obscure she might have actually been, her specialness made him feel special, too, and his sense of self-worth tingled at the thought of it.

Yoichi bought Sayuri a helmet the next day, and within three days, she was riding behind him as they drove out to the Miura Peninsula, where they spent the evening swimming in the night-dark sea. He helped the Wind Theater Company with their performance the following month, and the alcohol as well as the camaraderie he felt toward the troupe led him to accept their invitation to join up himself, opening a new path for his life to take. The unease and uncertainty he'd felt about his job search blew away in an instant. He'd been gripped by dissatisfaction at the prospect of spending the rest of his life as a salaryman. But he'd also lacked any other vision for his future. Meeting Sayuri and joining the theater troupe, however, gave him a sense of direction and determination. He redoubled his efforts at his part-time job and soon ended up moving in with her.

At first, living with Sayuri, he didn't notice her darker side. But as they spent more and more time alone together, his first impression of her as an eccentric young woman who sang like an angel began to change. He would catch glimpses of a deep instability hidden in the corners of her mind, unable to tell if it was something innate or something that resulted from some kind of experience. Yet, he couldn't deny that it was also part of her allure. Other women her age seemed so generic, so lacking in individuality. Sayuri's slippery, elusive nature made her stand out, as if she gave off a mysterious glow.

Sayuri owned a tidy two-bedroom apartment she'd inherited from her father after he passed away the previous year. Her mother was deceased, too. Yoichi got the impression that Sayuri had been no more than two years old at the time she lost her mother. But he decided not to pry, as she obviously didn't want to talk about her parents' deaths and what might have caused them.

It'd be easy to attribute the intermittent strangeness Yoichi saw in Sayuri's behavior to the fact that she'd lost both her parents. But that seemed too simple an explanation for the depth of her eccentricity. He felt like there was something more hidden in the bottom of her heart—not just loneliness, but something else...

"Save me."

This was what Sayuri uttered one night, having collapsed onto the carpet right after they'd come back to the apartment they shared in Yukigaya. He'd finished his shift and they'd gone to Shibuya to have drinks with some theater troupe friends, and she'd seemed perfectly fine right up to the moment they stepped through the door and said, "We're back!" But the color drained from her face with every subsequent step she took into the apartment, and ultimately, she collapsed to the floor.

"Save me."

She said it again, the exact same words. She didn't explain what she wanted him to save her from or how he might do it. Instead, she repeated those two words again and again, until finally, she added a new phrase, "I've got nowhere to run." Her voice was low and drained of life, almost unimaginable coming from someone who spoke in such an artificially chipper tone during rehearsals. Looking down at the carpet, he saw that her shoulders were shivering despite the intense lingering heat of the day.

"What are you running from?" he asked, but she remained tight-lipped. Instead of answering, she started to hum a melody, and her face brightened as she began to sing the lyrics as well. It was like she'd transformed into an entirely different person.

"How's this? Do you like it?" Her verve returned as she improvised. Yoichi couldn't make heads or tails of her rapidly changing expressions. He didn't know which version of her to believe.

Yoichi never heard the words, "Save me," pass Sayuri's lips again. But that didn't mean the sentiment behind them left her. Rather, the pent-up feeling would boil over from time to time, darkening her face as it bled from her eyes and mouth, even as it remained unspoken.

There were other incidents. For example, one morning in the early summer around a year after they'd moved in together, Sayuri began to do some fortune-telling using a deck of cards while Yoichi lay beside her in bed. Half asleep, he idly wondered what she might be trying to divine as he listened to her talking to herself.

"Oh no!

"Leave us alone!

"Love is a game—you have to give a little to get what you want."

She sounded like a typical girl in her twenties as she cut the cards. He watched her as she tried to find out what her future held, but she suddenly hunched over, her features hardening into an expression quite unlike her former girlishness.

"I see. Even you say so. A fifty-fifty chance..."

She appeared to be addressing the cards themselves as "you."

Yoichi raised himself up in the bed. "What're you trying to find out?"

"Nothing in particular..."

"What's a fifty-fifty chance?"

"Oh, you were listening?"

"I wasn't *listening.* You were making such a racket I couldn't sleep!"

Yoichi wasn't actually angry.

"That's the chance you and I will end up happy."

"Even odds, then?"

"Yes."

What bothered Yoichi was the way she addressed the cards when she said, "I see. Even you say so." He'd graduated from university, and, having decided to devote himself completely to acting and theater instead of entering the conventional job market, he had a keen interest in what lay in the hearts of people as they chose the words they spoke. Her sentences implied that she'd been told the same thing before. *A fifty-fifty chance.* Who would have told her she had a fifty percent chance of being happy?

"Did someone say that to you before?"

"Hm?"

"What you said...about the fifty-fifty chance..."

Sayuri looked at Yoichi with an indefinable expression. If it had been a play, it would have been impossible to predict what sort of line would come next. She could have been on the verge of passionate lovemaking or about to resign herself to death—it was an odd look that could be interpreted in a thousand ways. But her features quickly warmed into a smile and she gathered up the cards in front of her. "Gotta pee, gotta pee!" she exclaimed as she dashed into the bathroom. The next thing he heard was the sound of her urinating loudly, as if to wash away the tiny doubts from his head.

She was always evading issues like this. As soon as it would seem like they were coming close to reaching the heart of a problem, she would change the subject and put on a completely different face. It always left Yoichi hanging.

There was an incident one day when they decided to take time off work and see a movie together. The film, produced by a supposedly great French director, didn't really have a dramatic plot, revealing itself instead to be a meticulously observed portrait of two families living in the French countryside. But as they watched, Sayuri began to speak to the screen as if giving a monologue. Yoichi was at a loss and didn't know what to do. There were people around them, yet she was speaking in a normal voice.

"No, you're wrong. That's not how it is for me."

Sayuri said this while gnawing on her fingernail, and Yoichi wasn't the only one who responded. The man sitting right in front of them, perhaps to express his discontent, turned his head to the side, then quickly turned back to face the screen.

Heedless, Sayuri continued.

"I mean, that'd be too..."

She trailed off, falling deep into thought, and then sighed loudly.

A little while passed, and she spoke again.

"Why is that woman crying?"

She was asking about what was happening on the screen. Yoichi realized for the first time that her earlier outbursts had nothing to do with the movie at all. She wasn't so caught up in the action that she felt moved to speak to the characters. Rather, there was an entirely different scene playing out in her head. It seemed natural for someone's mind to wander while reading a book. But even if she ended up thinking about something else in the middle of a movie, there was no need to speak aloud.

"Just be quiet and watch—you'll figure it out," hissed Yoichi in as quiet a voice as he could.

"You're so mean."

Sayuri turned back to the screen. It was clear she was still consumed with whatever was happening in her head, though, and her disruptive outbursts continued. The man in front of them kept looking back in silent rebuke. Yoichi couldn't stop wondering what had Sayuri so preoccupied.

Thinking back, similar things had happened several times in

their everyday lives. Sayuri would abruptly change the subject in the middle of a conversation, making him question if she'd been thinking of something else all the while he'd been talking. And he couldn't help but wonder if her mind was going to the same place each time she'd watch a movie or converse with him...

Compared to other members of the theater troupe, they had little trouble making ends meet. After all, they lived in an apartment Sayuri had inherited from her father, and the life insurance she'd received after his death was no small sum. It was almost incalculable how much easier it made their lives not to have to worry about how they'd afford to live in a big city. But it was nonetheless true that they spent all the time between their thrice-yearly performances consumed completely by their part-time jobs. Yoichi, not wanting to be a freeloader, made sure he earned enough to pay his share of the rent, while Sayuri was so afraid of using up her inheritance that she ended up increasing her nest egg instead.

It was Yoichi who brought up marriage first. He could no longer conceive of a life without Sayuri. They would fight, of course, but after a few days, they'd forget their anger and be back at each other like cats in heat. They wouldn't stop touching each other's bodies even after the act was done. Filled with a sense of deep satisfaction, Yoichi would hold Sayuri's face in his hands and imagine himself as a successful actor. But even if he never made it big, he would still be happy as long as he was able to continue living with her like this. So he would also content himself by imagining their mundane life stretching out into the future. In other words, he didn't mind how his life might turn out as long as she remained by his side.

Sayuri was twenty-three years old and Yoichi twenty-seven when they ended up leaving the Wind Theater Company. During rehearsals one day, Yoichi reached his limit with the director, who was also the president of the company. The two of them had never gotten along. They began arguing about certain aspects of the performance, and the quarrel escalated to the point that the director threatened to kick Yoichi off his co-lead with Sayuri if he couldn't perform as instructed.

"If you put me off this role, I'll leave the company. And take Sayuri with me, of course."

The director felt real fear at the threat. Yoichi was easy enough to replace, but Sayuri was indispensable. Seeing this written across the director's face, Yoichi felt as though his worth was being further denigrated, and blood rushed to his head.

"Think for a second what I'm doing here—trying my best to make these stupid lines of yours work, at least a little!"

This led to Yoichi and the director fighting for real. He didn't remember much of it, just that the other company members eventually split them up. It was then when he noticed that the director was lying face-up and motionless on the ground, blood pouring from his nose. Yoichi, for his part, felt a sharp pain in his shoulder. As the other members looked on with grave faces, Yoichi took Sayuri's hand and exited the rehearsal space. Showtime was quite soon, which meant that leaving the troupe now would be fatal. The thought of all his castmates' hard work going down the drain made Yoichi feel incredibly guilty. They hadn't done anything wrong, after all, so it was a pity that the show they'd worked so hard to create would be destroyed by his fight with the director. But he felt he had no choice at this point but to leave the company.

"Hey, are you okay with this?" Yoichi asked Sayuri as he walked with her down Shibuya's Koen-dori shopping street, his body still fizzing with adrenaline. The Wind Theater Company's audience had grown steadily since they'd joined, and he couldn't help but ask the woman who'd become the troupe's marquee actress if it was really all right to make her leave for such a selfish reason.

"It's fine," she said and took his hand.

"Just promise me that you'll never leave me, no matter what."

Sayuri sounded oddly desperate, but Yoichi failed to notice. He was too consumed with thinking about his own future to pay attention to the tone of her voice.

"Why would I ever leave you?"

This didn't seem to reassure Sayuri, and she tightened her grip on Yoichi's hand.

"What are we going to do now?"

"Audition for some commercial theater troupes, I suppose."

"I hope it works out."

Sayuri's reply was curt, as if in her heart of hearts, she didn't believe it would.

"What, don't you have faith in me?"

She didn't answer him.

"Say something! You don't think we'll make it, right?"

But Sayuri still refused to respond. Yoichi dropped her hand and strode ahead. While he didn't regret leaving the Wind Theater Company, he was burning with anger. He felt like he was back at square one. There were thousands of small theater troupes just in Tokyo, and many thousands more people trying to become actors, but only a handful of these ever ended up making a living out of acting. Turning the Wind Theater Company into a major, well-known troupe would help his own career advance—that was the idea behind joining a small troupe, not just for Yoichi but for everyone in the company. It seemed like the only realistic way to make it. And now, he'd destroyed this path to success with his own hands. At a time like this, he might have felt better if the woman he loved showed confidence in him. Yoichi was a man who wanted to carve out a career for himself. If the director came to him and apologized, Yoichi would be willing to return to the troupe and bring Sayuri along with him. The prospect of joining a new troupe now, at their age, was daunting. He'd rather avoid it if he could. But apologizing himself was out of the question. If that was the only option, he felt he had no choice but to go through with leaving the troupe. Had there been a way for him to rejoin the troupe while still saving face, though, he probably would have taken it.

"Yoichi!"

Sayuri called out from where she trailed behind him. Turning around, he saw she was crying. Yoichi stood where he was and let her approach him.

"Yo, the truth is, I can never have a child."

It was the last thing he'd expected her to confess at this particular moment. Why now? Why here? He had no idea what prompted such an outburst. Yoichi looked down at Sayuri calmly.

"What does that matter?"

His tone was even and composed.

"It doesn't bother you?"

"I don't need to have a kid right now."

Yoichi said this firmly.

"I don't mean 'right now.' I mean, 'not ever.'"

"Either way."

"Good," said Sayuri, visibly relieved.

They began to walk together again, hand in hand once more. But Yoichi's heart was far from quiet. Something didn't make sense.

You can never have a child? But that's strange. Why are you always being so careful, then?

Sayuri blithely swung their hands back and forth, unaware of the doubts blooming within him.

What did she mean by that?

"I can never have a child."

He couldn't think of a way to interpret her words other than as a way to say she didn't *want* to have a child.

Does she really think I don't know that she takes her basal body temperature every morning?

Sayuri would check her temperature and discreetly record it on a chart in the morning every day. And whenever it seemed her ovulation was approaching, she would always rebuff his advances. He'd eventually noticed the pattern and begun taking it upon himself not to approach her during those times. If it was something biological preventing her from getting pregnant, surely she wouldn't be going to such trouble. Her words and actions weren't lining up. Yoichi decided it was simply a rather transparent lie.

Despite all this, around a year later, Sayuri's period was half a month late, a fact that clearly agitated her. "How could this be?" she muttered and bit her lip, seemingly on the verge of laughter that never came. Her eyes darted restlessly left and right. This was how she always acted when she didn't know what to do.

For his part, Yoichi was ready. If she was indeed pregnant, he wanted them to keep the baby. And he wanted them to get married. He didn't feel any resistance to the prospect of spending the rest of his life with her.

"Let's get you to a doctor," he said, his tone intentionally soothing. He hoped it conveyed his unspoken wish that she go through with having the baby.

"Nuh-uh."

But she shook her head as she glanced up at him, her face still downcast.

More than a year had passed since they'd last performed together.

She's forgotten how to be convincing.

From her expression, he could tell she was frightened. And that was why she'd lied. She'd claimed she could never have a child.

But what is she so scared of?

Yoichi refrained from speaking these doubts aloud and instead patted Sayuri lightly on the head, saying, "C'mon, why don't you go to the doctor?"

Sayuri's response was surprisingly swift. She put her insurance card in her purse and headed out the door with a quick, "Okay." But, as it turned out, it wasn't the gynecologist she went to.

Upon her return, Sayuri offered only the vaguest answers when Yoichi asked how it went. Her stubborn refusal to respond, coupled with the worried look on her face, pushed him over the edge.

"Out with it already! Are you pregnant or not?!" he yelled as he upended her purse, letting everything in it fall out. A patient registration ticket fluttered onto the floor, but it wasn't from the ob-gyn.

It read, *Naito Psychiatric Clinic.*

And it had today's date written on it.

"You didn't go see the gynecologist?"

Yoichi was at a loss. It came to him all at once that Sayuri might be hiding something shocking. Who would go to a psychiatrist after being told to go see the gynecologist? Unable to think of what to say or get any angrier than he already was, Yoichi looked down at Sayuri and felt an unexpected sense of pity. She was crawling on the carpet, gathering up the spilled contents of her purse, muttering, "What're you doing? You're so mean..." Perhaps it was the trembling in her shoulders that made him feel that way.

"If you don't want me anymore, just go ahead and leave," she continued.

Still disoriented, Yoichi tried to reassure her. He told her he wanted to be with her, to raise the baby with her. "So let's get married. Let's be together forever." There was no trace of dissimulation in his words—they came straight from the heart.

Sayuri drew her knees up to her chest and buried her face in them without answering. She seemed both happy at his marriage proposal and troubled by it.

"What do you think? Do you want to?"

He tried to ask this in his gentlest tone of voice, but to no avail—she still didn't reply. In the end, she went to bed that evening without speaking a single word.

Sayuri gave every indication that she was on the horns of some terrible dilemma, and Yoichi took pains to try and coax it out of her. If he pushed her too hard, he could see it would only make her more reticent. She spent the night sighing like someone torn between two options, tossing and turning, and keeping Yoichi, who was trying to sleep beside her, awake too.

The next morning, Yoichi asked her again.

"Why did you go to a psychiatrist instead of the gynecologist?"

But still, she didn't answer. Yoichi could see that to answer such a question would be to confront the dilemma head-on. He couldn't go to the Naito Psychiatric Clinic and ask them why Sayuri had come, either. After all, a psychiatrist would have no reason to break a patient's confidentiality like that. He'd have to find some other way to get to the truth. And then it came to him: he remembered hearing that her father's death the year before they'd met had likely been a suicide. He hadn't thought much about it at the time, but now that things were coming to a head like this, it seemed likely there was some kind of connection there.

What about your father's suicide?

He knew he couldn't ask her about it directly. It was a hard subject to bring up. But he had the feeling that there was a secret buried deep in her, one that involved not only Sayuri, but also her father.

That was when Yoichi ran into Keiko Nojima again. Every person's life has its pitfalls. It's easy enough to overcome them when you're healthy, but just as an exhausted body becomes more susceptible to viral infections, a weakened mind becomes vulnerable to all manner of unforeseen traps. And Keiko was, to an almost ridiculous extent, a trap like no other. She wasn't a bad woman or anything. It was just that he happened to meet her again at a moment in his life that seemed almost designed to make him fall into the trap she represented. At that time, his life was one of constant auditions and rejections. Everything would seem to go well, but then he would be eliminated at the last stage. And finally, he started to realize he might need something more—some sort of connection—to clear that final hurdle. It was then when he learned Keiko Nojima's father was an executive at the company—a former *zaibatsu* business conglomerate—that was sponsoring an upcoming musical. He and Keiko had previously co-starred in a small theater production, and while her acting and general dramatic prowess failed to rise above the level of a college production, she had the charm of a well-raised daughter, a sense of innocence and purity that endeared her to people. He couldn't help but compare her with Sayuri. They seemed so opposite in every way.

He ran into Keiko in the lobby of the Nissay Theater and was reminded of her sunniness all over again. She seemed unchanged by the two years since they'd last seen each other. The darkness lurking behind Sayuri was becoming a bit too much for him, and Keiko's uncomplicated good cheer was a balm to his spirit. Sayuri was certainly more alluring as a woman, but her elusiveness and unpredictability made him increasingly uneasy, and it was exhausting to be with her. Keiko was the opposite. Her bottomless optimism buoyed him.

Keiko approached him from behind, tapping him on the shoulder and exclaiming, "Hey, Yoichi! It's been so long!" He turned his head and found himself staring straight into her carefree smile. Her big, sparkling eyes, the pert roundness of her cheeks, the ample curves of her chest: every aspect of her being seemed to exude good health. Yoichi was dazzled. The softness, roundness, and warmth of a woman—she had it all.

Naturally, they ended up catching up over coffee and tea. When Yoichi mentioned that he'd been auditioning for commercial theater troupes but having no luck, Keiko told him she'd realized she lacked the talent to make it as a performer and had moved into the production side of things.

That was when she looked him straight in the face and declared, "Yoichi, you're so handsome and talented—you can't give up!"

"You always say such positive things. I've been trying and trying—if that's all it took, I would have succeeded long ago."

Yoichi said this bemusedly, a self-deprecating smile on his face.

"You know, Imada Productions is casting for a show right now. Why don't you give it a try?"

The smile left Yoichi's face.

"Are you serious?"

"Of course. My father's company is sponsoring it, and the producer's an acquaintance."

"You think it'd work out?"

"Just go in for an audition. I'll handle the rest."

Yoichi felt like jumping for joy. This was a production he was interested in, and he had never imagined he could clear the final hurdle so easily.

"Thanks for this."

His voice was strained. He even found he was bowing his head.

"Ah, but I wonder... You know, it's not that good a role. Maybe it'd be a waste of your talents."

"Look, I'm serious. As long as it gets me on stage, I'll do anything!"

Everything had always come easily to Keiko, so she had no idea. Yoichi was at the point where he'd take any role at all. He'd play a dead body. He lacked the luxury to pick and choose. Yoichi tried to make this as clear as he could.

"I'll play any role. Even a walk-on!"

"All right, I'll talk to my father."

Yoichi sighed in relief.

Their conversation then drifted away from theater.

"How have you been lately?"

Keiko brought her face closer to Yoichi's as she sucked on her straw and drank down the iced coffee. Yoichi knew Keiko had been aware of his relationship with Sayuri, and it was obvious to him that she was trying to find out if they were still together. But he didn't tell her. Or, to be more precise, he didn't mention Sayuri at all. He recalled that Keiko had had a bit of a thing for him two years ago, and he couldn't deny his ulterior motives now. Not that he was thinking of breaking up with Sayuri. But he would be lying to himself not to admit that his heart beat faster at the thought that he might still have a chance with Keiko. And he also had to confess that the prospect of being with Keiko, who was so bright and cheerful, and who held the key to unlocking his future, appealed to him on some level.

And so, Yoichi chose not to say anything. He didn't tell Keiko about Sayuri, and he didn't inform Sayuri about running into Keiko and the possible role that might come out of it, either.

Usually, Yoichi would tell Sayuri about his day, and he probably would have said something like, "You won't believe who I ran into today."

If he'd just done that, disaster might have been averted. But he didn't, and he went on several dates with Keiko in secret. These "dates" never went beyond meeting for drinks at a café somewhere, but still, he never quite got used to his own actions, perhaps due to a lingering sense of guilt.

In the end, Yoichi managed to get the part in the Imada Productions musical. When he told Sayuri, she was much more thrilled about it than he'd anticipated. Of course, she wasn't aware of Keiko's influence behind the scenes, so she took it simply as a recognition of his talent and celebrated it as if it were her own achievement. Seeing her so sincerely happy for him made him feel horrible.

"It's not such a big deal."

Yoichi tried to get Sayuri to calm down. But she kept jumping up and down, running around the room, and shouting, "You did it! You did it!"

"Can you be quiet?"

He took Sayuri's delicate body into his arms and covered her mouth with his hands.

"Didn't you hear me? I told you to shut up!"

Hearing him raise his voice and seeing his face contort, Sayuri finally shut her mouth. Her eyes were wide, and her lips bent into a lopsided frown as she fought the urge to cry.

"What's the matter, Yo? Why are you—?"

"Nothing's the matter. I just told you to shut up 'cause you were being so loud."

Yoichi's tone was low and threatening. Still trapped in his embrace, Sayuri began to tremble, her face growing steadily paler.

"What's wrong? Please, tell me. Don't you like me anymore?"

Her voice diminished into nearly nothing as she continued.

"You're acting weird, Yo. There's something off with you lately."

"If anyone's weird, it's you."

"Is there... I can't believe I'm saying this, but is there someone else?"

Sayuri looked up and peered into his eyes. Realizing what she was doing, Yoichi turned his head away and tried to soften the corners of his mouth. If he'd placed a mirror in front of himself, he would have seen what kind of expression he was making. The look on his face said he didn't want her to know, but its subtle nuances revealed the answer anyway. It was an expression that represented a lifetime's worth of skill for an actor. And just like that, in an instant, Yoichi communicated a series of truths to Sayuri. He'd wanted, in his heart of hearts, for her to see through him.

And she did. With the intuition of a longtime lover, Sayuri understood exactly what Yoichi's stage-honed look meant. Her chest heaved, and just when he thought she took a deep breath in, she cried out.

"No!!"

She pushed him away as she screamed, and her eyes began to dart back and forth again.

"Who is it?"

Sayuri's stance was challenging, as if bracing for a fight, but she stepped back a couple of steps as she spoke.

"Keiko Nojima. You know her."

Hearing himself, Yoichi regained his composure and instantly regretted saying the name.

"Keiko Nojima..." Sayuri murmured.

"No, forget that. This has nothing to do with her."

Yoichi's words made no sense as he tried to take back what he said just a moment ago.

"Nothing to do with her? You just said her name."

"No, believe me. It's not like that."

"But that's the name you said. Keiko Nojima."

"There's nothing going on between me and Keiko."

"You're not sleeping with her? Is that what you mean?"

Yoichi nodded.

"And I'm not in love with her. We just met a few times, that's all."

"Then tell me, why are you so upset? I don't understand any of this."

Her expression was filled with despair. It made him even angrier. This was the face that bound him to her. If he didn't free himself now, he'd be tied down forever.

"Stop acting like my wife. We're not even married. Why should you care who I meet?"

A deep, low sob ripped from her chest.

"No. We're not. It's not what you think. We can't be like that."

Yoichi didn't understand what she meant.

"We can't be like what?"

"I mean... I mean..."

Sayuri went silent. Then, suppressing her words, she ran to the sink and threw up. It was as though she was vomiting up the contents of her stomach in lieu of the words she couldn't bring herself to say.

She must be having morning sickness. I knew it, she's pregnant.

Watching Sayuri bent over, Yoichi suddenly felt pity for her, and he rubbed her back. His emotions were changing every ten seconds. One moment he was angry, the next he was full of kindness, then irritation, then sympathy...

"I just used her to get a part."

This was how Yoichi summed it up as he quickly described what had happened between them. Of course, he concealed his momentary temptation to leave her for Keiko. Sayuri listened silently. It was impossible to tell if she accepted his explanation or still doubted him. But it was clear the damage had been done, and no matter what he said now, he could never erase the mark it had left on her heart.

As it turned out, Sayuri's vomiting after hearing about Keiko Nojima wasn't morning sickness. It had simply been the intensity of her jealousy bursting up and irritating her stomach. Her much-delayed period arrived the next day, a fact that she communicated obliquely to Yoichi. He found himself indifferent to the news, neither relieved nor disappointed. All that had really happened was that now he knew Sayuri's body was able to conceive a child. The nature of the disaster she thought her pregnancy would bring remained unclear, still to be revealed sometime in the future.

Things between Sayuri and Yoichi became somewhat distant. They would try their best to find something to talk about, but the conversations would never last for long. Sayuri, for her part, wanted to talk about Yoichi's new role, but the specter of Keiko Nojima would appear in the back of their minds, and their conversation would dwindle into silence. They both knew the reason, which only made it more awkward. So the time they spent in the same room with each other slowly diminished.

The day came when Yoichi saw Keiko again. It was a meeting arranged long in advance, ostensibly to discuss the musical. They met at a café and then went for dinner, and while it was their custom to say their goodbyes at that point, this time, Yoichi proposed going for a drink. Keiko readily agreed. He threw himself into drinking to shake off the heaviness in him and ended up asking Keiko if she wanted to go to a hotel. He and Sayuri hadn't made love for weeks, and the alcohol was making his desire boil up. Yoichi didn't want to interpret his behavior any more deeply than that. He was acting on the instinct common to any man in this situation, he told himself.

Keiko's body was unyielding, and his affection failed to grow the way he'd expected as he touched her. She simply lay on the bed and made the typical cries of a woman in the throes of passion. With tears in her eyes, she didn't hide the joy she felt at being embraced by the man she'd admired for years, and it dampened Yoichi's ardor. He found himself longing intensely for Sayuri. Hers was a body that could elicit joy at the simplest of touches. He realized his deep bonds with her weren't just psychological, but physical, too.

Even as he embraced Keiko, he could only think about Sayuri, and he resolved that this would be the end of things with Keiko. He also decided that he should be more honest with Sayuri. Things would never get better between them if the both of them remained so stubborn. It would probably make everything simpler if he took it upon himself to be the one to give in and accommodate her more.

Filled with the resolve to breathe new life into his relationship with Sayuri, Yoichi took the last train home. Sayuri was still awake and waiting for him when he arrived. The apartment had two rooms, and one was floored traditionally in tatami. Sayuri had laid out a futon in the tatami room. They'd opted to take out a futon at night and roll it back up in the morning to save the space a regular bed would take. Yoichi smiled at Sayuri, intending it to break the ice after so many days of silence. He didn't feel any guilt about having just slept with another woman, and was instead filled with a sense of satisfaction at finally having made up his mind. He crawled into the futon with a look of contentment on his face.

It was a cold night in late February. He started drifting off almost immediately, helped along by the alcohol in his system. A strong breeze foretelling the coming of spring rattled the window in its frame. He felt something caressing his lower abdomen, and he jerked awake, looking down to see what it was. Sayuri's head was above his navel, and a few strands of her long hair tickled his bare stomach as she brushed her lips against what lay below. Since she was looking down toward his legs, he couldn't see her face. But the hair falling from the back of her head waved back and forth above his stomach. Wondering why she would choose to do this so late at night, Yoichi laid back and allowed her to do what she wanted, until he froze, suddenly realizing something. He'd made love to Keiko twice at the hotel. He remembered taking a shower after the first time, but after the second... He thought back, but he had no memory of doing so. And that was when he understood what Sayuri was doing. She was using her tongue to seek out traces of another woman—her smell, her taste...

"Stop it!"

Just as he shouted this, Sayuri turned and crawled up to his ear.

"You slept with her, didn't you? With Keiko Nojima?"

Yoichi didn't have the time to make something up or the energy to deny it. He lay awkwardly on his back, his pajamas and briefs still pushed down unceremoniously to his knees, unable to do anything but stare up at the ceiling to avoid the eerie light in Sayuri's eyes.

After that night, the fire of Sayuri's jealousy raged out of control. Yoichi thought time and again that they should live apart for a little while. But he never actually suggested it aloud. He caught glimpses of the thoughts she kept hidden tossing like waves inside her, and he was sure that she would break, like a body dashed against the rocks by the sea, if he brought it up to her.

At night, Sayuri often experienced hysterical seizures. Awakened by a scream and a shortness of breath, Yoichi would find Sayuri on top of him, beating his chest with her fist. One night, that same hand reached out to grab his throat. He slapped it away, yelling, "What are you doing?!" In return, Sayuri began to tremble uncontrollably, and she dissolved into heavy sobs. It was truly miserable, the way she cried. It was the sound of utter despair, and it drained the hope from him as well. No matter how many times he promised to never see Keiko Nojima again, Sayuri didn't believe him. Or rather, she'd reached a point beyond belief or disbelief—even if she accepted what he said intellectually, her body would reject it from its very depths.

There was no limit to the ways men and women could hurt each other. Once the gears stopped meshing, things could only go from bad to worse. Many times, Yoichi found himself hating Sayuri, whom he'd loved so much. But he would feel a surge of affection well up inside of him the very next moment. He swung dizzyingly from extreme to extreme, black to white to black again, unable to control his emotions at all. There was nothing more painful a heart could experience. How did things go so wrong? They couldn't find the cause and make things right even if they wanted to. After all, no matter how they tried to trace things back to the root, they could never identify the real reason for the rift between them. It was clear that something from before Yoichi met Sayuri haunted them, hidden from sight but ever-present. It wasn't just her father's suicide—Yoichi realized that he knew nothing about what kind of people her parents were, what sort of expectations they'd had of their daughter before she was born, or how they'd raised her. He had the feeling that he wouldn't ever understand Sayuri until he traced her life back to the moment of her birth. But her life before they met was a blank page. Yoichi had refrained from asking about it, and Sayuri had deliberately kept it from him and never spoken a word about her past.

During this period, Sayuri withdrew from both theater and music. Sometimes, she would absentmindedly hum snatches of "In the Mirror," her debut single, to herself, but the drive to create new songs seemed to have totally left her. Drowning in listlessness and absorbed in self-contemplation, she would take the tranquilizers prescribed to her at the psychiatric clinic and occasionally visit a nearby meditation center. One day, a friend she'd made at the center gave her a newborn black kitten. She named the kitten Mémé, and when he heard her calling it by that name, Yoichi couldn't help but think of the word *memeshii*—meaning effeminate and weak. The name was probably meant to be a reflection of her own womanly weakness.

March came, and Yoichi and Sayuri's relationship hadn't improved. Indeed, the tension between them seemed to only grow more intense. One evening, Yoichi was lying on the bed and reading his newly received script for the musical when he looked over at Sayuri, who was sitting at the vanity with her back to him, doing her make-up. Rehearsals had recently begun, and Yoichi's self-confidence had taken a severe blow as he witnessed the high level of talent among the cast. Many of them were trained in the foundations of acting, be it in vocalization or body movement, and it overwhelmed Yoichi since he had only learned how to act in a small theater troupe. He felt like the only way to overcome his disadvantage was to work hard, and he spent all of his free time reading the script and practicing his role. But this evening, he was having trouble focusing, and his attention kept drifting to Sayuri. He couldn't remember her ever doing her makeup at night if there wasn't a special event.

Yoichi felt Sayuri's eyes on him as she looked at him in the mirror. At first, it didn't bother him. But eventually, the sheer duration and intensity of her gaze rattled him, and he put the script aside to look back at her. She'd taken out a tube of lipstick and brought it to her lips. But her hand remained still, and instead of looking at her own face, her eyes were fixed on Yoichi in the mirror. He pretended to study his script furiously. Soon, though, he began to hear a tapping on the glass, and when he looked back up, he saw that Sayuri was banging the surface of the mirror with the lipstick. Its tip broke off and the metal base scraped the glass with an ugly screech. Through the mirror, Yoichi suddenly saw murder in her eyes. His concentration broken for good, he threw the script onto the tatami with a thump and left the apartment. Wandering aimlessly around the neighborhood, he resolved that it would be best if he and Sayuri lived apart, at least for now. He foresaw that if things continued like this, something truly terrible might happen.

We'll discuss it calmly tonight. I'll find an apartment, and we'll live separately for a little while.

Yoichi vowed to broach the subject with Sayuri once he returned home.

It was just past nine when he did, and her demeanor changed completely when he brought it up. With a docile look on her face, she responded with a simple nod and said, "Okay." She then began to talk not to Yoichi but to Mémé, who was curled up in her lap and softly mewing like a baby. Her voice was numb and listless as she spoke.

"It must be hard having me around. Fine, I'll give him his space. We'll live together, just you and me, Mémé... But Yo's busy with rehearsals, so we'll be the ones to move out instead. All right, Mémé?

Let's do that."

Partway through her monologue, Sayuri took two beers out of the refrigerator. Yoichi had to admit he could use a beer after hearing her speak in that eerie, pained voice.

"In exchange, take a bit of this."

Sayuri turned to face him, picked up her purse from where she'd thrown it on the floor, and reached into it to take out her tranquilizers. She washed a pill down with the beer.

"Here, Yo. Your turn."

"Why? I'm—"

"Come on. Please? Do what I say."

Yoichi could sense Sayuri's desperation. He'd just proposed to live apart, and she wanted to make a ceremony out of this evening. Perhaps he owed it to her to go along with it...

"What do you want me to do?" he asked, using the gentlest voice he could manage.

Mémé, who'd been playing on Sayuri's knee, silently slipped away from her.

"All you have to do is swallow this."

Sayuri held out her palm. It had several pills resting on it. Thinking that a tranquilizer wouldn't kill him, Yoichi willingly put one in his mouth.

"More, take more."

"Why're you making me do this...?"

"Just take them. You'll feel really good."

"You've done this before?"

Sayuri nodded. "Yes."

"And you feel like doing it with me?"

"Of course. I don't want to do it with anyone but you."

Yoichi put another pill in his mouth and swallowed it. She stared at him fixedly, her eyes wide and slightly uneven in size, to make sure he didn't covertly spit it back out, and she didn't drop her gaze until she was sure the pill had reached his stomach. Swallowing the pills obediently was an expression of love. It was no small thing to do something simply because someone asked you to do it, without asking why.

"Another."

Sayuri pressed him to continue. Yoichi placed one more pill in his mouth and then threw the rest away, showing her that he'd reached his limit. He tried to shake his head. He had the feeling that something was surging toward it... But in reality, nothing was coming his way. Rather, it was more like he was losing his strength. He lay down on the tatami and tried to shake his head again. It seemed that if he didn't do something to stop it, the strength would leave his body entirely. Was this what taking too many tranquilizers felt like? Or had she given him something else? He tried to raise his head to ask Sayuri about his suspicions, but sleepiness overcame him, and it was as much as he could do just to open his eyes. Doubt swirled in his mind.

What do you intend to do to me, making me take those pills?

He repeated the question in his head as Sayuri rose to her feet and, after looking down at him silently for a while, stripped off her clothes layer by layer until she was completely naked.

Do you think I can get hard in this state?!

Although Yoichi meant to speak aloud, his voice wouldn't really leave his throat. Some sound leaked out, but his tongue refused to work, and any words that did escape were garbled and blurry. His body, which had been so full of vitality, was slowly being robbed of its abilities.

Kneeling beside him, Sayuri stripped the clothes from his body, too, and started caressing him with a tenderness like that of a mother for a baby. Yoichi didn't resist and let her do as she pleased. *Ahh, this is what she wanted, wasn't it?* His thoughts became sluggish, but even as his consciousness grew murkier and murkier, he managed to realize what Sayuri was doing.

She wants to have me, all of me, body and soul. That's why she gave me those pills—so I wouldn't be able to resist her.

Abruptly, Yoichi imagined what might happen next. It was obvious where this was going, but he failed to summon up the appropriate horror—his mind had grown too muddy and dazed for that. Still, though, the shrill of an alarm sounded somewhere in his mind.

Stay awake! You can't fall asleep! If you do, that'll be it!

Picking up both of his legs, Sayuri dragged him across the linoleum and into the bathroom. She propped him up against the curved surface of the sink so that he was sitting up on the enamel flooring. The closed lid of the Western-style toilet acted as his armrest. Water overflowed from the washbasin and poured down over his head. Sayuri sat down on the edge of the bath in front of him.

Hey, what are you going to do to me?

Yoichi's drowsiness warred with his desire to stay alive. It would be easier if he just drifted off. He felt so tempted to. As his eyelids drooped again and again, his gaze rested on Sayuri, who sat on the edge of the bath. Her stomach was directly before him, and when he dropped his eyes, he saw that semen was dripping from within her pubic hair and running down her inner thighs. Yoichi had almost no recollection of them having had sex just now. Despite his incapacitated state, he'd somehow gotten hard and ejaculated. The fact struck him as funny, but it also, perversely, gave him a kind of confidence. It was as if he'd regained a bit of the energy he'd thought he'd lost. If he had it in him to come, then he also should be able to gather his remaining strength when he absolutely needed to.

Right then, Yoichi's eyes were struck by light bouncing off the edge of a stainless-steel blade. The next moment, he saw a gout of fresh blood. There was a gash on Sayuri's left wrist, and blood was spurting from the cut artery. Yoichi sensed her heartbeat even though he couldn't hear it. It was like he could see the very contractions of her heart in the rhythm of the spurting blood. *I have to do something!* He felt the last reserves of strength stir within him as he tried to rouse himself into action.

Resting her bleeding hand on the edge of the bath, Sayuri leaned forward to whisper in his ear.

I'm going to fill this bathtub with our blood, Yo. Then I'm going to stir it real well. Every one of our blood cells will mingle with each other. And then we'll finally be together, don't you think?

This was what he seemed to hear. Her words didn't enter through his ear and instead penetrated his mind directly. But her fantasies held no interest to him. What was important was the open wound on her wrist—something had to be done. He couldn't just watch this happen. He wasn't thinking of saving his own skin. The life of someone he loved was fading before his eyes, and his instincts kicked in.

It's fine, right?

Sayuri was enticing him. The prospect of death itself was not frightening. His body was drenched in Sayuri's blood, and she'd run the blade over his wrist again and again. The feeling of its edge, blunt and warmed by the blood, possessed a strange reality—there was a rawness to it, if only because it made the approach of death so palpable.

But Yoichi summoned his remaining strength and used it to resist one last time. He needed to cover Sayuri's wound first. That was what drove him. He could hear Mémé meowing forlornly from outside the bathroom. He'd seen the kitten's tiny black figure cut across the tall, narrow frosted glass several times, and it was now clawing at the door. Using the kitten's silhouette as a target, Yoichi raised his fist and pushed open the door. But that was the last thing he really remembered doing. He frantically crawled across the floor, and his last spurt of energy must have surpassed that of Sayuri since he managed to pull away from her. Everything afterward appeared in his memory as disconnected scenes. The feeling of the telephone receiver in his hand. A man's voice on the other end. The agonizingly long time it took for his blurry speech to be understood. In the end, though, an ambulance siren reached the depths of his fading consciousness. Listening to it approaching and hoping that it meant Sayuri's life would be saved, Yoichi finally fell into a deep sleep.

6

The videotape containing Sayuri's images had slipped between the waves, and the letter from Takeshi Sunako, after floating a bit on the surface of the sea, eventually took on enough water that it, too, sank out of sight. Yoichi's last memory of Sayuri replayed vividly in the back of his mind. He was looking out at the sea, and the color of its surface was replaced by that of the tiny bathroom's bloodstained walls. It flickered like a strobe light.

If she's pregnant, that must have been when it happened.

Staring down at the waves from where he stood on the deck, Yoichi cursed the dark humor of the gods. A woman making love for the last time before she killed herself naturally wouldn't use contraception. This meant that at the very moment she was attempting to take her own life, a new one was sprouting in her womb. And one thing he did remember clearly was seeing his own semen trickling from between her legs. Sayuri had been taken to the hospital in the ambulance soon afterward, and she was confined to her bed until morning. At some point that day, or perhaps the day after, his semen had fertilized her egg. This nascent baby had been struggling toward life in the womb of a woman who longed for death. And factoring in the month it took for the letter to reach him on the tuna boat, the baby was already seven months old. If all went well, Yoichi's child would soon be born.

It has nothing to do with me.

He wanted so much to deny it.

Sayuri ended up staying in the hospital for two weeks, but Yoichi didn't visit her even once during that time. Perhaps due to the overdose, or perhaps simply because of his mental condition, he spent the first few days after the incident in a lethargic state, drifting in a kind of trance. And then, as his consciousness gradually returned to something closer to normal, he found himself overcome with a terror that seemed to well up from the deepest reaches of his body. He was tormented with visions of Sayuri's slit wrist and the vivid blood that had spurted into his eyes. They haunted him whether he was asleep or awake. He now felt the sheer weight of his own life, which had almost been made to accompany another into the afterlife.

On top of this, he was sick and tired of the incessant questioning by the police, and since he had to take a week off from rehearsals, he was feeling even more left behind. All in all, he was becoming incredibly depressed. He had no appetite and, fearing that he'd lose control of himself completely if he drank, chose not to have any alcohol. He spent his days lolling about in bed, picking at the scabs on his left wrist from where Sayuri had sliced into him. No matter how at home he felt in this apartment, at the end of the day, Sayuri was the owner, and this fact pained him as he spent more and more time there.

A week passed, and Yoichi, having ignored the insistent ringing of his phone, decided to leave the apartment in the morning if only to take a ride on his motorbike. When he got to the parking lot, he saw Keiko.

"What's wrong with you, Yoichi? I call and call, but you never answer."

Thinking she'd taken the opportunity to drop by after she'd found out that Sayuri was still in the hospital after her attempted suicide, Yoichi became extremely angry. And seeing his reaction, Keiko, too, became upset.

"I know it's hard, but how long do you plan on skipping rehearsals?"

Her tone was condescending, even chiding.

"Don't you know how important this is for you right now?"

She sounded like a mother scolding her son for not studying hard enough for his exams.

Suddenly, Yoichi was gripped with an intense revulsion at the way his life, which he'd been trying to build for himself, was at the mercy of others. He was nearly killed by Sayuri, and now, Keiko wanted to act as his guardian. He didn't want anything to do with either of them anymore. He was turning twenty-nine this year, and soon he'd be thirty. Although he hadn't led such an irresponsible life, now that he was staring thirty in the face, he felt the need to escape from everything around him. So what if he lost this role he'd finally managed to get in a commercial musical, or if he ended up penniless, with nowhere to return to? He didn't care. All he wanted to do was throw everything away and start anew. His dreams of being a successful actor seemed ridiculous to him now. He wanted to work somewhere that tired his body until it gave out, until he could think of nothing else. Then, he'd be able to wash all the poison within him away with his blood and sweat, and finally be reborn as an entirely different person...

That thought turned into a desire. "Move." Yoichi pushed Keiko on the shoulder and jumped on his motorbike. But even then, he never in his wildest dreams imagined that he would end up on a tuna boat. But as he sped down the route he often took with Sayuri along the coast of the Miura Peninsula, he eventually reached Jogashima and, looking out into the bay, he saw a tuna boat returning. He could see various men standing on the deck. They were too far away for him to make out their expressions. But even though their bodies were the size of beans, he could still sense their joy. The deck glittered with their satisfaction of a job well done and excitement at seeing their loved ones again. That was when Yoichi, enticed by the vitality exuded by these men, rode out to the wharf, met Jukichi Takagi as Yoichi stood there looking up at a docked tuna boat, and ended up deciding to join the crew right there on the spot. He went back to the apartment, packed up his belongings, and then, leaving Mémé in the care of a friend, returned to the wharf to throw himself into preparing for his departure. Afraid his resolve would weaken, he ended up leaving without seeing Sayuri again.

The result was now spread out before his eyes: the open sea. It was an entirely different world from the one he'd gazed out at from the wharf in Misaki. There was no environment as harsh and cruel as the sea. The work itself was hard, but it was during the storms that things were truly life-threatening. So had he been reborn? Yoichi couldn't say. The true effects of his decision would be revealed only at some later point. But one thing he did know was that the longer he stayed out at sea, the further that last scene with Sayuri drifted from his mind. The shape of his body and, quite naturally, his taste in food changed over time. His way of dealing with his sexual desires and the way he treated his fellow crewmen were all different from how he'd behaved on land. And yet, despite this, Sayuri had still been able to find him and negate the changes he'd worked so hard to make. His heart was shaken once again.

Now that the necessary materials had been distributed, the supply ship prepared to leave. The steam whistle sounded. The brief respite as they traveled between fishing areas was coming to an end, and tomorrow the hard work would begin again. Yoichi, calling out, ran to the boat's stern and stood amongst his fellow crewmen as they unloaded the new supplies. Walking down the ramp toward the storage area, he said a little prayer. When they reached the new fishing spot, he hoped there would be so many southern bluefins waiting for them that the amount of work would blast any thought or hesitation from his mind for good.

PART III Wall Fruit

1

It was the beginning of October, and the weather had suddenly gotten cooler. The South Seas, where Yoichi was, were heading toward spring. But back in Japan, it was the winds of fall that approached.

Mochizuki's apartment was on the sixteenth floor, and simply leaving a window open let in a lovely breeze, making it unnecessary to use air conditioning even in the summer. Sitting with his family after dinner, Mochizuki was quietly reading the evening newspaper. But the coolness of the wind coming through the window began to bother him. He kept looking up at the clock on the wall. He slipped his wallet out of his back pocket and checked to see if the gym membership card was in it.

More than a month had passed since he joined the gym, but he'd yet to actually go and sweat through a workout there. His wife Naomi, however, thought he went once a week. No matter how he might smell of soap when he got home, he'd just have to tell her that he'd gone to the gym and she wouldn't suspect a thing.

Mochizuki was meeting Akiko Nonoyama at eight. With thirty minutes remaining, he was getting restless, and his mind wasn't processing any of the words he read. The plan was that he would meet her at a park about ten minutes away by car, and then they'd leave one of their cars at the parking lot there and drive together to their actual destination... This would be the third time they'd met this way.

"Okay, I'm going to the gym now."

Mochizuki spoke to his wife from behind the newspaper he'd raised to hide his face. Naomi had always chided Mochizuki about not getting enough exercise, so she was very supportive of him going to the gym and sent him off with a smile every time.

"Should I pack your underwear, towel, and things?"

Having just finished washing the dishes, Naomi dried her hands with a towel and began heading toward the bedroom.

"No, don't worry. I can do it myself."

Mochizuki answered almost immediately and stood up. He couldn't let her help him. He lacked the insensitivity necessary to permit his unsuspecting and trusting wife to pack his underwear and other stuff for him. Unable to stay in his home another moment, Mochizuki stuffed his duffel bag with the gym clothes, shoes, towel, and everything else that was destined to spend the evening completely untouched by sweat. He sat down near the front door to put on his shoes.

"I think I'll get back a little past ten."

He got back up and turned around, only to see Naomi standing right behind him. Kanae, their daughter, had appeared at some point to join them, and she was standing next to his wife. Glancing at both of their faces, Mochizuki felt more and more agitated. Starting from the tips of his toes, his entire body began to tremble uncontrollably.

I'll put an end to this tonight.

He'd told himself this so many times.

"Go for it, Daddy! Diet! Diet!"

His daughter grinned up at him, her fingers in a V sign. Mochizuki squeezed his eyes shut to block out the image of his wife and daughter and turned quickly to head out the door. His heart was racing. His suffering felt not only mental but physical. To divert his thoughts, he joked and told himself that he should look for a reliable mental health professional in case he ended up with a neurotic disorder. But his heart continued to beat so rapidly, it started to feel like much less of a joke.

Adjusting the rear-view mirror in his car, Mochizuki found himself thinking of a female patient he'd examined about a month earlier. It was plain after only a preliminary examination that she was suffering, but it wasn't the kind of thing that could be called a neurosis. She was simply a married woman who'd fallen in love with another man, and it was causing her much distress.

The patient was forty-two years old and lived comfortably with her husband, an executive at a major local business. Despite her seemingly ideal situation, though, she'd fallen deeply in love with her son's tutor, a man with no money, status, or reputation—but who did have a wife and child of his own. But their love was purely platonic, existing at the level of a quickening of the heart on days the tutor was scheduled to come.

However, one evening, the woman's husband noticed that she would put on makeup only on the days the tutor came, and he confronted her about it. It wasn't that he suspected them of having an affair. But she struggled to come up with an answer. And when her husband learned that his wife, in all her fading beauty, had apparently fallen schoolgirlishly in love with a home tutor, his response was to laugh at her. It was her husband's ridicule that had wounded her, and she'd been suffering from an extreme lack of appetite ever since.

Mochizuki knew of so many examples of this type of thing: the sudden collapse of an engagement, the morass of a love triangle, the result of an affair... It wasn't even all that uncommon for such things to escalate to outright murder.

A part of Mochizuki had always believed that the people in these situations simply didn't know how to live, that a person who lacked the ability to imagine what might be in another's heart would naturally also lack the ability to make others happy. He'd assumed that these were pitfalls troubling only those who didn't have such life skills, and someone who knew the workings of the human heart could easily avoid them.

But now, of course, he was in a car heading straight toward exactly such a pitfall. The racing of his heart as he'd lied to his wife and left the house told the truth. He simply had to refuse the tryst to stay out of trouble, but he found himself unable to do it. Why not? The answer was nothing more complicated than his sense of reason lacking the power to suppress his fleshly desires. He was about to meet his lover, but his heart was in turmoil.

Mochizuki pulled into the parking lot next to the park a few minutes before eight. The lot was completely empty, and Akiko had yet to arrive. He turned his headlights low and kept the engine idling. Sliding a cassette into the tape player and settling in to wait with both hands resting on the wheel, the faces of his various patients suffering from neurotic disorders that stemmed from romantic entanglements drifted one by one through his mind.

I'll put an end to this tonight.

How many times could he tell himself the exact same thing? It was as if he were one of his own patients, and he was attempting to use hypnotic suggestion on himself. Yet he kept repeating it—until he was interrupted by a beam of light sliding over him as it licked his car's interior from the rear window to the front. Looking out, he saw it was from the headlights of a small coupe turning from the parking lot's entrance. The dashboard's digital clock told him it was eight on the dot. Akiko got out of the car, her eyes hidden by sunglasses. She wore a beige dress that hugged her curves. Mochizuki watched in the rearview mirror as she approached, her high heels clacking against the asphalt. She knocked smartly three times on the passenger side window—*tock tock tock*—before opening the door and sliding gracefully into the passenger seat with her knees together. As soon as she was in place, she wrapped her arms around Mochizuki's neck and pressed her lips against his. Their warmth and softness, along with the natural smell of her skin—untouched, as always, by even a drop of perfume—lit up his senses like a torch, and the resolution he'd been repeating like a mantra flew from his head completely.

Akiko lay on the bed with the sheets wrapped around her waist and her arms folded behind her head, and she stretched so that her back arched, thrusting her ample breasts up toward the ceiling. She then slid her legs from beneath the sheets and sat up on the edge of the bed, plucking a piece of fruit from the paper bag on the sideboard as if just remembering it was there.

The fruit was a European pear, carefully wrapped in translucent paper.

"Do you know what this is?"

Akiko held the pear at chest level.

"It's a European pear. Why did you bring it?"

She laughed at Mochizuki's reply as he roused himself from the bed.

"He gave it to me before I left the house."

"You mean your husband?"

"I told him I was going to Reiko's, and he handed it to me saying, 'Then bring this along with you.'"

Reiko must be the friend Akiko had told her husband she was meeting when she left. But Mochizuki became a bit worried. Had her husband seen through her lie?

Seeing unease drain the color from Mochizuki's face, Akiko reassured him.

"Don't worry, he's not the kind to call Reiko to check up on me or anything. He'll be in the bath getting ready for bed by now."

"For bed? It's not even ten."

"He's an early riser..."

"Because of work?"

As the conversation drifted toward her husband's work, Akiko began throwing the pear back and forth between her hands like an *otedama* beanbag. It was clear she didn't want to talk about it, and she tried to change the subject. Mochizuki realized she'd never told him what kind of work her husband did.

"Did you know the European pear is a type of 'wall fruit'?"

"Wall fruit? 'Wall' as in...a regular wall?"

"Yeah. It's a kind of fruit that's sensitive to cold and wind. It won't ripen properly unless it's planted next to a wall."

Mochizuki had heard of the term "wallflower" being used for someone who couldn't find anyone to talk to at a party, but this was the first time he'd heard of a "wall fruit."

Akiko placed the pear in Mochizuki's hand.

"Eat it."

But Mochizuki ended up staring at it instead. A fruit that needed to be sheltered by a wall to protect it from the cold and rain. In other words, it was a fruit that would never grow if it wasn't properly loved. The faces of his patients appeared in his mind again. Matsui Hospital was filled with people who more or less resembled this fruit.

Seeing that Mochizuki wasn't interested in eating it, Akiko snatched the pear back with an impatient, "C'mon..." She took a bite and wiped her mouth with the back of her hand. The curved, golden surface of the pear was wet with saliva where she'd bitten it, and it reflected the room's pinkish light. It reminded him of a sea cucumber in shallow water, glistening beneath a full moon.

"The rest is for you, Doctor. Have it."

"Huh?"

Mochizuki flinched as she held it out to him, and he made no move to take it. He'd lost his appetite ever since he'd been reminded of his patients.

"I don't want it."

"Just take it."

"I'm fine."

"Is that so?" Akiko withdrew her offer with a flourish, throwing the half-eaten pear into the wastebasket. It made a dull thud as it landed, its fall cushioned by the soft mountain of tissues at the basket's bottom.

"Then instead of the pear..."

Akiko walked her fingers across Mochizuki's chest as she spoke. "Is there something else you could give me, Doctor?"

"Something else?"

He had an idea what she meant, but he asked anyway.

"Something from you..."

Her fingers worked their way down his chest toward his lower body, and she brought her face close to his ear.

"Your baby, Doctor."

It wasn't that he didn't know how to answer her, or that he hesitated because he was thinking about what to say. But he remained silent. It was the type of situation where silence seemed to communicate enough. In fact, it seemed like the only real option. He'd never felt as though he were on the typical course male-female relations took when he thought of Akiko, but in this moment, he couldn't stop himself from imagining their future.

"Don't worry, it'd be fine.. No one would suspect a thing. I'd never cause you any trouble."

Mochizuki kept his silence.

"I'm already thirty-three, so having a child wouldn't seem strange to anyone. But I don't want one from my husband! I want *yours*, Doctor."

"..."

"I'd never ask you to acknowledge it."

Mochizuki put a cigarette in his mouth, lit it with his lighter, and inhaled deeply. After only one puff, though, Akiko once again extinguished the lit end between her fingers.

"Your blood type is A, right? Mine, too. My husband is O, so a child of ours could only end up with either A or O blood. So that wouldn't give it away, either. And he won't suspect anything even if the child doesn't resemble him as much as it might. He's not exactly the sharpest tool in the box."

Mochizuki used his elbows to raise himself up a bit.

"It's easy to get pregnant with a lover's child and not get found out, trust me. I know I can do it. I take my temperature every morning."

A woman recording her basal temperature every morning could indeed track her ovulation with a certain degree of accuracy. If Akiko were to make love to her husband a few days after she ovulated, it would be easy to have another man's child without anyone suspecting it wasn't her husband's.

Seemingly unbothered by Mochizuki's lack of response, Akiko silently rose from the bed and disappeared into the bathroom.

A few minutes passed, but Mochizuki didn't hear any more water running. Had she picked this moment to take a leisurely bath? Having lain back down on the bed, he raised his head a bit and listened. The pinkish light shone down on him, but its gaudy color no longer seemed appropriate to the room's stillness. Was she intentionally being so quiet to draw his attention? Mochizuki tried to find the reason for the unnatural silence.

One thing Mochizuki knew for certain was that Akiko's wish to have a child was sincere. Or at least, her wish *not* to have her husband's was.

She has it in her to go through with it. She's clearly capable of having my child while keeping it a secret from her husband. She could probably even hide it from me.

This thought ran through his mind. The situation still lacked any sense of reality for him. He found himself letting his guard down and thinking, *If she promises not to cause any trouble, would it be so bad if she went through with it?* But even as he told himself that, he knew it spelled nothing but future disaster for him and his family.

Eventually, Mochizuki heard something through the slightly cracked bathroom door: the sound of Akiko softly humming to herself. Imagining her in the bath, neck-deep in warm water and merrily singing a song to herself with her eyes closed, Mochizuki became a bit embarrassed about his earlier overthinking.

He decided to change his mood by humming a little himself,

and a melody soon came to his lips. But he couldn't quite place it at first. Repeating the notes over and over to stimulate his memory, Mochizuki suddenly realized what it was: Sayuri Asakawa's song, "In the Mirror." She'd taken to singing it to herself during their regular consultations at the hospital, and at some point, he ended up memorizing it, too.

Sayuri's mental condition remained largely unchanged, but her body seemed to transform with every passing day. Her pregnancy was now entering its eighth month. Cradling her swelling stomach in her hands as she wandered the courtyard, she struck an almost comical figure. According to the information Takeshi Sunako had gathered, the baby in her belly was almost certainly Yoichi Maki's—meaning that he was the one man in the world who held the key to curing her. But he was apparently on a tuna boat somewhere off the coast of New Zealand, so the prospects of him actually doing so were dim. There seemed to be no other way to interpret his actions than that he went to sea expressly in order to leave her behind for good.

Mochizuki went back over all the information he knew about Sayuri in his mind. A patient's psychiatric chart customarily included details of not only their life but also those of their family members, adding up to a thick stack of pages. But in Sayuri's case, she didn't have any family, so he couldn't fill in the blanks, and her chart remained woefully thin. Thankfully, though, Takeshi had managed to uncover enough information that the outlines of her family problems, while still vague, seemed to be emerging at last. The key mystery was the reason why Shuichiro, her father, took his own life. When Takeshi met Shuichiro's former business partner Nagata, he confirmed that the death had definitely been a suicide, though the lack of a note or any clear motive meant that many unanswered questions remained. But one detail intrigued Mochizuki: that just before his suicide, Shuichiro had apparently visited a psychiatric clinic for a consultation. According to Nagata, Shuichiro's behavior began to change radically about three months before he took his own life. The first sign was him becoming alarmingly forgetful. They would meet to discuss work, and Shuichiro would have forgotten contracts that had been finalized only the day before, leaving Nagata baffled. Further, whenever he pointed out these discrepancies, Shuichiro would react with intense, uncontrollable rage. He seemed to be afflicted more and more with such bouts of reasonless anger, causing problems for everyone around him. His work began to suffer, and he lost his usual vitality. Everything about him had changed, from the expression on his face to the way he walked. People started to whisper about how something must be wrong with him, and Nagata suggested he see a psychiatrist to get checked out. Eventually, he agreed and went in for a consultation. Takeshi even uncovered the name of the clinic he went to: Naito Psychiatric Clinic.

This intrigued Mochizuki as a fellow psychiatrist. He wanted to know if Shuichiro was suffering from a mental health condition—if it was an officially recognized pathology, what was its name? Chronic outbursts of anger, extreme forgetfulness, all adding up to a sudden change in character... What could be the cause? Was it a neurotic disorder, schizophrenia, or an organic mental disorder? Or was he abusing a substance—could it be alcohol? Stimulants? Some other kind of drug? Mochizuki mentally compared the various pathologies that came to mind, testing their symptoms against what he knew so far. But there just wasn't enough information. He had another key factor to consider: that Shuichiro's daughter, too, had attempted suicide at least twice. Six years ago, she'd made her debut as a singer, but she started to come undone during the summer campaign, and two months later, she ended up canceling it—and, as it turned out, her singing career entirely—when she was unable to recover from the shock of her father's suicide. It seemed that she met this Yoichi Maki fellow the following year, and then, after living together for about five years, she attempted a double suicide with him this past spring. And two months ago, five months pregnant with his child, she attempted to kill herself again, walking into the surf off the Nakatajima coast. Thinking it over, Mochizuki couldn't help but wonder if there wasn't a hereditary component to whatever it was Shuichiro suffered from. Was that the thread connecting father and daughter? What was hidden in the blood that bound them?

Could it be?

A possibility floated to the top of Mochizuki's mind: a vanishingly rare and terrifying mental illness estimated to affect only one out of every five hundred thousand people. Mochizuki was overcome by the desire to go to Tokyo and visit the Naito Psychiatric Clinic to look at Shuichiro Asakawa's chart. The name of the illness recorded there could turn out to be a key piece of information. And the family history section could very well contain descriptions of Sayuri's condition and the weight of the destiny coming to fruition within her.

His train of thought, which had shifted to his work, was broken by Akiko's wet body as she emerged from the bathroom. Her skin was flushed from her long soak, and tiny beads of sweat glistened from her hips to her breasts to her neck. She was still perspiring even as she ran a towel across her skin. Though only half dry, Akiko slipped on her underwear, followed by her dress. Pulling the zipper up, she turned to face Mochizuki. What could lead a man to step into something he knew full well was a trap? The untamed passion in the gaze of a woman glancing back at him through a curtain of wet hair. Her ever-shifting eyes glowed with both an eerie light and a coltish naivety, drawing the man in her sights inexorably to her, enticing him to make her every wish come true.

2

Mochizuki attended the Japanese Society of Psychiatry's conference held in Tokyo, then took the opportunity to go out to Ota and visit the Naito Psychiatric Clinic. The world of psychiatry wasn't that big, and as Mochizuki looked into the clinic, he discovered that his former mentor at Hamamatsu University School of Medicine, Professor Tatsunami, had been good friends with Naito. Using this connection, he phoned ahead and introduced himself before heading to the clinic.

"If Shuichiro Asakawa's chart is vital to your patient's treatment, why don't I mail the summary to you?"

Naito's offer was kind, but Mochizuki refused, asking if it would be all right if he visited in person instead since he had a conference to attend anyway. The chart would be filled with details about the patient's life and that of his family, and Mochizuki wanted the chance to pore over every inch of the file with his own eyes.

Looking at his watch, he saw that it was just past seven in the evening. Naito had told him to visit him at home if it got later than seven, and Mochizuki had jotted his address and telephone number down in his notebook. Glancing at the address to confirm he was in the right place, Mochizuki then walked the five-minute route from the station to his destination.

Naito lived alone in a rented apartment near the clinic. Tucked into a two-story wooden building, it hardly looked like the home of a physician who'd founded his own medical practice. Perhaps business at the clinic wasn't as good as it seemed, or perhaps he didn't think it was seemly for a lifelong bachelor to live somewhere too luxurious—Mochizuki couldn't stop speculating needlessly about Naito's situation.

Seeing him in person, Mochizuki saw that his hair was pure white, his body skinny and a little bent. But if he was the same age as his mentor Professor Tatsunami, that would make him exactly sixty years old.

Naito greeted Mochizuki warmly at the door, saying, "Please, please, come in." He seemed happy to have a fellow psychiatrist visit him during an otherwise unoccupied evening. The two-bedroom apartment was airy and pleasant, the interior neat and well-appointed in a way that was hard to guess from the exterior. It faced a park, which lent it a peaceful quietude.

I see—this must be why he lives here.

Mochizuki looked around the tidy little apartment, no longer wondering why Naito rented such a place. A door to a Western-style room stood open, affording a view of its book-stuffed interior. Every nook and cranny of the home seemed to be thoughtfully designed and well-organized.

"What a lovely place. Have you been here long?"

"More than twenty years now. Lost the urge to move at this point, I'm afraid."

Naito led Mochizuki into a Japanese-style room, which wasn't crowded by books.

They spoke a bit about how their mutual acquaintance Professor Tatsunami was doing, and then Mochizuki broached the topic of why he'd arranged this visit: he had a young female patient named Sayuri Asakawa staying at Matsui Hospital, where he was the assistant director, over in Hamamatsu, and in the course of investigating her condition, it was revealed that her father, Shuichiro Asakawa, also suffered from a psychiatric condition, so he'd like to look at the father's chart if he could.

The name of the illness he'd guessed from the limited circumstantial evidence flickered like a lightbulb in Mochizuki's mind. The chart would show him if he was right.

"Do you remember having a patient named Shuichiro Asakawa?"

Mochizuki wanted to confirm this first, and the older man nodded slowly.

"Of course. That must have been, what, six years ago now?"

"Why do you say 'of course'?"

"Well, you..."

Naito stopped there and stood up.

"Why don't you take a look at this first? When I got your call, I dug it out and looked it over myself to make sure I remembered it right."

He handed Shuichiro's chart to Mochizuki.

Mochizuki straightened his back as he took it, feeling as if he were receiving a sacred tome, and steeled himself so that he would react calmly no matter what he might read. He opened the file to start leafing through its contents. And there it was, right on the first page: the name of the condition spelled out in English, passing through his eyes to sear itself into his brain.

HUNTINGTON'S DISEASE

Just as I thought!

Mochizuki raised his head and met Naito's gaze. His suspicions had been proven true. It seemed inappropriate in response to something so tragic, yet he couldn't hide the excitement that welled up within him.

Six years ago, Naito had experienced something similar upon diagnosing Shuichiro's condition.

"In all the thirty years I've practiced psychiatry, his was the first and last case of Huntington's I ever encountered."

In a calm, deliberate tone, Naito proceeded to describe his encounter with Shuichiro Asakawa.

It wasn't something he was likely to forget. After conducting several tests assessing Shuichiro's involuntary bodily movements, Naito looked into the medical histories of not only his parents and siblings, but also that of his grandparents in order to confirm his diagnosis. Shuichiro's mother died in an accident at the age of forty, while his father, though he was never examined by a psychiatrist, died by suicide after suffering from an unidentified mental illness. His aunt, too, passed away prematurely at forty-three and had reportedly exhibited clear signs of dementia before her death. Factoring in these findings along with his involuntary bodily movements, changes in personality, sudden forgetfulness, and general confusion, the diagnosis was clear.

Huntington's disease.

But even as he'd heard the word come out of Naito's mouth, Shuichiro could only stare open-mouthed and repeat it back to Naito. It wasn't a disease that anyone outside the medical profession could be expected to know, as it was extremely rare. Among the Japanese, it struck roughly one out of every five hundred thousand people.

Naito had proceeded to explain in simple terms what Shuichiro could expect as the disease progressed. Shuichiro's expression began to harden as he listened. Only his eyes still moved, darting back and forth. Naito could guess what was troubling him: what it meant for his only daughter, Sayuri. What if the cursed fate wouldn't die with him—what if it awaited his daughter as well? Shuichiro must have wanted to grind his teeth at the thought of it.

"Do you know if Shuichiro ever discussed his illness with Sayuri?" asked Mochizuki.

"It's something that affects her life directly, so he had to. We talked about that point more than once."

"But did he really do it?"

"His daughter absolutely knew. She even came to the clinic herself, beset with worry about the disease, and we explained the situation to her in detail. After that, she'd come again from time to time. She was particularly insistent in asking if there was a way to tell if she had it before symptoms appeared. From how she spoke, it sounded like there was a man in her life she cared about... It's so cruel, this disease."

It was during the summer campaign following her debut as a singer that she unexpectedly fell into a state of depression, eventually shortening her singing career prematurely. The reason was now clear: it was the shock from learning about her fate. Two months later, she sustained another blow with her father's suicide, and it ended up taking her more than half a year to recover from that. According to the family timeline Takeshi had created, she met Yoichi Maki in June of the following year. But was their relationship a cure for the sickness in her heart, or did it simply represent an even larger dilemma for her to face?

These were Mochizuki's thoughts as he leafed through the rest of Shuichiro's chart, until he reached the pages concerning Sayuri's mother, Yuko. Reading them, he was brought up short. He'd heard that Sayuri's mother had passed away while Sayuri was just a child, but that wasn't what was written in the chart.

At 28, Shuichiro Asakawa divorces his wife, Yuko (27)

When asked about this point, Naito consulted his notes and began to explain in more detail what had happened in the Asakawa household.

"Shuichiro was in the stage lighting business when he met Yuko, an aspiring actress, and they married soon after. She had Sayuri, but only two years after that, she left them and ran off."

"Ran off?"

"With another man."

"She did?"

"Yes. Shuichiro signed the divorce papers when they arrived, freeing him legally. But Sayuri was one and a half at the time, and he kept her to raise himself. It was her mother who was at fault, so he vowed never to let her go."

"I see... And do you know where Yuko is now?"

"Certainly not... I don't have any way of knowing that."

Mochizuki did some quick calculations in his head. If she'd been twenty-seven when she got divorced, she'd be pushing fifty by now.

"I forgot to mention it earlier, but Sayuri is currently eight months pregnant."

Mochizuki said this to let Naito know why he was interested in Yuko's whereabouts.

"I see." The older man understood immediately.

If Sayuri's condition didn't improve after giving birth, and if Yoichi continued to run away from his responsibilities, then her child would end up cared for at a baby-and-infant welfare institution. But it would be a different story if Sayuri's mother was still alive. She would be the baby's grandmother. Regardless of whether she was willing to take the child to raise herself, she at least needed to know of the child's existence. If Sayuri did end up improving enough to be discharged from the hospital, Yuko seemed to be the only person who could act as the guarantor.

"So you don't know Yuko's current address."

Mochizuki sighed in disappointment. Naito had no answer for him but to sigh as well.

"Perhaps you can speak to a caseworker? They can probably track people down in cases like these."

Mochizuki was already planning on contacting the city welfare office and doing the necessary paperwork once he returned to Hamamatsu. But, if circumstances permitted, he would just as soon have Takeshi look into things again. He'd gathered so much information and put together a detailed timeline in such a short time—he might be more skilled than an actual caseworker. Playing detective seemed to suit him, and he seemed to find it fun, even. Mochizuki knew Takeshi had formally resigned from his job in Tokyo, and he was doing nothing at the moment besides just staying at his parents' home. He had to be contemplating what to do next. Perhaps he should consider becoming a caseworker himself? Mochizuki decided to wait for a good time and bring it up to him next time they met.

It was eight thirty in the evening. Half the small stores around him were closing up. Naito had told him the taxi ride to the station would take less than thirty minutes, so he strolled around the shopping arcade and bought a small flask of bourbon before getting in the taxi to Tokyo Station. He would be fine as long as he made the Hikari bullet train leaving at nine twenty-five.

He wasn't all that hard a drinker, but this was a night when he felt like having something. He'd absorbed next to nothing from the conference in the afternoon. More than anything, his heart was heavy, and he was haunted by the specter of Huntington's disease. Sayuri had a fifty-fifty chance of inheriting the condition from her father. If her present state was due to the disease emerging, then there was almost nothing they could do for her besides somehow tracking down her mother so she could take care of her child. But of course, the baby would face the same cursed destiny as its mother and grandfather. It was when he felt powerless that he reached for a drink.

3

Eating lunch with Mochizuki at the café next to the hospital, Takeshi listened to the doctor explain his visit with Naito in Tokyo the previous day and how he was able to confirm the name of Shuichiro's illness. But Takeshi didn't understand what this had to do with Sayuri's condition, and his face clouded with incomprehension.

"Huntington's disease?"

After a few moments of silence, Takeshi repeated Mochizuki's words back to him. He'd never heard of it before, so there was little else he could provide by way of response. Takeshi readied himself to listen as he stuffed the remainder of his sandwich into his mouth.

Mochizuki began to explain the disease.

"It's a very rare condition, first described by the American physician George Huntington in 1872. What's cruel is that it's inevitable—while most mental conditions are caused by a complex mix of factors, both environmental and genetic, Huntington's disease is purely genetic. In other words, it's the result of an abnormality in the patient's DNA. Nothing else affects it."

Mochizuki opened his notebook on the glass tabletop and drew two pairs of circles on it with a pencil. One pair had a white and a black circle, and the other had two white circles. The nucleus of a human cell contains pairs of chromosomes, and a child receives one chromosome from each parent. Mochizuki was using the pairs of black-and-white and white-and-white circles to explain this law of inheritance as simply as possible.

"Have you heard of Mendelian inheritance?"

"I've heard the words... We learned about it in high school biology, but I don't remember what it actually is."

Mochizuki nodded anyway.

"Huntington's disease is transmitted as an autosomal dominant trait."

"Autosomal dominant...?"

"Genes can be either dominant or recessive. Some people think that dominant genes are the 'better' genes passed from parent to child, and that the recessive genes are the 'bad' genes, but that's not true. All it means is that the dominant variant of a gene will suppress the effect of a recessive variant. Huntington's disease is carried on by a single dominant gene, so if a child inherits it from a parent, that child will have the disease, too."

Takeshi hurriedly raised his hand to interrupt.

"Um, can you explain it a little more simply, Doctor?"

"Well, to make a long story short..."

Mochizuki drew lines connecting the circles he'd made and then sketched out four different outcomes. If the father had a black-white pair of chromosomes and the mother had a white-white pair, there were four possible combinations that the child could inherit: two black-white pairs and two white-white pairs.

"Suppose the black circles represent genes for Huntington's disease and the white circles represent normal genes. See here, two of the outcomes are a black-and-white pair. The black dominant gene, put simply, will override the white gene and express itself. That means that when one parent has Huntington's disease, the chance the child will have it is exactly fifty percent."

"What if the disease were recessive?"

"Then the abnormal gene would be suppressed by the normal gene, and a child with a black-white pair would merely be a carrier and not suffer from the disease."

"Then what if both parents have it?"

"It's so rare that it's hard to imagine such a thing, but if that were to happen, what do you think that'd mean for the child's chance of inheriting it?"

Takeshi hesitated a bit before answering with a look of uncertainty.

"Wouldn't it be…a hundred percent?"

"No."

This time, Mochizuki drew two black-white pairs of circles, then added lines branching out of each circle as he spoke. The resulting four combinations were: black-black, black-white, white-black, and white-white. In other words, there was still a pair that contained only normal genes.

"You see? When both parents have it, you end up with three combinations where the disease is expressed, but you still have one white-white pair that's free from the condition. So the chance is seventy-five percent."

"I see…"

Takeshi finally understood. It wasn't so hard to comprehend, after all.

"I get it now. Ah, there are still some things I'm confused about, though."

Mochizuki finally paused and took a sip of his coffee.

"But, listen. The truly scary thing about this disease isn't that."

He spoke after another sip. The serious expression on his face brought Takeshi up short.

"Most autosomal dominant disorders are expressed as abnormalities in the body and are detectable soon after birth. But Huntington's isn't like that."

"By which you mean…?"

"The disease usually waits until someone is in their late thirties to emerge, and until then, there's no way to know if it's been inherited."

"Late thirties?"

"That's an average, so individual cases may vary, of course. But yes, normally around then."

"In other words..."

Takeshi thought about it. He found that the easiest way to organize all of it was to imagine himself in the position.

"Let's say one of my parents was diagnosed with Huntington's disease right now. I'm twenty-four years old, but the disease doesn't usually emerge until your late thirties. So, that means I'd have more than ten years of living in fear before I might know if I have it?"

"Yes."

"Th-Then it's like Russian roulette—except the odds are fifty-fifty."

In his mind, Takeshi imagined putting three bullets in a six-shot revolver and bringing the muzzle to his head. Then, he pictured living for ten years that way. He felt a vein in his temple throb uncomfortably just at the thought.

"So there's no way of knowing? Really? Your destiny's just up in the air until you get sick?"

"For now. But recently, we found that the abnormal gene is located on chromosome 4. Soon we might be able to use PET—positron emission tomography—to detect atrophy or patterns of reduced glucose metabolism in the caudate nuclei and diagnose the disease before it emerges."

"I know I sound stupid asking again, but just to make sure: you're saying that Sayuri's father had Huntington's disease, but we still don't know if Sayuri's inherited the gene that causes it?"

"Yes, that's right."

"So that means there's a one-in-four chance that the baby in her belly has it, too."

"It does—that is, unless Sayuri actually has it. Then the odds go up to fifty-fifty."

Takeshi turned his head away from Mochizuki, who was sitting opposite him, and looked out the window at the gentle slope of the grassy hill outside. There was a small swamp at the bottom of the slope, its surface shining in the sun. The leaves of the trees around it were just beginning to turn. It was such a peaceful, familiar scene.

Takeshi looked back at Mochizuki.

"So what kind of disease is it, Doctor?"

"It involves both involuntary movement and psychological problems... Well, to put it simply, involuntary movement refers to patients losing the ability to move their body as they wish. It can be observed in a patient's face, tongue, mouth, or in their hands and feet. They can have trouble walking and can even look a bit like they're dancing instead. Also, their words can become slurred or unclear."

"I understand. What about the psychological part?"

"They'll find it more and more difficult to concentrate and remember things. They can also become irritable, depressed, or delusional. Basically, their entire character changes. Suicide isn't rare, either."

"Suicide... Because of the hopelessness of the disease?"

"No, I mean suicidal ideation is itself a common symptom."

"Then Sayuri's father..."

"Yes, that must've been the case for him."

Takeshi remained quiet for a moment, then pushed his glasses up his nose.

"And is there any cure?"

Mochizuki shook his head slightly.

"No."

It was clear from Mochizuki's expression that the prospect of a cure was out of the question.

"So how does the disease progress?"

"Eventually, the patient will no longer be able to stand or even sit up. Of course, they won't be able to walk, either. So nursing care becomes necessary."

Takeshi's face paled. He realized his heart was beating faster. While he didn't want to hear any more, he knew he had to learn everything he could.

"And the patient's personality?"

"Will be completely destroyed. Until there's not a trace left of the person they once were."

So Sayuri would end up "completely destroyed"? What would happen then?

"And then...?"

"Their dementia will advance...until death."

At a complete loss, Takeshi simply stared back at Mochizuki.

What is this?

Inchoate words were filling his mind, resounding in his chest.

What is this? This is crazy. The whole world's messed up.

Huntington's disease was no manmade disaster. Never in his wildest dreams did Takeshi imagine that the natural world would produce a disease so accursed, so cruel. It was as though the gene for the disease, created by chance during the long process of evolution, now sought to prolong its existence through malevolent intent. Its propagation could be prevented if it were detectable at a young age, but because symptoms don't usually appear in people until they're past their childbearing age, it's able to evade such measures. What cunning!

Closing his eyes, Takeshi tried to bring his emotions under control. He must be as honest as he could with himself. There wasn't a person in the world who truly knew their fate. Nothing was absolutely certain. He could leave this café right now and end up run over by a car; he could be diagnosed at any time with a cancer that would kill him. Nonetheless, the cold exactitude of the fifty-fifty chance Sayuri faced hurt his heart to contemplate.

Takeshi opened his eyes again with a look of resolve. The melody that Sayuri liked to hum to herself flitted through the back of his mind. He met Mochizuki's gaze with his own and nodded firmly, but Mochizuki didn't understand the meaning of it yet.

"It might be the case, though, that she's already suffering from the disease, right?"

Takeshi's voice was hesitant and halting as he asked this.

"Not necessarily. We still don't know anything for sure."

"But her condition..."

"The clinical manifestations don't match. The distinctive involuntary bodily movement hasn't appeared, for example, and her psychological condition looks different as well. Until we take her to the university hospital for a CT scan to look for signs of atrophy in the caudate nucleus, we can't really make a judgment."

In truth, Mochizuki hesitated to ascribe Sayuri's current unresponsiveness to Huntington's disease. Any evidence of atrophy in her caudate nucleus would be a telltale sign, of course, but the disease was so rare that Mochizuki lacked the clinical experience to confidently diagnose her with it. Sayuri was presently twenty-five years old. Symptoms were found to manifest before the age of twenty in five to ten percent of Huntington's cases, so it was possible she was experiencing something similar. There were also cases of patients being completely unresponsive, making it impossible to assess their mental capacity, and Sayuri's symptoms were not completely atypical in that sense, either.

But Mochizuki somehow sensed that Sayuri was making gradual improvements lately, if only slight ones. Perhaps because of a certain motherly instinct rising as her pregnancy advanced, Mochizuki observed that her expressions seemed to be becoming more distinct, even lively. She was able to nod and shake her head in response to simple questions, and her humming was occasionally accompanied by small snatches of lyrics. It was as though she was unconsciously preparing for the birth of her child, the will to care for it slowly rising within her... These impressions led Mochizuki to believe that her current state must be caused by something besides Huntington's, since that condition only ever gets worse; or at least, that's what he wanted to believe.

"By the way..."

Mochizuki casually shifted the conversation, explaining to Takeshi that Sayuri's mother, Yuko, had run off with another man twenty-three years ago, her current whereabouts unknown.

"She's not dead?"

Takeshi's brows were furrowed as he asked. He seemed to find it mystifying that Yuko could still be alive.

"She'd only be in her early fifties, so if she hasn't had an accident or an unexpected disease, it's reasonable to think she's alive and well."

Takeshi tilted his head. He'd always assumed that Sayuri's mother was long dead. But where had he gotten that information? He tried to remember, but all that came up was various instances of hearsay and third-hand accounts along the lines of, "I think her mother's already passed away." These vague indications had intertwined with his own unconscious wish for it to be true, eventually blossoming into unfounded certainty.

"Is that so?"

Mochizuki hadn't meant to chide Takeshi for the mistake in the information he'd gathered. But Takeshi seemed to feel some sort of responsibility for it anyway as he bowed his head at Mochizuki's words.

"Doctor..."

Takeshi looked back up.

"What is it?"

"If we figure out where this woman, Sayuri's mother, might be..."

"We would contact her right away and try to get her to come here in person, of course."

"And then...?"

"She would be designated her primary guardian, and in the happy event that Sayuri improved enough to leave the hospital, she would be released into her care."

Once again, Takeshi fell silent, his face clouded with dismay. Mochizuki couldn't help but notice. He realized Takeshi was worried that the appearance of a possible guardian would mean that Sayuri might get taken away from him. There was one other person who might do the same: Yoichi Maki, who was currently on a tuna boat off the coast of New Zealand. If he ever changed his mind and returned to land, he might well take both mother and child away with him.

Takeshi was the first to break the awkward silence that had descended on the table.

"By the way, do you think Yoichi Maki knew Sayuri might end up with Huntington's?"

"Who knows? We can't say one way or the other."

"I think he did. That's why he ran away. It makes sense that he might have reacted that way."

Neither Mochizuki nor Takeshi had any way of knowing if Yoichi had found out about Sayuri's father's diagnosis. It certainly appeared as though Yoichi's actions following the attempted double suicide were those of someone running away. Perhaps he'd escaped because he didn't want to share her destiny. But this was no more than a guess.

Takeshi had a way to test his hypothesis. It was easy. If Yoichi somehow didn't know about it, Takeshi would simply inform him. He would send him documents about Sayuri's father's Huntington's disease via the Wakashio Fisheries office the same way he'd mailed the videotape and letter before. If they contacted a supply ship and things worked out well, the new package would reach Yoichi in about a month. While the previous tape and letter had notified him of Sayuri's pregnancy, the new one would inform him of her father's disease. Takeshi was sure that if he found out that his lover might also be suffering from such a horrifying disease—and that the baby in her belly might be facing the same accursed fate—it would surely drive Yoichi to run even further away.

4

"Doctor?"

Mochizuki almost stood up reflexively at the sound of Akiko Nonoyama's voice. She waited at the door, giving no indication that she intended to enter any further. Normally, he would ask a visitor to come to his desk, but this time he rose to his feet and met her at the door. A young doctor and two nurses happened to be in the assistant director's office, and they could easily overhear anything Akiko might say. Young nurses were especially fond of scandals. Mochizuki took great care in the hospital not to give them any gossip fodder if he could help it.

Stepping into the hall and closing the door behind him, Mochizuki spoke to Akiko in a hushed tone.

"What is it?"

He suspected she wanted to talk about their rendezvous that night. Did she want to change the time? Or reschedule entirely? Mochizuki's expression was slightly irritated as he faced her. He'd grown fond of their once-a-week trysts, and he prepared himself for her to offer some sort of excuse for putting off tonight's plans. Last week, they hadn't ended up meeting at all. If that happened again today, he needed to stop indulging her caprice and stand firm.

Akiko seemed to have read Mochizuki's thoughts and smiled, causing a dimple to appear on her left cheek.

"I think you've got the wrong idea."

She took Mochizuki's left hand in hers, lightly poking the base of his index and middle fingers with the tip of her pinkie.

"We're still on for tonight," she whispered.

Mochizuki breathed a sigh of relief, and then, as he tried to disentangle his fingers from hers, she continued.

"Can you come with me for a moment? There's something I want to show you."

The tone of her voice had changed completely. She turned and began walking toward the Second Ward.

Her destination turned out to be Tomoko Nakano's room. Besides Sayuri Asakawa, she was the only patient at Matsui Hospital who was in a stuporous state. Tomoko had been unable to cope with the shock of losing her two-year-and-seven-month-old daughter; she'd fallen into a state wherein she couldn't even eat or go to the bathroom by herself, and she required constant care—a much more serious condition than Sayuri's.

Akiko knocked on Tomoko's door before entering the room. The Second Ward was all female, and the air was filled with feminine voices of all kinds. Not just flirtatious, womanly tones, but long bouts of loud laughter, endless streams of slurred words, random outbursts of fury, intense sobbing... Seemingly every sound that could gush forth from a human body swirled up around them. Having grown used to the din, Mochizuki found the silence that prevailed in Tomoko's room paradoxically chilling. She lay in bed on her back, completely still. Mochizuki looked down and saw that her eyes were slightly open. But her gaze was weak and unfocused, and her expression remained unchanged even when he leaned his face close to hers. The visual information registered on her retinas should have been conveyed by the optic nerve to her brain, yet there was no response. The world was the same to Tomoko whether she saw it or not. It always unsettled Mochizuki to be confronted with such bottomless indifference. Where was Tomoko's consciousness as it floated within her, cloaked in impenetrable silence? Mochizuki lacked the imagination to guess.

He didn't see any change in her condition. He turned to face Akiko, his eyes asking her why she'd brought him here.

"Can you take a look at this?"

Akiko tugged at the left sleeve of Mochizuki's shirt. There was a small sink mounted on the wall next to the bed, and above it, a metal-framed glass window. Looking at it, he understood immediately what Akiko meant. There were two white masses stuck to the glass, roughly the size of two palms, as well as the remnants of another two that appeared to have fallen onto the bottom of the metal frame.

Mochizuki picked up a piece of the fallen materials and examined it. It was nearly weightless and crumbled as he touched it, like soft sheets of paper that had been moistened, molded into the shape of something like a *senbei* rice cracker and then stuck to the glass until it dried out and fell. Its texture led him to believe it was toilet paper. After all, toilet paper was easy enough to get a hold of, as it was stocked in every room.

"I don't remember seeing it when I checked in on her yesterday afternoon," explained Akiko.

If she was right, then that meant Tomoko had performed the strange act of vandalism sometime last night or this morning. It couldn't have been the work of anyone else but her.

"What does this mean?"

Mochizuki tried to pull apart the material in his hand a little bit. At the very least, it meant that Tomoko had moved under her own power, which would be the first time she'd have done so since being admitted. Mochizuki wanted to know what the action meant, as it might hold the key to her recovery. Why had the woman, who had no interest in anything, even things related to her own survival like eating and going to the bathroom, felt the need to perform this small, strange prank?

He became completely absorbed in the mystery, forgetting that Akiko was even there. From time to time, he'd glance at Tomoko as she lay in bed, trying to imagine her standing next to the sink.

There were four clumps of toilet paper in total. Two were stuck to the window, and when he touched them, they were still a little wet. The other two were completely dried out, which meant that there was a difference in wetness. Between yesterday and today, Tomoko must have walked over to the sink four different times and soaked the paper in water. She didn't make all four at the same time. How much paper would it take to mold these white masses? Mochizuki decided to try it out for himself, taking a roll of toilet paper from the cupboard and wetting some in the sink. The water made the paper shrink, of course, which meant that it took around two or three meters to make clumps the same size that Tomoko had apparently made. He looked back again at Tomoko, trying to put himself in her headspace. It was late at night and when he woke up, he took some toilet paper and washed it…

Washed it?

Mochizuki had used the word unthinkingly, but retracing his train of thought, it struck him as strange. People don't wash toilet paper, after all.

This was no prank.

Which was obvious enough—it had been two years since Tomoko was admitted to the hospital, and this was the first time she'd acted spontaneously on her own. It seemed likely that it was a repetition of an action she'd habitually performed before she was hospitalized. Mochizuki squeezed the water out of the paper with both hands, and then stuck it to the glass in front of him. *Of course, she was drying it...* Tomoko's daughter had drowned in a reservoir and died. She'd been two years and seven months old at the time—just around the age when she would be transitioning away from diapers.

Mochizuki took his hands off the glass.

"Hey, do you know if Tomoko used cloth diapers for her daughter?"

Akiko shook her head.

"No, I don't..."

"Shiraishi was the attending physician, right? Can you get him?"

Akiko looked blankly at him in response to his request, prompting Mochizuki to remember that Shiraishi was presently on assignment at a hospital in Toyohashi. That was why Akiko had gone directly to the assistant director with her discovery.

"Oh, but he's not here at the moment."

Akiko gently wrapped her right hand around Mochizuki's upper arm as she answered him.

"Ah, of course. How careless of me."

"This patient used to use cloth diapers for her child, which means that she washed them nearly every night for almost three years. For some reason, this habit came back to her and, taking the strip of toilet paper for the cloth of a diaper, she washed and dried it.

Is that what you're thinking, Doctor?"

Mochizuki nodded his agreement, thinking back to his own daughter, Kanae, when she was between two and three years old. He had no memory of washing her diapers. Nor did he recall ever changing them. He didn't know how it felt or how it smelled. Yet the long, thin strips of cloth nevertheless symbolized a child's babyhood to him. His wife Naomi seemed to enjoy the smell and feel of them as she folded them once they were dry.

It was hard for Mochizuki to see a prospect of recovery in Tomoko's sudden activity, though. Everyone will face the loss of someone close to them, and in most cases, they will overcome the grief with time. But there are people who cannot cope with the loss. Such cases usually end in suicide, but in rare instances, the result is a total shutdown of mental processes, as seemed to be the case with Tomoko. The only cure for her grief would be for her daughter to come back to life, and since that was impossible, her only other choice was to immerse herself in the other world where her daughter was. Her flesh remained, but her mind was wandering on the opposite shore. And there, she continued to wash her daughter's diapers every night.

Many mechanisms of the brain are yet to be understood. Mochizuki had no explanation for why Tomoko would suddenly start washing toilet paper now. The neurons in her brain flipped like a switch and her body began to move, but it was impossible to say with certainty what triggered them. Did catching a glimpse of Sayuri's swelling belly here in the ward do the trick? Did she see a discarded doll in the piles of separated garbage during one of her outdoor excursions in her wheelchair and get reminded of her daughter? There was no way to predict what might or might not have an impact on patients like her. The same went for Sayuri—there was always the chance that something might make the gears inside her head turn again. Mochizuki was surer than ever that the key to unlocking that "something" lay in Yoichi Maki's hands.

5

The sounds of Field Day traveled across the crisp mid-October air and floated through the open window of the assistant director's office. Matsui Hospital sat atop a plateau, and midway down the hill leading to the wetlands at the bottom was a newly constructed junior high school. The breeze was carrying the noise up from the school's playfield. If Mochizuki listened carefully, he'd surely hear a few marching songs familiar from his youth. The sky was clear and blue, perfect for a field day.

Looking down at the courtyard of the hospital, Mochizuki caught sight of Takeshi sitting on a bench.

Has he mistaken the hospital for his own backyard?

Mochizuki laughed wryly to himself. He felt like he was seeing Takeshi more often than members of his own staff these days. The young man seemed to visit Sayuri at least twice a week.

Standing next to the window, Mochizuki idly watched as Takeshi conducted his usual one-sided conversation with her. He took out a square package that contained maybe snacks of some sort, lifted the lid, and offered what was inside to Sayuri. Takeshi always brought a present when he visited. But Sayuri never seemed particularly pleased by them and usually didn't take anything he offered. Her appetite was much the same as it had been when she was admitted, and Takeshi's well-intentioned efforts to feed the baby in her belly often went unrewarded.

According to the ob-gyn at the hospital affiliated with the medical school, though, the baby was growing at a normal rate. In two months' time, Sayuri would be transferred to the maternity ward and give birth there.

Tomoko Nakano's face appeared in the back of Mochizuki's mind. She'd passed away only the day before. While some patients were transferred to the hospital to give birth to new lives, there were also patients who lost their lives there. Tomoko came down with bronchial pneumonia and was brought to the hospital four days ago, but her condition took a turn for the worse on the fourth night, and she died. She was thirty-nine. Ironically, her mental functions had suddenly started to return since the day they'd discovered her toilet-paper washing, and in the space of three days, she was able to use the restroom on her own. After that, whatever switch that had been flipped within her resulted in a recovery speedier than anything Mochizuki could have predicted. She began to feed herself without help and eventually improved to the point that she no longer needed personal care. So it was all the more tragic when this miraculous recovery was cut short by a disease that robbed her still-weak body of the life that was just returning to it. It was almost as if she knew she would soon die, and it was this knowledge that made her mental functions blossom in the end. The expression on her face as she lay in her deathbed was satisfied and peaceful, and it reflected a tranquility within her. Watching over her as she passed away, Mochizuki felt a certain sense of relief. He prayed that she was now holding her daughter in her arms somewhere in the next world.

Gripped by a sudden urge to feel the fall breeze on his skin, Mochizuki descended the stairs and walked out into the courtyard. He'd just finished his last outpatient consultation of the morning, so he had a few minutes to himself before lunch. He passed by the bench where Takeshi sat and called out to him.

"Hey."

A nurse had just fetched Sayuri for lunch, and they were making their way into the West Ward. Takeshi was staring forlornly at her retreating back when Mochizuki greeted him, and he turned his head.

"Doctor..." he replied politely.

Mochizuki sat down where Sayuri had just been sitting.

"Have you observed any changes in her lately?"

"Uh, well..."

Takeshi trailed off vaguely. Seeing that the younger man had something on his mind but was having trouble saying it, Mochizuki placed a gentle hand on his shoulder and purposefully rose from his seat.

"Doctor?"

"What is it?"

"Can I ask you something?"

Mochizuki sat back down, turning his upper body to face Takeshi.

"Sure. What's bothering you?"

"There's something I feel like I need to discuss with you..."

Even the slightest sign of disapproval or irritation on the face of the person he was talking to was enough to make Takeshi shut down. Mochizuki knew that he was teetering on the edge, unable to decide whether to share his thoughts or keep them to himself. Mochizuki willed himself to smile as pleasantly as possible to draw whatever it was out of him.

"Um, I did some research, but I was wondering... Would it ever be possible for me to become Sayuri's primary guardian?"

"You?"

Takeshi nodded firmly. Mochizuki feigned surprise, but he had secretly been waiting for him to bring this up.

"Practically speaking, it's possible for the Family Court to recognize you as her primary guardian."

The Mental Health and Welfare Law recognizes the guardian or curator, the spouse, and then the person with parental authority as the primary guardian, in that order. However, in the absence of any such people, the municipal head of the region where the patient resides or is currently located becomes their guardian. In Sayuri's case, this was the mayor of Hamamatsu. The mayor's office was responsible for the cost of her hospital stay, and a percentage of it was paid by the Treasury. The Family Court, though, had the power to designate Takeshi as her guardian. In that case, the Court would have to make sure that he fulfilled his duties correctly. Mochizuki understood that beneath Takeshi's question lay his desire to marry Sayuri. Becoming a spouse would be an easier, more traditional way to become her primary guardian.

"For her, this would be—"

Mochizuki cut him off.

"I'd say the problem isn't with her, it's with you. Being someone's primary guardian is more complicated than you might think."

"But I..."

"You want to marry her, right?"

Takeshi raised his head.

"Yes, I do. Is that so wrong?"

"It's not *wrong*. The thing is..."

It certainly wasn't wrong. Sayuri was all alone, suffering from mental health problems, pregnant with the child of another man, and possibly afflicted with Huntington's disease—marrying such a woman would indeed seem like an unimpeachably humanitarian act. But Mochizuki wasn't convinced. Or rather, it made him oddly angry, and the irritation welled up within him.

"Why are you looking at me like that, Doctor?"

Noticing the change in Mochizuki's expression, Takeshi's resolution began to falter. Unease washed over him. Was there something wrong with what he wanted to do?

"All you're doing is selling yourself short, Takeshi."

Mochizuki spoke as forcefully as he could while he leaned forward.

"S-Selling myself short? What do you mean?"

"You think marrying Sayuri is an admirable thing to do, don't you? People should praise you for doing such a thing, right?"

Takeshi felt humiliated. He never expected Mochizuki to shower him with this kind of criticism.

"But...I love her. What's wrong with being honest with my feelings?"

"You love her? Sayuri?"

"Yes."

"Have you ever had a proper conversation with her? Shared your views on things?"

"Well, no..."

"How do you love someone you can't even communicate with? How can you know what she might be feeling?"

"..."

"You need to stop kidding yourself."

Takeshi opened his mouth, but Mochizuki raised his hand to stop him.

"What's really happening here is that you think the only person around who's on your level is Sayuri, with all her problems. Isn't that right?"

Contemplating the weakness within Takeshi—his lack of confidence, his attitude toward life in general—filled Mochizuki with despair.

He pictured Takeshi on one end of a seesaw and Sayuri on the other. Sayuri faced several difficulties. Each was a serious problem on its own, and all of them added up to an almost unbearably heavy load. Takeshi needed to have enough minuses on his end to balance it out. What Takeshi really needed was the strength to turn his minuses into pluses, but instead, he was preparing to use his minuses. He was looking for a partner who carried the same weight on their back. That was what Mochizuki meant by him selling himself short. And Takeshi saw it as an act of humanitarianism...

Takeshi slowly turned Mochizuki's words over in his mind. After thinking about it from as many angles as he could, he felt like he understood what Mochizuki meant, but he wasn't sure. He'd never been in a healthy, balanced relationship with a woman, and he didn't see that changing in the future. When he met an attractive woman, he immediately told himself she was out of his league and suppressed any feeling or desire he might have for her. So without really noticing, he'd tied himself down and, not wanting to get hurt, continually avoided any sort of engagement at all... Thinking about it that way, he realized why he found Sayuri so irresistible: in her current condition, she was a woman incapable of hurting anyone. But he still didn't see why that made loving her so wrong.

"What would you do with her child?" Mochizuki asked, his tone gentle.

"I'd raise it, of course."

Mochizuki sighed and shook his head rather theatrically.

"It's not yours."

"I know that!"

"It's easy to say you'll raise the child, but do you know how difficult a task that really is? It's no joke. And if Sayuri does turn out to have Huntington's disease, that means the baby..."

Mochizuki suddenly trailed off.

What right do I have to lecture anyone? he thought.

And indeed, who exactly did he think he was? Mochizuki reflected on his own recent behavior. He hadn't even properly responded to Akiko's wish to have his baby. His ambivalence about the entire thing had resulted in cowardly silence when she'd bring it up. And here he was lecturing Takeshi about the duties of parenthood. It was easy to see the faults of others, but when it came to one's own, it turned out to be not so simple.

Mochizuki wiped the cold sweat from his brow, then put his elbows on his knees and his chin in his hands, his eyes fixed on the ground. Feeling helpless, he'd lost the will to question Takeshi any further.

"Doctor, is Sayuri in any condition to be discharged? If there were someone to take care of her?"

Takeshi's voice sounded to Mochizuki as if it were coming from somewhere far away.

"Uh, well, yes..."

"She is?"

"Yes, I think she is."

There were no objective standards by which to judge whether a patient was ready to be discharged. Of course, patients could be kept in the hospital if they were a possible danger to themselves or others—that is, if they seemed suicidal or violent—but there was nothing cut-and-dry about the term "possible danger." Mochizuki knew of at least three cases where patients judged to be no longer suicidal were released only to jump from the roof of a department store the very next day.

Mochizuki occasionally regretted his choice to pursue a discipline like psychiatry, with all its vagueness and uncertainty. A surgeon who saves a patient's life by cutting the cancerous cells out of their body can experience unalloyed joy and satisfaction in a job well done. Mochizuki sometimes envied such unambiguous, clear-cut methods of treatment. Psychiatric care very rarely yielded results that could be assessed with that kind of objectivity. It wasn't a medication or a form of occupational therapy that was going to cure Sayuri Asakawa. He knew the key to healing her lay in the hands of one, and only one, person. A doctor was no more than a substitute. A patient like her simply needed the unconditional love of the person she loved. That would be enough to save her. And once that happened, hospitalization would lose its meaning entirely.

"It wouldn't be possible for Sayuri to stay here indefinitely anyway, right?"

It was Takeshi's turn to gently prod Mochizuki, who had suddenly become taciturn.

"But we still don't know where her biological mother Yuko is… And there's Yoichi Maki, too. We haven't heard anything from him."

Takeshi must have glared at Mochizuki at the mention of Yoichi's name.

"Do you think he has it in him to take care of her?"

"That's not really for me to say."

"But what you *are* saying is that I don't have what it takes, but he does?"

"Look, I don't know what happened between them, but they lived together for a few years. We should assume they loved each other, don't you think?"

"But he ran away."

Takeshi's antagonism toward Yoichi was coming to the surface.

"He's out on a tuna boat, so there's no real way to confirm his intentions. But whatever the case, there's no getting around the fact that he's the father of Sayuri's child."

Takeshi's face was the picture of contempt.

"Even though he deserted her?"

"Don't jump to conclusions."

"That guy ran away. Because he was scared Sayuri might have Huntington's disease. He's a coward."

"Maybe he doesn't know."

"About Sayuri's father's diagnosis?"

"That's right. It's not something that's so easy to tell a lover. Many actually end up hiding it from their partners."

"Either way, I've taken care of it already." Takeshi muttered these last words under his breath, as if to no one in particular. At first, Mochizuki couldn't quite tell what they meant.

Taken care of it?

Mochizuki thought for a while, then asked, "Huh? What do you mean?"

"Nothing. It's not important."

"Can't you tell me?"

"I sent the guy a couple of letters, that's all."

"Letters? How?"

"It's easy. You send them to the office of Wakashio Fisheries, the owner of the boat he's on, and they pass them along to the boat out in the South Pacific Ocean."

Takeshi confessed everything to Mochizuki: he'd sent Yoichi a letter and a videotape showing the swelling in Sayuri's belly, and then followed that up with a second letter about her father's diagnosis. Included in the package was an explanation of the disease, which he'd photocopied from a medical dictionary. Mochizuki thought about why Takeshi might have kept these actions from him—what was in the young man's heart? Most likely guilt, he decided. Takeshi had sent letters highlighting the faults of the woman he loved to his rival in an attempt to scare him off. He'd provided his enemy with every reason to run away and was now waiting for him to do so. A childish maneuver. Smearing minuses on top of minuses once again.

"I thought it might help with her recovery..."

Takeshi offered this excuse, perhaps sensing what Mochizuki was thinking.

Mochizuki felt less angry than disappointed. He regretted telling Takeshi about Sayuri's father's diagnosis. He'd shared it with him because he felt that the trust between them had surpassed the usual bounds of a doctor-patient relationship. And he'd figured it might not be so bad even if he turned out to be wrong. After all, he'd intended to tell Yoichi about Sayuri's father's disease if he showed up. So perhaps it was all the same either way. But the fact remained that it was his role as a doctor to decide when to divulge such information, not Takeshi's.

Mochizuki furrowed his brow. "When are these letters supposed to reach the boat?" he asked.

"The first one should have already arrived. The second... I think it should get there in about two months."

That was right when Sayuri was scheduled to give birth. Which meant the baby would be born the very moment the father learned about the possible curse it had inherited from its grandfather.

It was well past noon at this point, but Mochizuki had lost his appetite. He patted Takeshi's knee lightly, then stood up.

"In any case, I think you should reconsider. I'm sure you'll meet someone more suitable for you..."

These were Mochizuki's parting words as he walked away toward the ward building. Takeshi gnawed at his fingernail while he watched him leave, his heart a swirl of complicated emotions.

Takeshi was ashamed of what he'd done. By letting Yoichi know about the terrible disease that might be afflicting Sayuri, he might well have consigned her forever to a lonely, isolated life. Further, it was an act that betrayed the trust Mochizuki had put in him. He vowed to not rely anymore on the doctor he'd disappointed so much. Spitting the bitten fingernail out of his mouth, he stood up and began walking toward the main entrance next to the flower beds. But his legs felt heavy. It was so hard to leave. He still wanted to find some way to explain himself, to justify the things he'd done.

The music cheering on the teams of competing students had stopped, telling him that it must be lunchtime there, too. The sudden quiet made Takeshi stop in his tracks and look up at the sky.

What would life at sea actually be like?

The expanse of the ocean spread out across the sky in his mind's eye, somehow filling him with longing.

The sea has the power to change how someone lives their life, I'm sure.

It was a thought that had never occurred to Takeshi before, and it made him intensely jealous of Yoichi, who was out there in the middle of the ocean right then.

This feeling was immediately chased by another: the determination to change. Change how? Into what? He didn't know, but in any case, he had to stop messing around. Perhaps he should start by finding a new job.

He remembered something Mochizuki once told him.

Actually, I think you'd make a great caseworker.

In fact, Mochizuki's words had come right when he himself started to realize, after investigating Sayuri's past, that he might be suited to that kind of work.

Well, why not give it a try?

Filled with a sense of resolve, Takeshi began walking again. Field Day resumed as well, and the breeze carried the cheers and music up into the sky.

PART IV Chance Encounter

1

It was mid-December, and the streets of Japan were becoming more Christmasy with every passing day. Even in the little world of the *Wakashio Maru No. 7,* floating in the South Seas where December marked the beginning of summer, items from home brought pieces of Christmas with them. The week before, the boat had docked in Auckland as planned, and along with bait, fuel, food, water, and other supplies, the boat received packages for each crewman sent by those near and dear to them back home. While most of these had been mailed out around early November so they arrived just before Christmas, the thick envelope Yoichi found placed in his hands had begun its journey much earlier, near the beginning of October. The name on the return address was Takeshi Sunako.

The envelope's contents turned out to be rather grim for a Christmas greeting. This time, instead of throwing them into the sea, though, Yoichi spent the week poring over the pages until he properly understood their import.

There was a two-page letter explaining that Sayuri's father, Shuichiro, had been diagnosed with a condition called Huntington's disease. The remaining pages—twenty-three in total—were materials explaining the nature and symptoms of the disease. Three of these pages were actual clinical reports, and one of them showed a sequence of stills from a sixteen-millimeter footage of a patient attempting to stand and walk. The patient was shown pushing herself up with both hands, slowly rising to her feet only to lose her balance and fall back down again… There was a total of twenty-eight stills that documented her involuntary bodily movements. They were most likely copied out of a medical journal meant for specialists in the field. The sheer completeness of the materials assembled by this unknown actor struck Yoichi as creepy. Why would someone go to all this trouble? He couldn't figure it out. The surface politeness of the letters made it impossible for him to grasp the true character of this person, Takeshi Sunako. The malice of the disease overlapped with his perception of the man who sent the materials explaining it, filling him with disgust.

Yet, as he read through the letter and began to understand the nature of the disease, Yoichi's thoughts turned away from Takeshi and his possible intentions. His mind was filled with flashbacks of his time with Sayuri instead: Sayuri going to the psychiatric clinic when she thought she was pregnant; her face in profile as she read her fortune with playing cards, muttering that they had a "fifty-fifty chance of being happy"; the desperate expression that would sometimes cross her face; her intense jealousy; her suicide attempt… At the time, he couldn't understand her behavior, but now, knowing about her father's diagnosis, everything began to make sense.

Yoichi spent the week after he received the letter plagued with doubt and worry. He finally understood how Sayuri had been feeling. Once the motivations behind another's inexplicable behavior became clear, most people ended up accepting it. And accepting Sayuri's behavior made Yoichi all the more unsure of what he should do. He felt lost, and there didn't seem to be a way to reach any sort of resolution. Even if he understood now what she'd been going through, it was too heavy a burden for him to shoulder. Besides, their child's birth was scheduled to happen a scant ten days from now. The gene for the disease had already succeeded in finding a new host to carry it into the future. He would free himself from the chains of destiny if he could. That was how he felt, truth be told. He was haunted all week by the temptation to keep running, to take his initial escape onto this tuna boat after the attempted murder-suicide as a sign, and jump on another boat once he returned to Japan. All at once, as if in sympathy with his unquiet heart, the sky above him started to change. A week after leaving Auckland, the boat was on a northeast route toward the next fishing area. It was crossing the 10,047-meter deep Kermadec Trench at a diagonal when, contradicting the prediction on the faxed weather map, the atmospheric pressure began to drop precipitously.

2

It was the dead of night on the fifteenth of December when the extreme low pressure system struck the *Wakashio Maru No. 7*. Jukichi had already stopped the boat, as they'd reached the planned fishing spot that evening. The wind intensified, going from six to seven on the Beaufort scale, which meant they were in danger of capsizing if the storm waves struck the boat from the side. Jukichi stood at the wheel himself and steered into the wind. Once turned, the *Wakashio Maru No. 7* remained at a near-standstill, every mechanism ready to be shut down at a moment's notice, as it traveled windward ever so slowly. As if holding its breath, it waited for the low pressure to pass.

Akimitsu Miyazaki lay in his bunk as the boat swayed violently, tormented by fragmented dreams. Even a seasoned hand like him found it hard to sleep during a storm like this, and it was all he could do to remain in bed in an attempt to save his stamina.

Something would strike the bottom of the boat with a resounding bang, and the bed would dip so that his feet were higher than his head. Nausea rose from the depths of his body, a roiling feeling that might have been seasickness or something else entirely. More than the storm, he felt haunted by the bright red dream from which he'd awoken. It was obvious that the red was fire, but despite never feeling the heat, these were dreams that always left him drenched in sweat. Miyazaki knew what they meant, these dreams of fire.

He'd always known, ever since his late elementary school days, that his father had been killed during some sort of fight aboard a boat. His mother had told him he'd accidentally fallen overboard, but growing up in a fishing town like he did, he inevitably heard rumors about his father's death. Crewmen who'd been on board the same boat had loose lips when they drank, it seemed.

Miyazaki was four when his father died. Which meant he had almost no memories of the man at all. But there was one image that remained in his mind even now, clear as day. His skin remembered, too. How his father's body covered in sweat had felt, how he'd been wrapped in his father's thick arms, carried through the heat of the flames… It was right before his father had left on the boat. The storage room in their one-story house had caught fire, and it'd spread quickly to engulf the entire home. In the back bedroom where he'd been sleeping, his father had thrown young Miyazaki onto his back, pulled his wife along by the hand, and plunged out of the building right before the roof collapsed. The image that remained with him was of his father's bronzed back, glistening in the light of the flames. His nose was nearly pressed up against it as it heaved with labored breath, the skin running with sweat that smelled of alcohol. The three of them sat down next to the well, and his father doused his body with water from the aquifer beneath them. When his father looked back at their collapsing house, his suntanned face was obscured by the dark, and Miyazaki couldn't make out the expression he was making. The color of the flames was so clear in his memory, yet his father's face, which they should have illuminated, remained shrouded in mystery. His father had spent so much time every year away on the boat that he was hardly at home, and the outline of his features had faded from Miyazaki's memory.

During the short periods he was at home, his father was terror itself. His mother told him later that he'd been a drinker, spending every night out till dawn gambling and brawling. In particular, his constant violence ensured that his mother's wounds never got a chance to heal. Other people's accounts of his father's behavior largely matched his mother's, painting a clear portrait of a man with major faults in his character, but it never really matched the image Miyazaki had of him. The father in his head was probably the result of wishful thinking; it overflowed with strength and masculinity.

So when he heard that his father had been killed during a fight, he didn't believe it at first. It was one thing to have died on the job from an accident, but during a fight? That did too much damage to the image he had in his head. Anyone could die in an accident, but his father would never lose a fight, much less die in one… Miyazaki was irrationally sure of it. As he pursued the mystery further, he found out that he hadn't been buried at sea, but rather taken to a desert island and cremated. And now that he thought about it, he did have a faint memory of seeing an ossuary. Remembering his mother dispiritedly bowing her head before it, he realized that the rumors he was hearing weren't entirely without substance.

Ever since then, Miyazaki had been plagued with dreams of fire. In his dreams, a burning man would slowly crouch forward and raise his fists like a boxer ready to spar. At the last second, a loud sound would ring out, and all the bones in the man's body would shatter into bits. The burning man was neither his father nor Miyazaki himself. Miyazaki would regard the flames dispassionately in his dream, as if watching a scene play out on a movie screen, but when he awoke, his body was always drenched in sweat.

As waves tossed the boat up and then brought it crashing back down, Miyazaki woke up, having dreamed for no more than twenty seconds. As always, he was soaked in sweat and breathing hard. His chest hurt. He sat up in bed and bowed his head to avoid hitting the low ceiling as he endured the shudders passing through his body. This had happened to him before. He'd been in his second year of junior high when he first felt his body shiver and his heart race like this.

The trigger then was no mystery. It was his hatred for the man his mother had remarried. This stepfather stumbling into the house he shared with his mother was a middleman in the tuna-selling business. He cut an abject figure and was completely different from how Miyazaki, as a four-year-old, remembered his father. While he was never violent with his mother, he'd drink from morning to night and would tell the boy to go buy more whenever he ran out, even in the middle of the night. Miyazaki always regarded him with undisguised contempt. Aware of his stepson's lack of respect, he didn't hide his hatred toward the boy, either. However, sensing the superior physical strength Miyazaki possessed, he would slowly pull back his raised fist and pretend to scratch behind his ears. It irritated Miyazaki even more to watch him do that, and he marked him as a man not even worth confronting directly. But that didn't stop him from wishing, from the bottom of his heart, for the man to disappear. *I could do it—I could kill him right now.* The thought came unbidden to him almost every day, and it got harder and harder to fight it. But in the end, there was no need, as his drunk stepfather suffered a fatal heart attack in the bath. Miyazaki, walking into the bathroom when it was his turn to bathe, was half undressed before he saw the body in the water. The man's sparse hair waved back and forth like seaweed in the shallows, and Miyazaki approached the bath and looked down at it for a while without calling for anyone. An indescribable pleasure welled up from deep within him, and he could feel it cleanse his body of every bit of irritation and hatred. He felt purified, and he never forgot that sensation.

Three years ago, Miyazaki had found himself plagued by an oppressive tightness in his chest and tormented by fiery nightmares every night. He was on a tuna boat that had departed from Yaizu and was in the middle of the Indian Ocean at the time. Bathed in cold sweat, he desperately tried to recall his stepfather's submerged corpse, but to no avail—the healing power of his imagination had its limits, it seemed. Without realizing it, he'd wandered barefoot all the way up to the boat's bridge, so he poked his head into the wheelhouse to see who was on watch. It was a newbie, just graduated from a fishery-related vocational high school. Slender and boyish, he heard Miyazaki's soft footsteps and turned around, and Miyazaki didn't fail to notice the boy's face briefly coloring with fear as he did. He hadn't come with any particular ill intent, but there was something strangely provocative about the delicate lines of the boy's shoulders, the way his lip curled slightly when he spoke. The newbie's look of terror was brief, and he covered it quickly with a rush of meaningless small talk, but Miyazaki gave only the most perfunctory responses while he persuaded the boy to go out onto the deck.

The night ocean was calm. The surface of a quiet sea was often compared to a mirror, and the cliché was proven true once more as the lustrous black surface spread out before them in all directions.

After exchanging a few more words as they leaned against the deck's railing, Miyazaki made his move—less as a consequence of his will than a sort of physical impulse. He took the boy from behind, reaching with his right hand between his legs as if to grab his testicles, and then lifted him up. The newbie did a half turn in the air, and then he plunged headfirst into the water and disappeared.

After some time, his head popped back up. He tried to scream, but water filled his mouth, and he sank again. He came back up and treaded water for a while, waving his hands above his head and yelling, but he was too far away for his cries to reach the crewmen sleeping in the cabins. And soon enough, the darkness that lay beyond the boat's wake swallowed his delicate frame for good. Miyazaki remained on the deck, staring at the ocean that had engulfed the young man, enjoying the thought of him being stranded at sea all alone, well beyond the normal shipping routes. He reveled in the cold air passing over his body as it extinguished the burning dreams within him.

The thought of repeating this act now arose in his mind. But he knew he couldn't do it the same way. The first time, it was a case of a man on watch disappearing in the middle of the night, and without proof, the Japan Coast Guard couldn't touch him. But if someone disappeared from boats with Miyazaki on board twice in a row, people would get suspicious. The boat three years ago had been from Yaizu, while this one was based in Misaki. Still, the world for seafarers was small, and rumors spread in the blink of an eye. Miyazaki thought it over, searching for a way to drown a person without arousing suspicion. The low pressure system currently rocking the boat led him to his answer. After it passed, the sea would be somewhat calm again, and they would drop the longlines into the water early the next morning. That would be when he'd have his chance. Miyazaki wiped the sweat from his forehead. But who should it be...? He knew that Jukichi Takagi was the man who killed his father. But he regarded the skipper with a mixture of hatred and reverence—his death was something he'd have to build up to, something for the future. Besides, a boat that lost its skipper would have to return to port immediately, and the freezers on board were just shy of half their capacity of tuna at the moment. As a fisherman, the thought of returning to port with only half the expected catch was too humiliating to contemplate. So it would have to be someone who could be easily replaced, like a newbie. Now that Mizukoshi had been sent back to Japan because of his bullying, there was only one such new crewman left: Yoichi Maki.

Miyazaki tried to tamp down the excitement that rose within him as he imagined pushing Yoichi into the sea over and over again. He would try to pick a time when Yoichi wasn't wearing a life jacket, but in truth, he didn't think that would make much of a difference—anything swallowed by the rough sea would never come back up. Any aid a life jacket would provide would add up to nothing in the end.

3

The next morning, the sea began to calm. The low pressure seemed to have passed.

But Jukichi regarded the dark water with suspicion, weighing his options as he contemplated casting the longlines to begin fishing. The newest weather forecast that had been faxed to the boat claimed that the worst was over. But something didn't feel right. The intuition he'd built up over his many years as a seaman noted subtle changes occurring in the sky above him, and it kept sounding a faint alarm in his head. He remembered numerous years back when he'd been in a similar situation and had cast the lines after a low pressure system had passed, only to have a second one blow in almost immediately, forcing them to cut the lines and flee. Once you put longlines into the water, it was no simple matter to haul them back in. If things went badly, you could end up losing them. Even worse, men could fall overboard if a storm hit while they were processing a catch. With these thoughts swirling in his head, Jukichi contemplated the sea and the sky from his perch in the wheelhouse and found himself unable to reach a decision.

"C'mon, old man! Let's drop the lines already!"

Standing next to him, Miyazaki seemed to have lost his patience.

"Wait."

Jukichi uncrossed his arms, glancing briefly at the small shrine in the corner.

"If we stop fishing every time there's a little storm like this, we'll never make any money!"

Miyazaki's angry voice resounded in the cramped space of the wheelhouse.

The truth was, Jukichi was feeling restless as well. They'd left the port at Auckland ten days ago, and despite being fully restocked with fresh bait and fishing supplies, the weather had prevented them from taking in even one catch so far. It was just as Miyazaki said: if an ordinary storm like this was enough to keep him from throwing the lines in, he was no seaman at all. Everyone on board wanted to fill the freezers with tuna and head back home as soon as possible. Finally making up his mind, Jukichi left the wheelhouse without saying a word and ordered the boatswain to prepare the longlines.

Longlines are made up of three parts: mainlines, branch lines, and float lines. Float lines are spaced about three hundred meters apart, an interval referred to as a "basket." Five branch lines dangle from the mainline within each basket, and a hook is attached to the end of each branch. The float lines are buoyed up by glass floats, which have flags that stick out of the water. In other words, longline tuna fishing involves casting mainlines between one hundred and one hundred and fifty kilometers long, with thousands of hooked branch lines hanging from them, out into the ocean to wait for tuna to latch onto them, then pulling the lines back in with haulers, and processing the tuna on the deck. Throwing out the longlines took around five hours, pulling them back in took about seven hours, and the wait in between for tuna to take the bait was usually about three hours, which meant that from beginning to end, a day's catch took upwards of fifteen hours to complete. This was why dropping the lines into the water was a process that started early in the morning before sunrise.

As the white spray thrown up by the waves began reflecting the dull, gray light of the sky, five crewmen—with Yoichi among them—were busy attaching branch lines to the mainline as it unspooled from the automatic caster, quickly baiting each hook before it went out into the water. The mainline stretched farther and farther out into the sea. They had no time to think about anything, and there was nothing for them to think about, either. Yet, as Yoichi went through the motions that had by that time become routine, he couldn't help but contemplate the dilemma that had been weighing on his mind since ten days ago. Should he continue fleeing Sayuri, or should he accept her and take her back? As he mulled over his conundrum, his mind drifted away from his tired body and split into two warring selves, one on each side of the issue.

Nature seemed to be as conflicted as his heart. The calm eastward wind that had arisen died completely, and the northward wind began blowing again, its force gradually rising. The clouds above moved faster, and they formed a thick leaden curtain across the sky. The *Wakashio Maru No. 7* continued on its course nonetheless, heading north-northeast at a speed of ten knots.

The casting of the longlines finally ended just past ten. The five crewmen descended into the galley to have an early lunch before heading to their cabins for some well-earned sleep. The time spent waiting for the tuna to bite was their precious opportunity to rest, but Yoichi felt that the boat was rocking more and more.

It wasn't his imagination—the pressure was dropping precipitously. While the wind in the morning had been about four on the Beaufort scale, it had increased to six, and then seven by noon. The surface of the ocean was now covered in whitecaps as far as the eye could see.

Yoichi had barely started to drift off when he felt himself shaken awake by the boatswain.

"Get up! We're hauling in the lines!"

Yoichi couldn't hide his irritation, asking, "What? Already?"

They were supposed to wait much longer than that. And he hadn't had a chance to rest properly. But the boat was rocking violently, and even before the boatswain answered him, he quickly understood what this premature end to the catch really meant.

"There's a big storm coming. If we don't get them in now, we might lose them. Now hurry!"

And with that, the boatswain turned and rushed out of Yoichi's cabin.

Save for the watchman making sure they stayed on route, all hands were on deck to haul in the lines. The middle deck had become a battleground. Yoichi strapped a life jacket on over his raincoat and joined the melee of crewmen shouting and running around. The raindrops blowing into his face at a near-horizontal angle weren't huge, but they'd mixed with the seawater and tasted salty on his lips. Indeed, there was no real difference between the rain and the ocean spray, as plumes of seawater thrown up by the crashing waves were caught by the wind and blown across the boat.

This was not the time to process any of the tuna they'd managed to catch. As the crewmen's bloodshot eyes attested, they needed to haul the lines in fast or they'd be in trouble. Even a newbie like Yoichi could understand the gravity of the situation.

It was hard to hear in the roar of the storm, but Jukichi's booming voice reached his ears.

"Stop hauling in the line!"

A few men clung to the boat's lifeline, desperate to keep their balance on the slick deck as it listed steeply beneath their feet. They barked the skipper's orders down the line to pass the message along.

"Stop hauling it in!"

"Let the line go!"

By three in the afternoon, the air had turned white with spray, limiting visibility to three or four meters. Yoichi could no longer tell who was giving the orders, much less which orders to obey and which to disregard. His breathing was ragged, and his heart beat furiously in his chest. Yet, for Yoichi, the experience was as intoxicating as it was terrifying. All of his own thoughts had been blown away in the wind, and it felt perversely comforting to let himself act solely according to the needs of his body or the orders of men stronger than him. At the very least, all thoughts of Sayuri had finally left his mind.

He could hear a war of words being waged somewhere beneath the bridge.

"Floats—"

"Radio buoy—"

Only fragments and isolated words reached his ears, making the meaning impossible to parse. But judging from the two voices, one shrill and harsh, the other low and booming, it sounded like an argument between Jukichi and Miyazaki. Yoichi guessed that Miyazaki was objecting to Jukichi's order to stop hauling in the lines.

"Yoichi!"

Hearing his name called, Yoichi walked a few steps in the direction of the shout.

"Yoichi!"

There it was again... It was Miyazaki's voice.

"What?!"

"Bring...radio buoy...storage hold..."

The storm stole bits and pieces of Miyazaki's words, and only fragments reached Yoichi's ears. But he didn't need to ask Miyazaki to repeat himself. It was obvious he wanted Yoichi to go to the storage hold in the quarter deck and fetch the radio buoy.

Pressing his back against the cabin wall, Yoichi edged sideways toward the stern of the boat. He knew that in a storm like this, no one would be able to save him if he fell overboard. Inch by inch, he carefully crept his way to the hold. But as he reached out to open the hatch, a chill went up his spine, his body tingling. Even amid the chaotic din around him, he sensed there was a fleeting moment of silence. Glancing sideways, he saw a dark silhouette—someone was standing next to him. The shadow was alone; there was no one else around. His hand still on the hatch's handle, Yoichi looked up only to be confronted by Miyazaki's long, narrow face just a meter away, framed by the black hood of his raincoat. He was like a ghost, always popping up where you least expected him. To end up here, Miyazaki would've had to walk along the opposite side of the deck from the bridge.

But why would he do that?

Yoichi froze mid-motion. Miyazaki's lips curled into a devilish grin, his bloodshot eyes shining unnaturally.

What's he smiling at?!

Yoichi cursed inwardly. The chill he'd felt had surely been him somehow sensing the malice glittering in Miyazaki's eyes. *Malice*—but in truth, he had no idea what Miyazaki might be planning. Yoichi decided to swallow his fear. Perhaps Miyazaki had simply come to help him carry the radio buoy. He turned away to face the hatch.

Just when Miyazaki reached his right hand toward Yoichi's back, the boat tilted wildly starboard. The wind had surpassed ten on the Beaufort scale by then, and the waves were cresting at eight meters high. When waves converge and build on each other, they can reach up to four times their original height. The wave that crashed into the *Wakashio Maru No. 7* at that moment had reached well over twenty meters. The boat floated in the air for a split second and then dropped into the trough of a wave. That was when the gigantic gray wall of the wave came crashing down over the deck.

Instantaneously, Yoichi's vision was swallowed by darkness. He was thrust against the hatch at first, but then he was immediately pulled the other way, and the force ripped his body away from it. His hand, which he'd extended reflexively, closed only over water, and he had no way of stopping himself from being carried away by the wave.

The huge wave came over the starboard side of the stern, and it washed over the hull from the quarter deck, drenching the bridge. When the water receded, Jukichi let go of the lifeline and looked around to see if anyone had gone overboard. The stern seemed to have taken the brunt of the hit—had there been any men back there? If so, they were the most likely to have been carried away. It then came to him: Miyazaki had ordered Yoichi to go fetch the radio buoy, which was stored in the hold at the stern.

Jukichi ran up the stairs to the bridge, yelling, "Keep steering into the wind!"

Then he dashed toward the stern, calling for Yoichi. Seeing no one on deck, he immediately looked out into the white-capped ocean. His eyes picked out two arms sticking up from between the waves.

"No!"

Jukichi immediately lowered the inflatable life raft into the water. The raft fell onto the roiling surface of the sea, and it bloomed like an orange flower, tossed this way and that by the waves. Then, he racked his brain to remember whether Yoichi had been wearing a life jacket. He always ordered his men to wear them, especially during storms, but many—like Miyazaki—thought they were a bother and never did. Jukichi was about to head back toward the wheelhouse when he caught sight of something else. He couldn't believe his eyes—there, in a different area, another arm was reaching out of the water.

There're two *men overboard?!*

During all the time he'd spent at sea as the skipper, this had never happened before. Two men were overboard at the same time, and not only that, they were out there during a storm.

We can't save them.

A man as familiar with the sea as he was knew good luck wasn't enough to save anyone who'd fallen into the water at a time like this. Fighting back the despair of losing two men under his watch, Jukichi ran up into the wheelhouse and ordered the boat to make an abrupt starboard turn. He then instructed his men to cut the mainline and informed a radio officer of the situation. The officer who received his message immediately sent telegrams to the other boats in the area, informing them of the accident and requesting any aid they could provide to search for the overboard crewmen. The radio officers on four tuna boats in the region—*Hoyo Maru Nos. 5* and *3*, the *Shoei Maru No. 2*, and the *Wakashio Maru No. 8*—answered and confirmed the location: 24°07′ S, 175°58′ W. That was where Yoichi and Miyazaki had fallen. The four boats turned as sharply as they could away from their planned routes and headed south-southwest toward the rescue point.

It was only four in the afternoon, but the clouds above were less like leaden strips than heavy brushstrokes in a largely black ink painting. The ringing in Jukichi's ears hit hard now that he was cut off from the roar of the waves, making him dizzy. The world outside was drained of color save for the flashy orange of the life raft, but more often than not, even that was hidden in the shadows of the roiling waves. There was no sign of the two men in the water. The one grain of hope he had for them to be saved was if they managed to reach the life raft themselves and clamber up onto it. There was a transmitter on the raft that emitted an emergency signal. Even if they turned hard to the right, the boat's movements were rather imprecise, and it was a very hard thing to locate two men in the water and bring them up to safety. If they weren't on a raft that emitted a rescue signal, it was well-nigh impossible. Further, the storm showed no sign of letting up, and it was going to be night soon. Too many negative factors were piling up. Jukichi estimated the chances of rescue were close to zero.

Nonetheless, the skipper couldn't help but pray that Yoichi would find the raft.

But the other man—who could it be?

He realized that he hadn't given much thought to who the second man might have been. That man had been clinging to Yoichi. Immediately, Miyazaki's face appeared in Jukichi's mind. Only about two minutes had passed since the men had fallen, but in that time, Jukichi had raced all over the boat and seen many of the crewmen present. Yet he didn't remember seeing Miyazaki, despite his presence being one of the strongest on the boat.

"Is it you out there, Miyazaki?"

Jukichi addressed his question to the sea.

I killed a man with my own hands, and now I'm watching the sea try to swallow up his only son.

Out here in the South Seas, the father went up in flames, while the son was carried away by the waves—Jukichi's heart hurt as he considered the irony of their destinies.

But what was he doing back there in the first place?

If it really was Miyazaki who'd been swept away along with

Yoichi, Jukichi couldn't help but wonder why he'd followed Yoichi into the stern.

4

During the first few moments, Yoichi didn't realize what had happened. The sound and force bearing down on him were like nothing he'd ever experienced. He spent a full minute or more struggling, flipping over and over until he didn't know which way was up, unable to breathe, and gulping mouthfuls of seawater. Finally, he floated back to the surface, but just when he popped his head above the sea, a wave broke over him and filled his mouth and nose with water again.

Treading water, Yoichi did a 360-degrees turn and spotted the starboard side of the *Wakashio Maru No. 7* in front of him. Seawater was pouring like a waterfall from the stern where he'd just been standing. It finally came to him what had happened. A huge wave had swept him overboard into the sea.

He tried to swim toward the boat, but he sank into the trough of a wave, enclosed on both sides by walls of water. Gasping for air, he tipped his head back and looked straight up into the thin strip of sky visible above him. The dread that he felt from seeing its sheer narrowness was overwhelming. The water buoyed him up again, though, and as he floated in momentary peace on the wave's crest, he felt like the boat was getting closer. But then, he was plunged again into another trough, and the boat disappeared from view. When he bobbed up once more, it was nowhere in sight. Terror struck his heart. Something was gradually rising within him, threatening to strangle his consciousness completely. As the reality of what had happened sunk in, it felt like the very blood vessels in his head were swelling and about to burst.

Calm down!

Yoichi fought to quell his panic. If he lost himself to it, that would be the end. The battle he needed to win was with himself. He had to suppress the chaotic feelings rising in his body and focus his mind on a single, fixed goal. Yoichi twisted in the water, and the boat came into view once more.

"Just remain calm!"

He vocalized his thoughts aloud this time. The distance between himself and the boat was not unswimmable. It was just a matter of the huge waves beating him back. Every time a wave was about to break over his head, he took a big gulp of air so that he could wait for it to pass. But he never knew which way he was facing when he re-emerged on the other side. Whenever the boat slipped out of sight, terror gripped him, and he could feel himself panic. He needed to float better—and that was when he realized he was wearing a life jacket. Jukichi had taught him what to do with it: he simply had to pull down on the two straps dangling from it. He groped around in the water for them, and when he found their ends, he pulled with all his might. The jacket ballooned as it filled with carbon dioxide, and he felt his body buoyed up almost instantly to the surface. Now he could keep his head and shoulders above the sea even without treading water, and relief washed over him. He no longer needed to stretch his mouth open so wide his jaw hurt just to breathe.

Now stay calm! All you need to do is stay calm!

If he could use this moment to control his panic, then he'd be able to overcome his first challenge.

Moving his limbs constantly to keep the boat in sight, Yoichi spotted a bright orange object fall down its side. Someone had dropped a life raft. He saw it inflate into a circle as it fell, but after that, he could only catch glimpses of it when it happened to bob up onto the crest of a wave. Now he had another clear target, which was to swim to the life raft floating between him and the boat.

Suddenly, something tugged him back—a force clearly distinct from the waves. His body, which had become so stable on the water, sank until his nose barely cleared its surface. Seawater gushed down his throat and into his stomach. Something was pulling him. Two hands clawed at his torso on both sides, and he heard a ragged breath behind his head. As terror flooded him, Yoichi desperately tried to push back against the hands, and in the midst of the struggle, he found himself looking into a pair of bloodshot eyes mere centimeters from his own—eyes that, of course, belonged to Miyazaki.

The bastard's trying to steal my life jacket!

That was the first thought that crossed his mind. Miyazaki was frantically trying to hang on to the closest object he could find to remain afloat, and he had no intention of stealing anything. But Yoichi was struck by panic again, and for him, Miyazaki had emerged from the depths like Death itself. The life jacket wasn't sufficient to keep both their bodies afloat. Yoichi realized this and tried to push Miyazaki away with all his might. There's a passage in Article 37-1 of the Penal Code that specifies what happens in the case of an emergency evacuation. Suppose two people who've fallen overboard are confronted with a single plank of wood floating in front of them. The plank can only hold one person—it would sink if both held onto it. So they fight over the plank, and one pushes the other away and clings to it until help arrives. The question is: should the survivor be charged with murder? According to Article 37, the answer is no. So what Yoichi was trying to do right now was not considered a crime. Miyazaki was the one who failed to wear a life jacket during a storm in the first place, so Yoichi was in no way responsible for this.

Tossed to and fro by the gigantic waves, the two men desperately fought over the life jacket. Yoichi's intention to swim over to the life raft was completely derailed by this unforeseen turn of events, and he was losing precious time and strength in this battle.

Suddenly, Miyazaki froze. Yoichi stopped as well, letting his limbs float free in the water. His breath was rough in his throat, and every muscle in his body hurt. With his hands still on Yoichi's shoulders, Miyazaki looked around frantically and turned a full circle. Seawater bubbled out of his mouth, and he seemed to be saying something, but Yoichi couldn't understand him. He imitated Miyazaki's movements and turned twice, then finally realized what Miyazaki was trying to tell him: the *Wakashio Maru No. 7* had disappeared completely. It wasn't hidden by the waves—rather, the current had carried them so far away that the boat was no longer visible. Yoichi cried out in frustration and despair. His sense of time was numb. He had no idea how long he might've been struggling with Miyazaki amid the waves. All he knew was that in their present depleted condition, being so far away that they could no longer see the boat surely meant that the chances of them being rescued were close to nil. The terrible feeling in his stomach rose again as he grew more and more conscious of the imminence of his own death.

After drifting for a while with Miyazaki clinging to his back, Yoichi felt his life jacket regain its former buoyancy, and it soon lifted his head well above the water once more. He realized that Miyazaki had let go of him. Treading water, Miyazaki turned around so that he was facing Yoichi, then fixed him in his burning gaze. Yoichi saw madness in his eyes. It didn't take long for a seasoned seaman like Miyazaki to realize when it was time to give up. He'd decided in that instant that his life was over, it seemed. After staring so hard at Yoichi from several centimeters away that he nearly bore a hole in his head, he flashed Yoichi a mocking smile, raised both hands above his head, and then sank to the bottom of the sea.

The sky had begun to dim. His nerve endings screaming as if brushed by the edge of a knife, Yoichi felt nausea rise within him, but he fought to keep it at bay. If he vomited what remained in his stomach, he'd lose what meager reserves of strength his body still had.

I've got to conserve as much energy as I can. There's still a chance I'll be saved, he told himself.

But Miyazaki's ironic smile just before he slipped beneath the waves haunted him.

What did it mean, that smile?

Was he mocking Yoichi's vain struggle to stay alive? With the life jacket, he could hold out for a bit longer, but that smile seemed to say he'd just be prolonging his own misery.

The gray sky grew darker and darker until he was engulfed by inky blackness. It seemed that this was all there was in the world, just layers of darkness painted one over the other... Shoulder-deep in an indifferent ocean that mocked his very humanity, Yoichi understood that Miyazaki's smile had been no empty pose. The torture to his senses would continue unabated and there would be no respite as long as he was out here.

If this continues much longer, I'll go crazy. I'm sure of it.

Yoichi knew it would be his mind, not his body, that would break first.

5

Sometime in the night, the low pressure passed and the storm died down. The roiling surface of the sea calmed and smoothed out.

What day is it?

Yoichi tried to calculate the date in his head. December 17. Only twelve hours had passed since he'd been swept overboard the *Wakashio Maru No. 7*, but this night felt like the longest he'd ever spent in his life. He'd been certain again and again that he'd lose his mind in the span of the next few minutes. He marked every minute, every second this way until, at long last, he saw the first light of dawn... He couldn't believe he'd managed to stay sane through the night.

The early morning sea stained the sky purple. Its color foretold good weather for the day. The absolute calm of the sea after the storm was almost chilling, and the abruptness of the change felt like a nefarious plot. Yoichi lay back on the waves, and his head occasionally dipped in the seawater as he gazed in the direction of the rising sun. It was barely above the distant horizon and only the longest waves of light could reach his eyes, so the sky looked purple as it stretched above him.

As long as there's light...

The steadily rising sun gave him hope that he would survive. His chances of being discovered were higher now that visibility had improved. Other boats must have joined the search as well. Perhaps they couldn't look for him during the storm last night, but now that the weather was calm again, they should be able to swing into action. He was sure they'd recorded the spot where he'd fallen, so reading the current should give them a reasonable idea of where he might have drifted.

Yoichi worked hard to remain optimistic. Pessimism only led to despair, and despair only to madness, then suicide... There were plenty of examples around the world of people who'd fallen overboard and ended up adrift like him. In ninety percent of those cases, they wound up killing themselves in the span of three days. It wasn't thirst or hunger that drove them to death. The flesh placed in extremity ends up breaking the mind, which in turn ends up destroying the flesh.

Having decided to pursue a life at sea, Yoichi had devoured various books on the subject, and there were plenty of accounts of marine accidents. He tried to mentally organize all the survival skills he could remember from what he'd read. What were the most pressing necessities to stay alive? Fresh water, for one—thirst would be the need that would plague him most acutely. He didn't feel terribly thirsty at the moment, but as the sun continued its path across the sky, he knew that would change in a hurry. He had read various opinions about whether or not to drink seawater. Most argued that drinking even small amounts of seawater was dangerous. But others said that as long as one didn't drink too much, it was better than nothing. He needed to make a plan. Would he drink some when he got too thirsty, or would he fight the temptation? There was an inexhaustible supply, and he had the feeling that if he held out until he finally succumbed, he wouldn't be able to control the amount he'd end up swallowing. And if that happened, there was no question that it would hasten his death. Therein lay the dilemma. Would drinking less than a liter a day allow him to live longer than abstaining completely? He thought it might, but he also doubted his ability to control his intake. And so he made a vow.

I won't drink seawater.

Though there were individual differences, people could apparently go without water for eight to ten days. Yoichi decided to hold out for at least the first three. The face of Miyazaki as he gave up so quickly lingered in the back of his mind, strengthening his resolve not to end up like him. He forbade himself from mocking the thought of survival. Fortunately, he was just below the Tropic of Capricorn in December, which meant that the temperature of the water was over twenty-six degrees. He could easily live three days or more submerged in that. If it had been below twenty, he would already be dead. He was not picturing the faces of his family, nor that of Sayuri, in these moments. His mind, bolstered by his sheer will to live, was focused entirely on supporting his flesh.

As the sun rose, shorter and shorter wavelengths of light reached the afternoon sea, returning it to its proper color. Fearing heatstroke, Yoichi pulled the hood of his raincoat over his head to cover himself from the sun. A raincoat and a pair of tall boots were *de rigueur* for the crew of a tuna boat. The thickness of the rubber was itself reassuring. Fish swam past his legs and waist, sometimes brushing against them, and had they been exposed, he surely would have felt vulnerable—or rather, his skin might have been broken and his blood could have attracted the attention of sharks.

As his thoughts turned to sharks, Yoichi realized that his life jacket seemed to be losing buoyancy. Looking around, he saw that it wasn't his imagination—his head was closer to the sea's surface than before. He ran both hands along the jacket, thinking that, God forbid, it might have sprung a leak. But he couldn't find any place where air seemed to be seeping out.

Is it just my imagination?

Yoichi then remembered the long, thin tubes that hung from the jacket at about chest level. They were for adding more air to the life jacket's chambers to keep it inflated. Yoichi put the tubes in his mouth and blew into them until it regained its buoyancy. The jacket tipped him back, and he looked up into the sky.

An airplane was passing high above him. It was the first sign of human life he'd seen since falling into the sea. He waved his hands and kicked his legs, yelling up into the sky, but the plane simply kept on its course as if he wasn't there. He knew it was next to impossible he'd be noticed. It would have been hard even if he'd been on a bright-colored life raft and setting off flares. There was no reason to believe that a pilot would notice a single person submerged up to his shoulders in the middle of the sea.

He scolded himself for wasting his energy and moving unnecessarily.

I'm just tiring myself out doing things I know won't work.

Above all, flailing his limbs and roiling the water around him might make him seem like food to any sharks in the area. His mind was preoccupied with visions of their razor-sharp teeth. Even when he tried to think about something else, his thoughts would circle back almost immediately. There were definitely sharks present in the deep South Seas, but his terror stemmed from movies he'd seen as well. His legs froze up at the very thought.

Think of something else!

Yoichi decided to try banishing the sharks circling in his mind by recalling the cases he'd read of people who were rescued after being stranded at sea. As he thought about what separated the survivors from the dead, the discovered from the lost, he couldn't keep one terrible word from returning again and again to him: *despair*. Almost all of the cases he could think of involved a life raft. A raft at least had emergency supplies on it, including water and food. It had a small tent for the people to shelter from the sun and a transmitter that emitted a rescue signal. And, of course, the raft also protected them from sharks. He couldn't think of an example of someone rescued while floating in the water in just a life jacket. Was there any chance at all that they would find him?

He was gripped, then, by a gut-wrenching terror and profound loneliness. He'd been floating for almost twenty-four hours, causing his skin to crack, his nails to turn white. His entire body no longer felt his own—it was as if his senses were leaving his flesh. His neck hurt, and as he looked down to stretch it, he caught sight of his black boots dangling below him in the clear water. During the storm, the sea had been an opaque and leaden gray, but now, it was almost transparent. If he slipped off his boots, he'd probably be able to watch them sink for quite a long time before they disappeared from view. The point they disappeared would be the depth where light could no longer penetrate. Running north to south about 2,000 kilometers, the deepest point of the Kermadec Trench reaches a depth of roughly 10,047 meters. Yoichi was presently floating directly above it. A vast, dark world slept beneath him, closed off by a dizzying amount of pressure from the sheer volume of water atop it. Just picturing the enormity of what lay beneath him made Yoichi feel like he was being dragged down into its yawning chasm.

He'd already counted three boats. They'd appeared at the horizon where the sea met the sky. Had he drifted into a regular fishing route? In any case, there seemed to be more boats than usual. But none of them had noticed Yoichi. They'd remained far in the distance, and he couldn't even see their sides—they'd only been visible from the bridge up.

Why did they leave? I'm right here!

Overcome by desperation and fury, Yoichi cursed out loud. Had they given up looking for him? He couldn't keep himself from dwelling on what might have happened. Perhaps they had declared him lost at sea. They might have already contacted his mother back home. Even as he drifted here, alive, they might be planning his funeral, his brother rushing from Hiroshima to Kosai. He pictured their weeping faces. His imagination slipped the bonds of reason and ran wild, one scenario leading to the next with no end in sight.

"I'm still alive!"

He screamed and screamed, but to no avail. The 360-degrees view around him was as lonely as before, nary a ship in sight.

Yoichi's attention turned inward, and he wondered if there was any way to survive by himself. If there had been an island anywhere in sight, he was confident he could swim to it. He'd always been good at swimming, and he had more stamina than the average person.

He told himself to remain calm and picture the currents that flowed through this part of the ocean. The South Equatorial Current flowed south until just above New Zealand, where it bent west. That meant that if he rode it, he'd more likely than not end up running into one of the Kermadec Islands. If he somehow ended up threading between them, the next dry land he'd encounter would be the eastern coast of Australia. That was around three thousand kilometers away, and it would take more than a year to reach it. There was, of course, no chance that his body would hold up that long. His white bones would wash up on the beach dressed in a black raincoat and a life jacket and scare the locals.

Yoichi laughed aloud at the thought. It was a tight, pinched laugh, the kind that would inspire doubts about his sanity if anyone were around to hear it.

A skeleton in a black, hooded raincoat? I'd look like a cartoon Grim Reaper!

But his laughter was interrupted by the sight of the prow of a ship appearing on the horizon. That made number four. And if he was looking at the prow, that meant it was slowly coming his way. Yoichi floated open-mouthed, watching the ship's outline get bigger and bigger, rubbing his eyes to make sure it wasn't a mirage. Then, he began readying himself for its approach.

I have to control myself. No matter how loudly I scream, there's no way they'll hear me from here.

The boat was approaching him straight on. It was a cargo ship, its bridge located toward the stern, and from the volume of water it seemed to be displacing, he estimated it to be around ten thousand tons in size.

It's too big!

The larger the ship, the farther the bridge is from the water, making anything floating out there that much harder to see. Yoichi had a bad feeling about his chances, but he kept moving anyway. He positioned himself to the front starboard side of the ship, out to where he would be visible from the bridge, then waved his hands and shouted. He needed to make sure he didn't get sucked into the ship's propeller.

The huge mass of metal began to pass mere meters from where Yoichi floated. He looked up at the bridge, searching for people there, as if supplicating the heavens. He caught sight of a human head moving behind the glass of the wheelhouse windows. It didn't look like a Japanese person. The name on the bow's starboard side was in English, too, and Yoichi guessed that it was a cargo ship registered to a non-Japanese nation.

"Hey, over here! *Help! Help!*"

He propelled his upper body as far as he could out of the water, calling out in a mixture of Japanese and English.

Notice me! I'm right here!

But the figure passing in and out of sight in the wheelhouse never seemed to look over in his direction.

What are you doing? I'm over here!

The cargo ship continued its agonizingly slow passage past Yoichi as he screamed and screamed. The ship's bridge had reached a point where he was no longer visible at a forward angle from the wheelhouse, lessening his already meager chances of being discovered. Yoichi kept calling out even as the person in the wheelhouse disappeared from his view entirely, leaving him to bob in the ship's wake. It was obvious if he thought about it calmly. What were the chances that someone standing watch on the bridge of a ten-thousand-ton cargo ship would actually see someone floating in the ocean? Yoichi had forgotten his own experience on the *Wakashio Maru No. 7.* How much time had he spent during his watches scanning the water's surface? Almost none. He'd spent most of that time drinking coffee and leafing through whatever magazines and books he could get his hands on. So it was only natural that this cargo ship would pass by without noticing his existence.

Nonetheless, the sight of the ship disappearing into the distance left Yoichi shaking with rage. He was angry at the ship's negligent watchman, and he resented the cruelty of a god that would bring hope so tantalizingly close, only to snatch it away. His powerless, limp body trembled as he dissolved into tears.

Abandoned!

He felt completely forsaken.

Why is this happening to me?

Faced with a reality so indifferent to reason, he was left to make sense of it however he could.

What have I done to deserve this?

Rage clouded his mind for some time, but it eventually subsided and he was able to start formulating answers to the questions that bedeviled him.

Almost all castaways ended up tying their misfortunes to incidents from their pasts. Thinking they deserved what was happening to them because of something they did in the past allowed them to make sense of their situations.

Yoichi only began to think of Sayuri once an entire night and day had passed since falling overboard. The cargo ship had disappeared from view, and he had managed to calm down. It was a calm brought on by thinking about his relationship with Sayuri and the chains of cause and effect connecting it to his current predicament. He put himself in the place of that cargo ship that had passed right by him. And he put Sayuri in his own position, as the abandoned castaway.

Isn't it the same?

He pictured himself as objectively as possible, passing Sayuri by without offering her any kind of help.

If I had only known about her father's condition!

If he'd known, would he have tried to help her?

No. I would have done the opposite—I'd have run. Even earlier than I did in reality.

The parallels between himself now and Sayuri then suddenly seemed so clear, leaving him in a state of shock.

Huntington's disease?

He understood the true horror of the condition thanks to the materials Takeshi Sunako had sent him. If a parent had it, there was a fifty-fifty chance the child would, too.

That's just like what's happening to me.

There he was, half of his body sticking out of the water and the other half submerged, never knowing when or if he would ever be rescued.

It's exactly the same.

It was like living with one foot in the grave.

No doubt about it.

It was clear to Yoichi now. Why this cruel fate had befallen him. The very same thing he'd done to Sayuri was now being done to him.

Settling on this interpretation allowed Yoichi to regain his will to survive. If Sayuri's fate had now fallen upon him, that meant his fate might affect hers as well. If he survived this, then there was a chance that Sayuri might miraculously recover, too. The song they once sang together floated up in his mind, and he began to sing it aloud.

From that point on, Yoichi's mind was occupied in large part by memories of Sayuri. How must it have been, living with a fifty-fifty chance of having Huntington's disease? Sayuri learned about her father's condition right after her first single came out, and that was when she found out about her fate.

That's around when we met.

Yoichi tried to imagine things from Sayuri's point of view. He could do so now, finally. Living six years in the shadow of a cursed destiny that had a fifty percent chance of coming true would surely have broken him as well. After all, look at how close he came to losing it during just the past twenty-four hours! What if he'd had to endure this kind of life-and-death uncertainty for six years? It was all clear to him now. Why Sayuri had ended up in a psychiatric hospital. Why she'd tried to kill herself twice. Why she'd been so mad with jealousy when they were together. Why she'd gone to the psychiatric clinic when she thought she was pregnant. Why she'd muttered, "I see. Even you say so. A fifty-fifty chance," when she told her own fortune. Why she'd blurted that she had nowhere left to run as she begged him, a desperate look on her face, to save her. Thinking back, Yoichi was overcome with sympathy for her, and with love. The tears streaming down his cheeks were different from when he'd been forsaken by the cargo ship.

A baby flashed before his eyes. A mirage?

That's right, it's already December 17.

Takeshi Sunako's letter had mentioned that Sayuri's due date was in the latter half of December.

Our baby's about to be born. Or maybe it's already here.

Even if he died, his genes would live on. It no longer really mattered to him if the baby ended up with Huntington's disease or not.

I can hear it—I can hear its voice.

Somehow, he could hear it. His child crying, healthy and alive.

6

December 17, 1:00 p.m., Japan time.

Having just returned from lunch, Mochizuki picked up the

ringing telephone and put the receiver to his ear.

It was Sugiyama, an ob-gyn at the university hospital. He was a close friend of Mochizuki's from medical school and two years his junior.

"She had the baby just now. A girl. Both mother and child came through just fine."

After going into labor the previous evening, Sayuri Asakawa had been brought to the university hospital and spent the night on the delivery table. And now, she was finally free of the labor pains that had passed over her in waves, successfully giving birth to her baby. Mochizuki breathed a sigh of relief when he heard that mother and child were both healthy.

"Is that so? Wonderful. Thank you for everything. And how long will she stay there?" Mochizuki asked.

"I'd say about a week."

"I see... All right, thanks again."

Mochizuki placed the receiver back into its cradle.

One week.

That was the entire length of time that mother and child would spend together. After that, the child would be brought to a baby-and-infant welfare institution, and Sayuri would be returned to Matsui Hospital, and they'd go off on their separate journeys. It would only be possible for them to stay together if Sayuri's mother, Yuko, agreed to put an end to her nomadic lifestyle and become her guarantor.

But what will Yuko say?

The rough-edged, indifferent voice he'd spoken to on the phone hadn't left a particularly good impression on him. She sounded unsurprised, even emotionless, at the news, yet she was guarded in her answers—Mochizuki couldn't help but feel disappointed as they spoke, and he told himself not to get his hopes up.

The welfare office had discovered Yuko's whereabouts about seven days previous. After having run off twenty-three years ago with a failed actor named Eiji Kawai, Yuko and her new husband ended up in Okayama, where they opened a hostess bar called Shizuka. Their business was doing well until Eiji passed away from cancer three years ago, after which Yuko seemed to lose any passion she might have had for running a business. Perhaps out of heartbreak over the loss of the man she loved, she sold the bar, which had been thriving, and used the substantial chunk of cash to embark on a nomadic life on the road. She flitted from one hot spring town to another, passing her days meeting up with old friends around the country. Among them was a friend she'd known since elementary school, and Yuko kept in touch with her more regularly than with anyone else, checking in with her about once a month. The caseworker from the welfare office found out about this friend and asked if she could pass a message to Yuko, who eventually called the Hamamatsu office a week ago. Two days after that, Mochizuki was finally able to talk directly to her on the phone.

Yuko was in Matsue at the time, and she seemed reluctant to come to Hamamatsu at first. Mochizuki couldn't understand why she wouldn't want to see her own daughter after finding out she'd been hospitalized, and he urged her strongly to come. To his surprise, she gave in rather easily.

"I guess I'll go, then. After all, I've never been to Hamamatsu..."

She was scheduled to arrive the next morning at ten. Mochizuki had provided her with Matsui Hospital's address, so naturally, she would end up coming directly to his office.

That's not good.

Sayuri wouldn't be here tomorrow, even if she came. After all, Sayuri had just given birth. He had no way of contacting Yuko to inform her of her grandchild's birth or to tell her which hospital Sayuri was staying at.

The cry of a newborn sounded in Mochizuki's mind. It made him nostalgic.

How many years ago was it, when I heard Kanae's first cry?

Mochizuki hoped that the experience of childbirth would have a positive influence on Sayuri and her mental state. At least in biological terms, a woman's body tended to be stronger after giving birth.

Is there any data on the psychological effects?

Mochizuki flipped through the medical journals lining his shelves, but couldn't find anything.

7

It was coming up on thirty hours since he'd fallen overboard. Multitudes of stars shone their delicate light upon him in the oppressive silence of the night. It was a world of illusion. The previous night had been overcast and pitch black, but the sky today glittered brightly enough to make him hallucinate.

Yoichi found himself slipping again and again into something like an ecstatic trance. If there was a framework holding his autonomic nervous system together, then that framework was definitely loosening. As he lost himself in the shimmering starlight of the southern hemisphere's night sky, memories tumbled through his mind without apparent rhyme or reason. Where was he? The world around him never seemed to change, whether his eyes were open or closed. He could no longer tell if he was asleep or awake. A part of his mind remained alert. *I think you've finally reached the end,* it said. The face of his father, who'd died when he was still in high school, floated before him, and he smelled the smell of home. It filled him with longing.

Home.

He wanted to go home so badly. Yoichi fought to keep himself from falling into a trance, clinging to his consciousness.

I want to go home. That's all I want. To go home and be with Sayuri, with our child. I can't stand this loneliness anymore. Please. Let me go.

Part of him was also picturing glasses filled to the brim with water and bowls of ice cream, while another part was scolding him, saying, *Stop wishing for the impossible!* He felt as though his consciousness had split into pieces, throwing his thoughts into chaos. A death wish began to take root in the deepest recesses of his heart. The desire to die while surrounded by sweet illusions grew like a snowball rolling through the darkness within him. If he died here, bathed in starlight, his soul would surely be carried away beautifully. It was a seductive thought. At the very least, it was better than being gradually beaten to death by waves.

At midnight, mist began to rise from the water, obscuring his vision.

Yoichi began to contemplate the existence of God.

Drifting somewhere between dream and reality, Yoichi suddenly felt something he hadn't experienced before. It sent a convulsive shudder through his body. He opened his eyes wide and tried to concentrate. It hadn't been a hallucination, nor just his imagination. He was sure of it. Dawn was beginning to break, and he could see its light through the white mist still rising around him.

A shark?!

His body froze in fear. He'd definitely felt it—something had touched the back of his head just now. He could still feel the sensation in the nape of his neck. Afraid to find out exactly what had touched him, he didn't turn his head, and instead reached backward with his hands to explore the area beneath him.

Nothing.

Right at that moment, he felt the exact same sensation again, this time just above his right ear. He gulped and tried to swallow his fear. Telling himself that a shark attack would be a bigger ordeal than this series of small shocks, he slowly turned his head.

He didn't cry out. Rather, he squeezed his eyes shut to make sure he wasn't dreaming and then opened them again. There it was, still floating in front of him. An object so orange it glowed in the white mist.

Overcome with elation, he felt himself go weak and almost lost consciousness. He managed to remain alert, though, and used both hands to cling to the life raft as he waited for the strength to return to his body. When he felt ready, he pulled himself into the raft. His body still wouldn't stop shaking.

It's a miracle!

Lying there inside the life raft, he couldn't believe his luck. He'd seen an inflatable raft drop from the *Wakashio Maru No. 7*. But it had disappeared from view almost immediately in the storm. It seemed hard to believe he'd run into it thirty-eight hours later. It must have been drifting along on the same current. If he and the raft had been floating at a constant distance from each other this whole time, it was even more unbelievable that they hadn't run into each other earlier.

Yoichi immediately looked for the emergency rations that should be on board. There were three one-liter bottles of water. He opened the lid of one and slowly poured its contents down his throat. He'd never tasted anything more delicious in his life. He could feel the water reach his stomach and spread throughout his body. He didn't know how long he'd end up adrift on the raft, so he forced himself to stop after just a few gulps, then turned his attention to the food.

His entire world was now a circle one hundred and fifty centimeters in diameter, but compared to how anxious he'd been when he was floating in the water in just his life jacket, he was feeling much better. However small the portions, he now had food and water. There was a canopy for him to shelter from the sun. Above all, his skin would have a chance to dry.

And...

One by one, Yoichi went through all the equipment on board, hoping he would find the emergency locator transmitter that should, by law, be on every inflatable life raft. He found it in a sturdy waterproof pack stowed against the edge of the floor along with some other supplies. He'd never used a transmitter like this before, so he looked over the instruction manual that came with it to figure out how it worked. It seemed simple enough—all he had to do was insert the battery and switch it on.

Sitting on the raft's round, seawater-slick floor, Yoichi lifted the transmitter with his right hand high above his head and flipped the switch. A red light came on, telling him that it was working. The electromagnetic waves carrying Yoichi's location began their journey, traveling two hundred kilometers in every direction. If a ship was in that area, it would be able to pick up the signal and hear his cry.

Here I am! Save me!

It was 6:46 a.m., December 18—thirty-nine hours since he'd fallen overboard.

8

10:10 a.m., December 18.

A plain face, completely untouched by any sort of make-up, presented itself across the table from Mochizuki. It belonged to Yuko, who was sunk deep in the leather sofa adorning the assistant director's office at Matsui Hospital. She'd told the doctor that she'd hardly slept at all, having taken the night train from Matsue to arrive in Hamamatsu that morning. Naturally, there was no chance for her to take a proper shower, but she wore her hair in all its disarray as if it were her regular hairstyle. Her present unkemptness seemed to be nothing out of the ordinary for her. Her entire body reeked of a disordered day-to-day.

Yuko rustled around in the bottom of a paper bag she'd brought with her, finally withdrawing a box of short Peace cigarettes. She tapped one out and put it in her mouth to light it. Mochizuki noticed that her gaze remained fixed on the curl of smoke rising from the end, her eyes studiously avoiding meeting his. It bothered him.

"You say this, but..."

Her manner of speaking was distressingly casual. She closed her eyes as if she was about to fall asleep, then slowly opened them again, smoke rising from her mouth. All without meeting Mochizuki's gaze.

When he broached the subject of whether she was willing to take her grandchild into her care, Yuko simply gave a small, derisive laugh without looking his way. She didn't reply. It was obvious from her expression that she wanted to avoid taking on such a heavy burden. She had no wish to alter her current responsibility-free lifestyle.

Mochizuki, for his part, had no intention of lecturing a woman nearly ten years his senior. He had plenty of elderly patients who had clearly been abandoned by their families. Figuring that the hospital was cheaper than a nursing home, these families dropped their relatives off for good, using it as a new home for them—even in these cases, Mochizuki never lectured anyone. He never told those family members to take better care of their parents or anything like that. He knew all too well how futile it was to tell someone to "care more" about anyone or anything. This was especially true in today's Japan, where almost all mental illnesses stemmed from interpersonal relationships, including those of family. He'd treated so many patients who never would have had to be admitted to a facility like this if there had only been someone close to them to give them the unconditional love they needed. Love and care weren't feelings you could direct another to have. This was the difficulty of his work in a nutshell. Even as he despaired for humanity, he could never truly give up on it. It was no easy thing to save another. A wounded heart could only be healed through encounters between living, breathing people. Mochizuki had taken a special interest in healing Sayuri Asakawa. He'd spent more energy on her treatment than, admittedly, those of his other patients. He knew it wasn't fair, but he wanted to test his hypothesis. If he spent enough time with a patient one-on-one, what would be the result? How much better would things turn out than with simple medication? But even as he conducted his little experiment, everything he did would be in vain the moment she presented with symptoms of Huntington's disease.

"You tell me this now, but I just don't know..."

Yuko repeated herself, more smoke leaking slowly from the corners of her mouth. Mochizuki had quit smoking during the past month at the behest of Akiko, who hated cigarettes, and he found himself recoiling as he watched Yuko smoke in front of him. He had never heeded his wife's wishes that he quit smoking, but he easily gave it up to please his mistress, and now he'd become someone who looked at smokers in disgust.

Akiko's face flashed before his eyes. Why was that? He wondered about it until it came to him: there was a certain resemblance between the two women's expressions. Their faces were completely different, of course—Akiko's voluptuousness couldn't have been more different from Yuko's slender, meager appearance. But there were moments when a look would cross Yuko's face that was exactly like one of Akiko's.

"Will she get better?"

Yuko changed the subject. Her tone made it sound like Sayuri's hospitalization was somehow Mochizuki's fault.

Yuko knew nothing of her daughter's life. She had no interest in imagining what might have happened to her during the past twenty-five years, and no way of understanding what might have caused her present condition. Having left Sayuri behind at one and a half years old when she ran off with her lover, Yuko was surely unaware of Shuichiro's disease. Even Shuichiro himself had only found out about it right before his suicide six years ago.

"Well, about that..."

Mochizuki knew he needed to explain clearly to Yuko that if Sayuri started showing symptoms of Huntington's disease, that meant there was a fifty-fifty chance that Sayuri's daughter had the disease, too. She was a baby now, but one day she would grow up and be able to have children of her own. She needed to know the truth to make a proper decision at that point.

"We need to talk about Shuichiro's illness..."

At the mention of his name, Yuko's body stiffened, her brows furrowing. She looked wary.

"Shuichiro's...illness?"

Now that the conversation had turned to Shuichiro, Yuko was at sixes and sevens. Mochizuki sensed that there must be some sort of secret related to the three and a half years they spent married that she wished to keep hidden.

"Yes, he suffered from Huntington's disease. I think you might not have been aware of that."

Yuko stubbed her cigarette out in the ashtray, then reached up to tuck her hair behind her left ear. A vein in her temple was twitching. Mochizuki could almost see the thoughts racing through her head.

"Huntington's disease?"

Everyone confronted with the name of this rare disease simply repeated it back. Yuko was no exception.

Slowly and carefully, Mochizuki explained the disease to her. He laid it out point by point: that the disease was carried on by a single dominant gene; that Sayuri currently had a fifty-fifty chance of having it; that if she lived the rest of her life without ever showing any symptoms, that meant the child would be safe. And then he went over the nature of the condition itself.

Yuko's reaction was different from what he'd imagined. He had been describing the symptoms and the main things to watch out for when caring for someone afflicted with the disease when Yuko began to mutter to herself. Her eyes darted around in all directions, and she eventually cut Mochizuki off.

"Are you saying Sayuri has this disease?"

Wasn't she listening at all? Mochizuki's tone had an edge to it as he replied.

"As I said before, we don't know yet. The chances are fifty-fifty."

"It's just that... How should I put it? What I want to know is, could she get this disease any other way than by inheriting it?"

"You mean, does it occur naturally? The answer is no."

It was clear that the disease had emerged at some point in history due to a mutation in a gene. But the chances that a normal gene would mutate in the exact same way now were so low it could be considered statistically impossible.

"I see. So, in other words..."

Yuko's mind was clearly somewhere else, but Mochizuki pressed on with his explanation anyway. Returning to where he'd left off, he was about to give some examples of the disease's symptoms when he stopped himself, having noticed the edges of Yuko's mouth curling up into a faint smile. It chilled Mochizuki to the bone to see her smiling as he described the terrible disease that could very well afflict her daughter, and it sapped his will to continue.

Yuko's expression grew quizzical when she noticed Mochizuki had abruptly stopped speaking. He felt a stiff pain in his neck as the pressure bore down on him.

"Is there something wrong, Doctor?"

Yuko's tone was oddly lighthearted, in a way that seemed out of sync with the matter at hand.

"No, not really... It's just that it seemed like your thoughts were elsewhere."

As Mochizuki voiced his suspicions, Yuko bent over in her seat, and a strangled sound broke from her throat. He couldn't tell if she was crying or laughing.

"How ironic," mused Yuko.

"Ironic?"

She appeared to be staring into the distant past, and she closed her eyes, as if her memories were too painful to look at.

"Doctor, there's no way that Sayuri has this Huntington's...or whatever disease."

Indignation rose inside Mochizuki.

How many times do I have to explain it to this woman?

Shuichiro's chart left no doubt—only the gods knew Sayuri's fate at this point. How could Yuko pretend to be so sure?

"But Shuichiro's diagnosis was clear."

Raising his head as he spoke, he found Yuko staring right into his eyes. They were filled with absolute confidence.

Oh!

It came to him at last.

Who would have guessed?!

The fact was, Yuko had every reason to be sure, every reason to believe that Sayuri's chances of having Huntington's disease were absolutely nil. And out of everyone in the world, only she would know why. Because the fact of the matter was, *Shuichiro wasn't Sayuri's father.* There was no other possible reason for Yuko to be so confident. She must have been sleeping with another man even before leaving Shuichiro, and when she became pregnant, she kept Shuichiro in the dark, passing the baby off as his. And if that child grew up to be Sayuri...

Right then, Akiko's figure appeared in the back of his mind. It was now even clearer why talking to Yuko had made him think of her. They were the same sort of woman. He could smell it on her—Akiko's scent, which wafted from her body to prickle his skin and ended up soaking into his entire body. How many men out there had been deceived by their wives and were unknowingly raising children unrelated to them?

Mochizuki nonetheless found himself laughing a little. He finally understood what Yuko had meant when she called the situation "ironic." She'd secretly given birth to the child of another man and then left that child in her husband's care when she ran off. She probably felt a lingering guilt over what she'd done. Whether she'd intended to do so from the start or it was just how things had ended up, her crime had likely haunted her for years. And yet, here she was twenty-five years later, learning that—irony of ironies—her crime was actually a stroke of genius. The devilish trap laid by the Huntington's gene to insure that its existence continued in the next generation was foiled in the end.

"Sayuri's father is someone other than Shuichiro, is that right?"

The issue was much too important not to be absolutely sure.

"Yes."

Yuko nodded.

"There could be no mistake?"

As he expected, Yuko nodded again.

It no longer really mattered who Sayuri's father was. All that mattered was that she hadn't inherited a drop of Shuichiro's blood. Her actual father might be Eiji Kawai, the man she ran off with, or it might be someone else. Yuko's seeming lack of affection for Sayuri made it hard to imagine she was Eiji's, though.

Terror of this disease had eaten away at Sayuri's mind for six long years. Now that Mochizuki knew there was no chance she was suffering from Huntington's disease, her present condition seemed explicable as a mixture of this intense fear and her deep love for Yoichi Maki. There was no way to erase what she'd experienced from her mind, but at the very least, this new development promised the possibility for her to get better.

Mochizuki hoped against hope that he would one day be able to meet Yoichi. He wanted to tell him that the light of morning had returned, that it had begun to shine once more upon the dark sea before him.

9

6:23 p.m., December 18.

Yoichi was preparing to meet his third night as a castaway. That morning, after miraculously encountering the life raft and finding it stocked with a small amount of food and water, he'd been filled with joy. Flipping the switch to activate the transmitter, he'd felt as if he'd already been rescued. As the day progressed, though, that feeling of relief left his body like air slowly leaking from an inner tube. Nothing sapped a person's will to live like disappointment after a glimpse of hope. He couldn't accept it. He'd been broadcasting the signal for the past twelve hours—why hadn't a ship shown up to rescue him? He found it hard to believe there wasn't a single ship searching for him anywhere in the two-hundred-kilometer radius around him. He switched the batteries around in the transmitter, and even exchanged them for the backup pair included in the pack. But the horizon remained totally empty. The search for him would surely be called off once this third night fell. As he resigned himself to never being rescued after all, he sensed the ten-thousand-meter-deep ocean rising beneath him like a dark entity, its malice something palpable for him to behold. The pattern of the waves around him that had appeared so peaceful that morning now seemed to take on a sinister air. The face of the ocean was like a Rorschach test reflecting the beholder's heart.

The sea's putting me through hope and despair over and over again. It wants to make me suffer before it snuffs me out.

As if in answer to his thoughts, the sound of the waves seemed to bring a message from the depths below. They were calling for him.

It'd be so easy, you know? There's a simple solution for all your woes right here.

As his mind grew blurry, he began to lose consciousness, and he was getting closer and closer to casting his flesh—the source of all the suffering and pain he was experiencing—at last into the darkening sea. This was the brink of death. His body had been fortified by the food and water he'd had that day, but his mind was not following. The transmitter had enough battery power to last three days at most. He'd only used a third of it, but he was beginning to panic anyway. Should he turn the signal off at night, since it seemed more likely he'd be rescued in the daytime? But a ship might pass while he was sleeping. The seemingly unresolvable dilemma bedeviled him, even made him angry. One part of him was hitting his head with his fists, shouting at himself to calm down, while the other part thought about his mother in Kosai and his brother working in Hiroshima. Even if he disappeared into the vastness of the sea, they wouldn't give up looking for him, would they? His mother, especially, might never give up. It was a terrible thing for a family when someone disappeared and no body was ever found.

He made a vow right then: that he, at the very least, would resist the temptation to plunge into the water and become fish food. He needed to leave his body behind to be found. He owed his family that. So he told himself this over and over, trying to instill the message in his heart. He needed to prevent himself from giving in to this killing urge inside him.

Scenes from his past drifted through his mind, fragmented and disordered. Even when he recalled events from the time he'd spent aboard the *Wakashio Maru No. 7*, they seemed impossibly distant. So memories of his life in the big city trying to make it as an actor with Sayuri felt like they'd happened to someone else entirely. Why had he thrown that life away? Even now, he had trouble coming up with a clear answer. He couldn't believe it. What had dissatisfied him so? Had he left out of boredom? Irritation at dealing with others? Nothing seemed like a good enough reason, looking back. He'd led a trivial life, it seemed. His existence was small, insignificant, yet still he didn't want to die. He wanted to try again, to see if he could do better this time. Pleading for another chance, Yoichi prayed.

Gradually, he began to calm down. He heard a melody coming from the depths of his memory, the sound of someone humming that eventually turned into words. It was Sayuri. He let her sing there, deep inside his head, for a while. But the song stuck in his mind, and even as he shook his head, it clung to the sides of his skull, refusing to go away. So he gave in and began to sing along. His voice grew louder every time he repeated the song, and his will to live grew with it.

The face of the ocean reflected the movement of the clouds above. A mountain range of thick cumulonimbus clouds were piling up where the sun was sinking into the sea. The sunlight illuminated them from behind, dyeing them a bright vermilion, and the color gradually spread across the surface of the untroubled sea. Yoichi leaned forward with his elbows propped on the upper part of the raft so he could get a better view of the changing scenery. The previous night, he'd been so absorbed in the hallucinatory beauty of the starry heavens that he'd been able to forget his predicament, if only momentarily. It had been the opposite of the previous hellish night he'd spent fighting the storm-roiled sea, and it looked like tonight would be another night of blessed calm.

At that moment, Yoichi caught sight of a metallic flash on the vermilion horizon that seemed to belong to neither sea nor sky. The tiny shape grew steadily larger as he watched. As soon as he was sure it wasn't a mirage, he swung into action. He'd mentally rehearsed this moment again and again during the long hours he'd spent adrift on the raft. There were six parachute rocket flares on board. He knew he had to use them wisely so as not to waste them. He took one out and fixed his gaze on the approaching ship, steadying his focus. This was no dream. The prow of the ship was pointed straight at him. He could even see the crimson waterline on the ship's hull as it rode high in the water. It was a tuna boat of the same type as the *Wakashio Maru No. 7.* No mistake this time—they'd picked up his rescue signal. Sobs of relief racked his body, but he managed to steady himself and hold the flare high above his head as he pulled the pin. The rocket flew straight up, making a sound like a firework, and then exploded in a great flash, briefly changing the color of the sea below. He still couldn't read the name emblazoned on the boat's bow, but he could now make out the shape of the anchor hanging from the port side. He grabbed another flare.

There was no doubt about it. The approaching tuna boat had noticed his raft. The encroaching dark and the tears streaming from his eyes blurred his vision, but the night sky made the flares shine all the brighter.

He caught sight of someone standing on the deck.

"Hey! Over here!"

Yoichi waved his arms, screaming as loudly as he could.

I survived! I'm going home!

He felt a joy and relief like nothing he'd ever felt before. It was sweet enough that he was almost willing to become a castaway again just to feel it once more.

Rejoice!

The ocean hid its malevolent face and instead smiled broadly as it stretched in all directions around him. Yoichi reached his arms out toward the approaching tuna boat as if to embrace it.

When I make it back to Japan—

He had so many things he had to do once he made it safely back home. First, he needed to see the most important person in his life. These forty-nine hours spent as a castaway was the springboard he needed to face Sayuri's destiny alongside her. Together, they would deal with whatever might befall them and their child. The same god that had determined Sayuri's fate was also whispering in Yoichi's ear. Life was cruel, he realized. There was no escaping it, no matter where in the world you might run. Turning your back on life's difficulties, denying them by chasing illusions, and wishing for an ideal world only led to your soul rotting.

Yoichi grabbed a third rocket flare and pulled the pin. It exploded in a flash high above his head.

10

Mochizuki had no knowledge of what Yoichi was like before he boarded the tuna boat. The doctor also didn't know that he'd fallen overboard during a storm, or that he'd spent his first thirty-eight hours adrift only in his life jacket and the next eleven hours floating in a life raft he'd miraculously bumped into before being saved. If he'd known, he might have become interested in how an experience like that, of spending so much time on the knife's edge of life and death, might change a person. The experience of someone who went through such an ordeal and came out stronger could be valuable research material for a psychiatrist. If it could ever be known exactly what it was that could induce real change in a person's character, such a thing would be an invaluable addition to any psychiatrist's toolbox.

Sitting there before Mochizuki, Yoichi looked much older than his actual age. After spending a mere two days being examined in a hospital in Auckland, Yoichi disembarked from the airplane in Narita two days ago, and now he was sitting in the assistant director's office in Matsui Hospital. There was a forcefulness in him, an almost intimidating energy. Mochizuki had felt it from the moment they met. The body of this silent young man exuded the steadfast air of someone much more mature. He'd even felt it over the phone when Yoichi had called from the airport. His voice sounded *adult*. He'd calmly explained that he intended to visit the hospital in two days' time and then, as if knowing already the passion with which Mochizuki had pursued Sayuri's care, economically expressed his deepest thanks in a few well-chosen words before quietly hanging up. Mochizuki couldn't help but compare him with Takeshi. At Mochizuki's suggestion, Takeshi had begun studying to become certified as a caseworker, and he'd become noticeably more optimistic and proactive. Still, he'd yet to fully overcome his native weakness. Yoichi exuded a certain quality from the very depths of his being—from each and every cell in his body—that Takeshi might never acquire during the course of his entire life.

Mochizuki had just finished explaining that they now knew Sayuri's chances of having Huntington's disease were zero. But Yoichi's expression remained unchanged. It was almost as if this piece of news didn't matter to him.

"Oh, I see," he replied, unruffled. It was the attitude of a man who knew in his bones that there was nowhere in this world that was truly safe in any absolute way. Everyone's life was subject to the indifferent, irresistible forces of chance. If his head hadn't happened to bump against that life raft in the early hours of dawn, he surely would have ended up sinking to the bottom of the ocean. His rescue was nothing short of a miracle. His experience drifting on the boundary between life and death had rendered him something of a fatalist. What had happened to Sayuri was as arbitrary a stroke of luck as that chance encounter at dawn.

"They're late."

Mochizuki looked at his watch. It had been more than ten minutes since he'd asked Akiko to go bring Sayuri to his office.

"I'm in no hurry."

Yoichi's stoicism disappointed Mochizuki. He'd expected him to seem a bit more jubilant at the news about Sayuri.

"Do you plan to marry her?"

Yoichi answered Mochizuki's question without hesitation.

"Yes, right away. I'll assume the responsibilities as the father of our child."

A new life as a family... Yoichi didn't have a job, but he did have the three million yen he'd earned during his eight months at sea. He'd fallen overboard halfway through the voyage, but Jukichi had arranged for Wakashio Fisheries to pay him for the labor he'd performed until then. Yoichi recalled Jukichi's face; it was a warm memory. Embracing Yoichi on the deck after his rescue, with uncharacteristic tears in his eyes, Jukichi was the very picture of an ideal father in Yoichi's mind.

"I heard it's a girl."

Mochizuki changed the subject to Yoichi's newborn child to fill in the silence.

"Yes."

"I have a daughter myself. She's really adorable."

"...Is that so?"

Their conversation stopped there.

Yoichi waited. He strove to maintain his composure as he anticipated Sayuri's appearance. Would it be now? Or now? The day he landed in Narita, Sayuri had been transferred back to Matsui Hospital, her yet-unnamed child sent to a welfare institution. Yoichi couldn't wait to see them both.

There was a knock on the door. Yoichi started, then reflexively jumped to his feet.

"Come in."

The door opened even before Mochizuki spoke.

Sayuri stood at the threshold, dressed in blue sweats. Next to her stood the carefully made-up and put-together Akiko. The contrast between her and Sayuri, unadorned and small-statured, couldn't have been starker.

For a moment, Yoichi simply looked down at Sayuri from his comparatively great height, but his face began to distort. He was losing his previous cool. Something was rising within him, and it was twisting his face.

Sayuri slowly raised her eyes until they discovered Yoichi's face, and then she closed them tight. Hesitantly, she opened them again... And as she did, they grew wider than ever before, providing a clear view of the light that was beginning to shine somewhere deep in the fog of her mind. She tried to speak, but no proper words came out, and only sobs—*Aaah! Aaah!*—bubbled up from her throat as she ran up to him. Yoichi took her hands in his and gently pulled her into his arms, patting her back as if burping a baby and nodding his head.

"I'm sorry, but is there any way we could spend a little time alone...?"

Mochizuki was slightly relieved to see tears in Yoichi's eyes as he made his request.

"If you go down the stairs and turn right, you can go out into the courtyard."

Yoichi bowed his head to Mochizuki, and he and Sayuri left the office. As if to take their place, Akiko slipped into the room, shutting the door behind her.

"I can't take it—what a moving reunion!" she exclaimed dramatically, blowing her nose into a tissue she'd pulled from her white coat's pocket.

Mochizuki went to the window to look down at the courtyard. Akiko joined him, and the two of them stood side-by-side watching Yoichi and Sayuri make their way slowly toward a bench. Mochizuki wanted to believe in Sayuri's chances of recovery. He expected that the combination of her childbirth and her reunion with Yoichi would be catalyst enough to trigger a significant change in her condition. He had faith that Yoichi would be able to help her—to remain by her side and peel away the layers of terror, which had built up in her heart over the past six years, at the prospect of having Huntington's disease. It was a process that might well take as long as the period of her traumatization.

Standing next to him, Akiko placed her hand lightly on Mochizuki's shoulder.

She spoke in a whisper.

"I'm a week late."

Mochizuki's breath stopped in his throat.

There below them, bathed in the light of this unseasonably sunny winter day, Yoichi held Sayuri's hand in his as they sat down on the bench. Mochizuki couldn't tell from where he was standing if they were having an actual conversation. He was filled with the desire to shut out the din of the world around him and watch over the two of them forever.

But Akiko's voice continued whispering in his ear.

"Did you hear me? I'm telling you I might be pregnant."

The hand on his shoulder slid slowly down and softly gripped his elbow. Still, Mochizuki didn't respond.

Life didn't move in a straight line. Every step along the way was a step further into a world ruled by unfathomable chance. Yoichi and Sayuri rose from the bench and began to walk toward the fountain in the middle of the lawn. Sayuri would likely be discharged in the near future. And the very first step they'd take together would be to bring their daughter home from the welfare institution. Living with Sayuri and her condition would be no simple thing. But no life was ideal—paradise was an illusion.

Mochizuki shifted his gaze upward. The surface of the gourd-shaped lake changed color with the seasons, and its present hue was impossible to put into words. A realization began to wash over him: that perhaps what he lacked was the resolve to face the world straight on, in all its vast uncertainty.

Translator's Note

The Shining Sea was first published in 1993. It is Koji Suzuki's third novel, following his debut, *Paradise* (1990), and the blockbuster success of his second novel, *Ring* (1991). As fellow novelist Yusuke Kishi points out in his afterword to its paperback edition, *The Shining Sea* represents a continuation of Suzuki's oeuvre, like *Paradise* before it or *Seize the Day* (2001) after it, that are more novels of adventure and romance than the novels of suspense and horror that became his trademark following the success of *Ring* and its sequels. Yet, as Kishi also points out, there are thematic consistencies tying his paranormal novels to his more realistic ones, allowing readers to get a fuller picture of Suzuki's authorial vision.

The central predicament in *The Shining Sea* has to do with a genetic condition that threatens to destroy the happiness of its main characters, much like the supernatural virus in *Ring* threatens the characters in that novel. Like *Ring*, too, *The Shining Sea* shows its age in the technologies it references. Much like the VHS tapes in *Ring* that became superseded by DVDs and other digital technologies during the course of the 1990s, the understanding of the genetic condition in *The Shining Sea* has become superseded by subsequent medical technology allowing Huntington's disease to be diagnosed in patients before symptoms develop.

However, also like *Ring*, the thematic power of the novel is not dependent on the timeliness of its technological world; rather, the deep existential questions presented by both novels remain potent and searching even now. The idea that there are vast, indifferent forces shaping our destinies allows Suzuki's novels of the supernatural to speak to his novels of adventure and romance. The predicament confronting Yoichi and Sayuri in *The Shining Sea* finds itself echoed in the predicaments faced by the other characters as well; everyone in the novel must navigate the push-pull between free will and fate that forms Suzuki's larger vision. Even more clearly than in *Ring*, the ethical dimensions of the human condition are put into stark relief in this novel as he plunges his characters into extreme situations not of their own making. The test for these characters lies in how they respond to the arbitrary role of chance in determining their destinies. This forms the thematic core of *The Shining Sea*, as well as its power, showing it to be a key part of Suzuki's literary project as it emerged in the early 1990s, one that continues to entertain and provoke readers up through today.

Brian Bergstrom
January 2022, Montréal

ABOUT THE AUTHOR

Koji Suzuki was born in 1957 in Hamamatsu, southwest of Tokyo. He attended Keio University, where he majored in French. After graduating, he held numerous odd jobs, including teaching college-prep courses. A self-described jock, he holds a first-class yachting license and has also made a motorbike trip across the U.S. from Key West to Los Angeles. The father of two daughters, he has written a number of books on childrearing, having become quite the expert in his days as a struggling writer and househusband.

In 1990, his first full-length work, *Paradise*, won the Japanese Fantasy Novel Award and launched his career as a fiction writer. *Ring*, written with a baby on his lap, catapulted him to notoriety, and its multimillion-selling sequels *Spiral* and *Loop* cemented his reputation as a world-class talent. In the U.S., his novel *Edge* was acknowledged with the 2012 Shirley Jackson Award. *The Shining Sea*, which was nominated for the 11th Seishi Yokomizo Mystery Award, is his third novel and his eleventh work to be translated into English.

KOJI SUZUKI

EDGE

When a team of scientists tests new computer hardware by calculating the value of pi into the deep decimals, the figures begin to repeat a pattern. It's mathematically untenable—unless the physical constants that undergird our universe have altered, ever so slightly... *Winner of the Shirley Jackson Award.*

PARADISE

In the arid badlands of prehistoric Asia, a lovelorn youth violates a sacred tribal taboo against representing human figures by etching an image of his beloved. When the foretold punishment comes to pass, the two must embark on a journey across the world, and time itself, to try to reclaim their destiny. A mysterious spirit guides them toward a surprise destination that readers may indeed find quite close to home.